Erin's Daughters

Gina Robinson

Gina Robinson
SEATTLE, WASHINGTON

www.ginarobinson.com

Publisher's Note: This is a work of fiction. Names, characters, places, and incidents are a product of the author's imagination. Locales and public names are sometimes used for atmospheric purposes. Any resemblance to actual people, living or dead, or to businesses, companies, events, institutions, or locales is completely coincidental.

Book Layout ©2014 BookDesignTemplates.com
Cover by Cormar Creative

Erin's Daughters/ Gina Robinson. — 1st ed.
ISBN 978-0692410066

Excerpted from *Molly's Girls,*
an unpublished manuscript by
Maggie Burdan Becker

Bitterroot Mountains
March, 1884

Snow obscured the world, weighing down the cedars
and white pines barely visible in the onslaught of wind
and cold, obliterating Mariah's fellow travelers from
view. The storm threw reality out of perspective, lead-
ing instinct to beckon Mariah to set down her load, to
fall asleep forever with little Lizzie cradled against her.
But her mind railed against such treachery; screamed
at her to keep moving. Why should instinct and rational thought be at such odds?

The blizzard made no more sense than the rest of
life. Back in Thompson's Falls, their guide had assured
Mariah that the mountain crossing was safe. By foot, a

simple matter of thirty miles, two days of travel. Nothing she and the child couldn't handle. Snow? Foul weather? No danger. Don't worry, pretty miss. *Liar!* Yet he had seemed so straightforward and knowledgeable.

Poverty had prevented Mariah from hiring a packhorse in Thompson's Falls. Poverty forced her along on foot wearing a coat too thin and shoes too worn to give protection against anything but the mildest squall. If she weren't very careful and clever, or exceedingly lucky, poverty would kill Lizzie and her.

The tiny two-year-old rode on Mariah's back, cheek pressed against the worn nap of Mariah's coat. The child grew increasingly heavy and hard to carry as the miles inched by and Mariah slipped and slid in the snow, fighting for footing, wanting to rest. Her arms ached from the weight of their bags and from pressing tightly onto Lizzie's feet to keep her from sliding off. Not being able to use her arms for balance only added to her fatigue. It had been hours since she'd felt any sensation in her feet and hands. Her cheeks were wind burned and brittle with cold from taking the brunt of the wind.

Mariah worried about Lizzie getting frostbite. She was slight, and her fingers and toes so delicate and slender. Sheltering Lizzie with her body and taking the sting of the wind was the most Mariah could do for the clinging little imp. And it was precious little.

Lizzie's mother had died but a week past, on the trail to the gold country to join her husband. Losing one parent was tragic, as Mariah could attest, losing two, devastating. So she'd vowed to take Lizzie to her papa. Mariah was headed to the Idaho gold rush anyway. But what a pathetic, pitiful attempt at heroism this business was! Oh, to be strong and rich, well fed, well dressed, and warm.

Without either physical strength or money to rely on, her only asset was mere determination to survive. And it seemed a meager tool and little comfort in the wild mountains of Idaho in the midst of a blizzard.

All around them, those also headed for the gold camp of Murray struggled on—hearty men without the burden of a child on their backs. Blast them! Though Mariah swallowed her pride and lowered the scarf shielding her face from the wind and pleaded for help, no one offered assistance. *Just carry Lizzie a step or two. Offer a kind word.* But the brutes marched by, deaf to anything but the gold dust dreams filling their heads.

It was late afternoon of their second day out. Five, maybe ten miles left to go—white, cold, frozen miles that separated them from their destination. Soon darkness would fall, and with it the already frigid temperatures. She and Lizzie needed warmth and food. Mariah rubbed her shoulder against the small, round scar of the smallpox branded on her cheek since early childhood, when the disease had taken her family, trying to battle the fear overcoming her. She'd never felt more alone or scared in her life, frailer, more vulnerable.

Suddenly her eighteen years felt as eight and she longed for the comfort and protection of the loving grandpa who'd raised her. He'd been old. His death last winter expected, but it still didn't seem fair that she should be left to face the world alone. And now here she was, death beckoning her.

In the desolate cold, denying the inevitable appeared almost foolish. The wind seemed to whistle a question: *Why struggle against fate?* All of nature urged her toward an eternal rest.

Keep going. Keep moving. Keep walking—for Lizzie.

Mariah staggered forward.

A group of packhorses overtook them from behind, seemingly coming from nowhere. With the wind screaming, Mariah hadn't heard them approach. The first rider crowded her off the trail. As Mariah scrambled to get out of the way, she hit ice and slid back into the horse's path. Lizzie screamed. Hooves danced above them. The rider cursed and maneuvered the horse past, somehow managing to avoid crushing them.

"Horsey," Lizzie said, fear wavering in her baby voice.

"Yes, horsey."

Horsey could have killed us, Mariah added silently. She pulled off the path to let the horses by, up into brush that snatched at her skirts.

Please, God, let me have the strength to keep going.

Lizzie cried.

"We're making way for the horses to go, baby. That's all." Mariah might have said, *Joining the angels like your ma*, because as well as Mariah could tell, she and Lizzie straggled behind all the others on foot. Once the horses disappeared, she and Lizzie would be left behind, lost in the woods.

"I hungwy."

"I know, baby, hush." Mariah swayed, trying to rock the child on her back.

Just as Mariah prepared to take the path again, a slender figure wearing a full fur coat and riding a fine mare emerged through the swirling white world as from the depths of a dream—obscured at first, gradually coming into focus. Surely, by the way the rider sat the horse, a woman. Mariah's heart pounded.

A woman might take pity on us. A woman might at least save Lizzie. A woman might...

Before her thought finished, the rider pulled over. Speared by conscience or led by God's hand?

A second horseman joined them, but before he could come even, the first rider dismounted. Mariah saw her now with the clarity of one desperate. As the woman came toward them, the moment etched itself on Mariah's memory. Forever after she would be able to recall her emotions at the time, the indistinct impression of time standing still, and the fairytale quality of the scene—the woman's beauty, her kindness.

An instant later the rider wrapped Mariah in an embrace, steadying her against the incessant winds of fate and shattering the illusion of her otherworldliness.

"I'm here to help." The voice sounded soft and feminine and carried the slightest hint of an Irish burr over the wind. "I'm Molly. Hand me the child."

CHAPTER ONE

Present Day

Four hours and forty-five minutes ago, I left Sean, my
husband of thirteen years.

I know pretty much the exact time because that's
how long it took to drive the three hundred miles from
my home on Sahalee Lane in the suburbs of Seattle to
Gran's Neoclassic early 1900s mansion in Browne's
Addition on the west side of Spokane. Nonstop. No pot-
ty breaks. No pit stops to restock the tissues. Straight
through. I was cried out and dried up and ready to just
blow away—from everything.

And no, Sean wasn't the lying, cheating scumbag
having an affair. I was the unfaithful one.

Tired and used up once my anger ebbed, I'd gone about as far as I could go without collapsing. I wound my way by instinct from the freeway to First Avenue.

Clear, starlit sky stretched above. Barely past the longest day of the year and the days were long. Night was only just falling, leaving a dusky aura clinging to earth in day's wake. Streetlights lit Gran's street in orbs and, despite their modern intrusion, did little to disturb the antique feel of the turn-of-the-twentieth-century neighborhood. I felt a little of my tension slip away. Stepping into another time and place was exactly the escape I needed.

Gran's house, with its three-story Ionic portico fa-çade and broad entry steps, stood aloof from its sur-roundings. But a welcoming light burned in the front parlor, even though I'd insisted Gran not wait up.

I pulled into the circular drive where Gran's ten-year-old Cadillac sat in its usual spot beside the con-verted carriage house. Only Lucy drove the car now.

Gran had been born into money in this very house at a time when it was the most posh address in town. Ex-cept for a short stint early in her marriage, she'd never left it. Not even during the calamitous years when drug lords ruled the neighborhood. Fortunately, although most of the old mansions had been converted to apart-ments, the neighborhood had regained its respectabil-ity thanks to a bit of urban renewal and a renewed public interest in historic preservation.

I grabbed my laptop, suitcase, and cosmetic bag and headed for the house, letting myself in with my key.

Gran's warbly voice called out to me from the parlor. "Dani! That you?"

"No, it's a burglar, Gran."

"Well, burglar, you'd better get a move on because I own a shotgun."

"Yeah? Locked in your gun safe. I think I can beat you to it in a foot race, old lady."

Gran laughed.

I found her and her nurse and companion, Lucy, sitting in the parlor in front of the empty fireplace with its brilliant gold leaf mantel. Gran was snuggled into a Victorian sofa with rose-colored upholstery, looking like a relic herself among the gold and rose moire curtains, enhanced by the golden glow of an ornate period lamp. Despite the heat of the night, Gran had an afghan pulled snug around her lap. Lucy sat in a chair next to her. Yellowed papers, old news clippings, aged books, and spiral notebooks surrounded them.

"Whoa, it looks like the historical society exploded in here," I said, taking in the scene.

Gran smiled.

I walked over and kissed my grandmother, then gave Lucy a hug. "I told you two not to wait up."

"Since when do you get to boss your gran around?" Gran squeezed my hand, looking me over critically. Her eyes may have been weak from age, but her mental acuity hadn't dimmed in the slightest. It wouldn't be easy to hide the truth from her long.

"Since never." I forced a smile. "Just don't blame me if you're cranky tomorrow."

Gran waved down my concern. "I'm never grumpy."

But Lucy winked her agreement at me.

To divert Gran from asking any penetrating questions about my sudden decision to drive over a day early, I nodded toward the pile of detritus around her. "I arrive a day ahead of schedule and you're hard at work till all hours on the book without me?"

"If you think we can just pause and wait to get things done around here, you've got another think coming." Gran shook her head. "No siree, girlie. At my age, the future's just a notion. There's only the present. And I don't have near enough of that."

I picked up a notebook. "How far along are you?"

Gran patted the seat next to her and I sat. She took the notebook from me. "We'll talk about the book tomorrow, dear. Lucy and I are awfully glad you're here. Neither our eyesight nor our minds are as sharp as they used to be." Gran gave me her soul-piercing look. "So. Are you going to tell me what brings you here looking like you've been crying for three hundred miles?"

Her old eyes were still sharp enough.

"Three hundred? No, it couldn't have been more than two hundred. I swear."

"Dani."

"Marital woes." Gran knew Sean and I had been having problems for the last several years.

"Men!" Gran said. "They're a pain in the ass." She patted my knee soothingly. "You can tell me all about what that bastard Sean has done tomorrow when we're both fresh and thinking clearly. Right now you need your rest." By which she meant she and Lucy were tired, too.

But bless Gran. She knew when not to push.

"Your mother will want to see you while you're here," Gran said.

My mother was quite possibly the last person I wanted to see, but I didn't feel like arguing now. I simply nodded.

"Lucy made up the green room for you, dear." She turned to her companion. "Lucy, help Dani take her bags to her room."

Gran could be a little too imperious sometimes.

"Lucy's tired, too, Gran. I can manage myself." I stood and helped Gran up. She was sprightly enough for a woman in her eighties, except when she'd been sitting too long. Lucy took over for me then, coming to Gran's aid. I wished them both sweet dreams and headed to bed.

The first fluttering of my eyelids brought the weight of my present circumstances crashing back to me. Even the brightness of the morning couldn't chase it away.

Being on the west side of the house, the green room caught little early morning light, but even so the window was lit brightly today. Probably another scorcher in the making.

When I saw the time, my senses came back to me. I'd slept like the dead. I grabbed my cosmetic case and headed for the bathroom.

By the time I'd showered and dressed, I still hadn't decided how to tell Gran. She wouldn't be shocked or judgmental. But I wasn't proud of what I'd done. Especially how I'd thrown it in Sean's face. How had I reached the point of becoming so cruel?

I also had to call Dad and get in touch with the family lawyer, Reed Wiesburg. At the very least, he'd be able to recommend a good divorce lawyer. My stomach lurched at the thought. I needed the comfort of my grandmother.

In her homey kitchen, I found a plate of breakfast warming for me in the oven—a nice gesture. But I couldn't face anything heavy. The sausages—long, fat, and rigid—seemed to stare at me accusingly. I wanted no part of them. Instead, I grabbed a cup of yogurt from the fridge, snagged a muffin and spoon, and set off in search of Gran.

I found her and Lucy in Gran's study, back in the suite of rooms that had been converted from servants' quarters and still carried an informal, casual air. Gran had moved into them several years ago when her arthritic knees began rebelling at using the stairs too often. She preferred them to the formal, ornately decorated, themed rooms at the front of house, still preserved as architect Kirtland Cutter designed them a century ago.

Lucy, fifteen years my grandmother's junior, had come to live with Gran over twenty years ago, after Granddad passed away. It stunned me to realize that Lucy was in her late sixties now, older than Gran had been when Lucy first came to live with her. To my amusement, I found them huddled around a desktop computer. Lucy sat in front of it, typing one-fingered. Though funny, it was painful to watch.

"Good morning," I said, bucking up my courage. "What's that you've got there, Gran? A new toy?"

"Good morning, dear." Gran looked up and took in my sundress with an up and down scan. "Oh, for the days when I could wear a sundress. I had a stunning figure when I was your age. Before I became as wrinkled as an old elephant." She sighed wistfully. "How are you this morning? Do you know, Lucy and I were just saying that you're an answer to prayer."

"I don't think so, Gran."

"Sure you are." Gran tapped the computer. "We've been praying for a computer expert to come help us get all our new voice-recognition and book-formatting software installed properly." She looked triumphant. "And here you are."

I sauntered in, picking at my muffin as I did, and took a seat next to Gran. "Don't tell me you've been doing everything longhand until now?"

"Don't knock it. Pen and paper have served me well for over eighty percent of a century," Gran said.

"Luddite."

Gran smiled. "I prefer traditionalist. But anything for the book."

The book—our family history that Gran was preserving for posterity. She'd cajoled me into using precious vacation time to come help her research and write it. Gran had assured me it would be good for me to get to know my ancestors, saying every girl should know where she came from. I groaned inwardly, remembering vague snatches of stories of long-dead ancestors that Gran used to tell me as a child. Surely I got brownie points somewhere for being such a devoted granddaughter. I needed something to balance out being such a shitty wife.

Gran put on a glove and held up a yellowed journal. "This is older than I am and crumbling just as fast. Every piece of our collection has to be handled carefully. Lucy and I decided that when we've finished, I'll donate our research materials, the originals, to the Cowles Museum." She looked at me for confirmation of her decision.

In the early sixties, Helen Campbell had died and left her mansion just a few houses down to the Eastern Washington Historical Society. It was the Cowles Museum now. Gran had an inclination to do the same with her home, though she worried about cheating me out of my inheritance. "Good idea, Gran. They can probably store it in an archival vault or something, where it will last much longer."

I couldn't tell whether Gran was relieved or disappointed with my ready agreement. I took a seat on her little sofa across from the desk and ate a spoonful of yogurt.

Lucy took the heat off. "When the book's finished, we're going to self-publish it and order copies for everyone in the family."

"That's right." Gran patted her computer. "And we bought the very best software for my magnum opus. It's probably easy for someone familiar with computers to use." She eyed me meaningfully.

She was crafty with her manipulation, but I refused to dive in and offer to be her lackey. "You know, Gran, you can hire someone to type that in for you." I pointed my spoon at her pile of papers.

Gran laughed, an aged, crackling, but definitely amused sound. "Didn't I tell you? We've already done that." She paused and bit her lip. I couldn't believe that Gran could look self-conscious, but she did. "I didn't explain this right. We're not merely *copying* things. We're piecing the whole history together from journals and letters and writing it out like a novel."

Lucy nodded along with Gran's statements.

"A novel! I thought this was nonfiction?" I was enjoying ribbing Gran. "The truth, the whole truth, and nothing but the truth."

"Well, it is. It's nonfiction written like a novel."

"You mean narrative nonfiction?"

"That's it." Gran looked sheepish.

"Any thoughts about sending this off to New York to a publisher when you're finished?" I was teasing with the ulterior motive of finding out just how far Gran intended to carry this new mania of hers.

Gran actually giggled. "Don't be ridiculous! Of course not. But I think my great-grandchildren would rather read a story than a dry historical account, don't you?" She gave me an arch look that cut directly to my heart without intending to.

Gran was the kindest of souls, but she didn't understand. I was her only grandchild and, if past history was any indication, I was barren. Not to mention on the verge of divorce. Unless a miracle occurred, there would likely be no great-grandchildren.

I wondered if Gran thought, like so many others, that all these years I'd just happily continued using birth control and pursuing my career. Oh, she knew I'd been to see doctors. But I didn't think she realized the scope of my problems, or lack thereof. The doctors could find nothing wrong with me. Or with Sean.

In thirteen years of marriage we hadn't conceived. At times, I'd really wished there had been something wrong, some concrete reason I couldn't make a baby. Problems have solutions. But if something's not broken, it can't be fixed.

If you got right down to it, not being able to have a baby is what started Sean and me down the path to ruin. The blame, the pressure, the sex on demand, the loss of intimacy regarding our sex life, the loss of passion, and the sense of failure and inadequacy all took their toll on our marriage.

"Yeah, sure," I said.

Gran's smile crinkled her already lined face. "We had all the original letters and journals typed, so they're digitally preserved for future generations. As well as all of the story that we had written when we hired the typist. But the tale isn't finished yet."

Gran became suddenly serious. "I'm not a spring chicken, Dani. I won't be around forever. Who knows how much time I have left? I want this story finished before I go." She paused, and reiterated her latest mantra: "I want you to know who we are, Dani. I think it might help."

For a moment I thought Gran had forgotten her promise to talk. I should have known better.

"You know, Dad could've helped you install and learn the software," I said, putting off the inevitable discussion.

Gran frowned and shook her head. "He's busy. And he doesn't understand or care about our story."

I set my yogurt and spoon down on the desk. "What do you want me to do first?"

"Get this software installed properly and teach us how to use it. Second—help us with the remaining research. You have a logical mind, Dani. Maybe you can help us put together the final, puzzling pieces of the story."

With the two of them looking at me so expectantly, what could I say?

"Good." Gran turned to Lucy. "You can go now, Lucy. With Dani here to help, I'll be fine."

Lucy looked relieved. "Good, Maggie. I'll be off, then. I was hoping to go strawberry picking and make some jam today. If I start right out, it may not be too late, yet."

"Get enough for a pie," Gran said. "You know how Dani loves your strawberry glacé pie."

CHAPTER TWO

Gran spoke almost instantaneously with the door latching closed behind Lucy. "Sean called early this morning. I didn't want to wake you, dear. Obviously, you needed your rest."

"Sean called the house?" My surprise was genuine. "Is that why you sent Lucy away?

Gran nodded. "Airing dirty laundry."

"She's practically family," I said. "What did Sean want?"

"He was upset." Gran paused, probably for effect. The old dame had a hint of the dramatic in her. "But you know Sean. He doesn't air laundry either."

Yes, I knew Sean. He would be stoic. His inability to share his emotions had been a barrier between us.

"About those marital woes, child." Gran's eyes were filled with curiosity. "How serious are we talking?"

"I told him it's time to call things off and divorce." I was amazed at how calm I felt talking to Gran.

"Yes, that makes sense. I'm sure he was trying to be stoic, but I could tell he was broken up."

"His vanity was wounded, that's all." With the little emotional attachment left between us, I couldn't honestly imagine it was more. "Did he want to talk to me?"

Gran shook her head. "No, the call was very brief. He wanted to make sure you'd arrived safely. I take it you were in an emotional state when you left? I had the impression he didn't think you should be driving."

"I made it here." I sounded defensive.

"I told him that." Gran reached across the desk and patted my hand. "Out with it. What made you use the D-word? What did Sean do?" Gran liked Sean, but she loved me. And would still, even when she found out that I was the wronging party.

"It's what *I* did, Gran." The whole sordid story tumbled out. "I had a one-night stand two weeks ago in Vegas with a coworker named Rand." I sighed. "He's handsome and hot. And damn it, Gran, passionate. He paid attention. Listened to what I was saying. Made me feel sexy again." I took a deep breath and tucked a strand of hair behind my ears. "Sean's been sleeping in the guestroom for the last six months. Our marriage has deteriorated into a bad roommate situation." I stared Gran down. "Was I so wrong to want a little fun? It just happened. I didn't plan it."

"No, no one does." Gran smiled weakly and shook her head ever so slightly. "I wonder sometimes, though, if there isn't more cause to the effect?"

Gran rose slowly out of her desk chair and came to sit next to me on the sofa. "You told Sean about this Rand person yesterday? That's why you came last night instead of today?"

I nodded.

"Whatever happened to the code of the road," Gran muttered.

"You don't think Sean had a right to know?" I was defensive again. No one likes censure.

Gran gave me a seriously skeptical look. "Why did you tell Sean?" Her tone had become gentle.

"Because he shrugged."

Gran frowned, confused. "You going to explain that?"

I sighed heavily. "I came home from a horrendous day at work. I was trying to get everything cleaned up at the office before I went on vacation. There were a million little forest fires to put out. Including a rumor about Rand and me. I was furious with Rand, wondering if he'd been boasting.

"Sean was in his study, working." I rolled my eyes to emphasize the point. Sean was always working. It was his way of avoiding me and our relationship issues. A way of avoiding talking and feeling.

"I don't know," I said, remembering the situation. "He was sitting in his chair and, from the back, he looked youthful. I guess I had a flashback to the way things used to be when we were young and in love. To the way we used to comfort each other. Be each other's best friend. I needed a little support.

"So I popped into his office. He turned and looked at me. And before I could speak, he said I looked horrible. And maybe I should take an ibuprofen. I told him I wasn't sick. He shrugged. Like I was inconsequential. I exploded. And it all came tumbling out."

"You wanted to hurt him," Gran said.

I shook my head. "I...I don't know. I wanted something. A reaction. Something more than apathy."

She leaned over and kissed me on the forehead. "You'll get through this. You come from strong stock."

"There's so little left between us, Gran. I don't think it's a matter of getting though it."

"Dani—"

"You don't think I'd have slept with another man if Sean and I had any emotional intimacy left between us, do you?"

Gran sighed. "I know I hear pain in both of you, Dani. That gives me hope that you can still make the marriage work."

I ignored her comment. Okay, so we both ached, but that wasn't the same thing as coming back from where we were. Sean and I would have to be less than human not to feel some sorrow that a once beautiful thing had died. I changed the direction of the conversation. "What I'd really like to do is kill Rand. But I'd be suspect number one and I'm not up for jail time just now."

"Don't joke about that, child. Don't."

I stared back at her. "I was kidding, Gran."

"I know." But she looked pale.

"What should I do now?" I asked. Gran always had an answer.

"Let it sit awhile." Gran nodded approvingly at her own idea. "Yes, let it sit. Working on the book will keep you busy while this sorts itself out."

Sort itself out? I am not a big believer in things just sorting themselves out. It may have been my own logical bent, or maybe my engineering training, but I knew that boards and nails left alone didn't build a house. Like the second law of thermodynamics stated, things tended toward disorder.

Without either Sean or me, or both, putting some energy into our relationship, it wasn't going to get better. The hurt would just fester. Gran was a wise woman, but maybe age had caught up with her. Maybe she'd come to a point in life where inaction seemed attractive. On any account, I felt too tired and drained to argue with her. If she wanted help with her silly book, I'd help like I'd promised. That was why I'd come.

"I don't know about letting things sit, Gran. But I'm here to help with the book. Let's get that new software installed and working."

I moved around to Gran's desk chair and began loading her new programs and apps. Gran pulled a chair around, too, and sat at my elbow, watching me work.

Lucy returned home, poked her head into the study, and smiled. Then she left to bang pots and pans around in the kitchen as she made jam and pies. I gave Gran a rudimentary lesson on how to open her new software and access the help guides. She had me print out a copy of the incomplete book for myself. I insisted on putting a digital copy in the cloud, too, so I could access it from my tablet.

A few minutes later, Lucy called us to lunch.

A large white pine and an old weeping willow tree shaded the back terrace. Through the trees to the west, you could see the Spokane River Canyon. The day was hot and balmy. The weather nearly always came in from the west. Looking that direction, I watched billowing thunderheads stacking up. It looked like we wouldn't be eating dinner outside.

I'd always loved eating on the terrace. Gran had an old wrought iron table and matching chairs that had undergone numerous iterations of new cushions. Lucy came out with a tray of sandwiches she'd picked up at the deli of the local grocery store and a large pitcher of iced tea.

"Help yourself." Gran reached across to pat my hand. "You know, Dani, you really are a computer genius. You've saved us weeks, maybe months of frustration in just a few hours."

She exaggerated, but what the heck? I could use a little praise. I smiled back at her and reached for a sandwich. Lucy remembered my favorite, a nice spicy Italian combo. Lucy and Gran bantered on, singing my praises, talking of the splendid, abnormally sweet and large strawberries this year. I sat silent. I guess they realized that I wasn't up to conversation. When I was upset, or ill, I retreated into myself. Gran knew that.

Lucy passed around a bowl of sour cream and onion potato chips. I took a few to be polite. Though usually a weakness of mine, today they didn't tempt me. I bit into one anyway, tasting only grease. Hormones always affected my taste buds, making them ultrasensitive. My stomach rolled. I took a bite of sandwich, but could taste the plastic wrap it had come in.

Reflexively, I glanced at my watch—a silly gesture considering it didn't have a date feature. I counted back in my mind. Yup, just as I suspected from this onset of symptoms, thirty-four days since my last curse.

Okay, it may not be politically correct to call a menstrual cycle a curse. But that was exactly what it was to me. For the last ten years, the onset of the flow each month put me into a mild depression. I was a failure, unable to do the most natural thing in the world—conceive. Even though I had logically given up, my emotional side still mourned each month.

Worse perhaps than the painful cramps I suffered, which would be eased, so my friends said, by bearing a child, was the way my body taunted me. During my teens and early twenties my periods had been regular and predictable. But once I decided to try to have a child, my body became a great, sadistic comedian. Many months, in many variations and differing intensities, I get all the symptoms of pregnancy—enlarged, tender breasts, nausea, extreme tiredness, you name it.

And while once I had a regular, predictable thirty-two day cycle, now I was often late by as much as ten to fifteen days. During those first hopeful months and years, I discovered that taking a pregnancy test and learning of the negative result could bring the flow on within hours. So was it my mind or my body that betrayed me? All I knew was that I didn't consciously will such deceit. I grumbled to myself. I was already two days late. I hoped this didn't continue. I was in no mood to run to the pharmacy for a pregnancy test.

"Dani, are you feeling all right?" Lucy asked.

No, quite possibly I'd never feel right again. But I didn't say that. "I'm fine."

"You look a little peaked," Gran added. "And you've barely touched your lunch."

I shrugged. "I'm just not very hungry today."

The two exchanged a "poor darling" kind of look, probably attributing my poor appetite to my problems. Lucy stood and cleared the dishes. Gran rose almost in unison.

"You look tired, dear. Perhaps you should rest this afternoon." She shook her head knowingly. "Let me just get you that printout of our manuscript. You can sit out here and read. That shouldn't be too strenuous."

She laughed at herself. "Not if we've done a passable job with the writing." She patted my knee as she walked past. "If you get too tired, you can put it down and nap awhile. We really need your sharp mind to help us piece the whole thing together. Reading what we have will get you started."

Ten minutes later I was settled into a reclining lawn chair with Gran's boxed manuscript on my lap, even though I would have preferred to read on my tablet. Gran insisted paper was better on the eyes. Lucy and Gran had both ambled off to their own rooms to nap and escape the heat of the day. I felt tired; maybe I should have slept. But I had to admit to a certain amount of curiosity about Gran's book. Reading it beat stewing on my problems. So I opened the box, pulled out a loose sheet, and began to read.

By morning the nightmarish white world had disappeared, replaced by the strong presence of sun and clear blue overhead. Mariah felt elated, victorious as the three of them rode Molly's rented mare into Murray. Between them, they had cheated death. Lizzie would join her father. Mariah would make her fortune. And Molly, well, she'd do whatever it was she did. She seemed capable of anything.

Molly rode in front, carrying the thumb-sucking Lizzie. Mariah took up the rear. She peeked around Molly to get a view of the forming crowd. Mariah glimpsed one or two members of their party. Hypocrites and cowards! Eagerly awaiting their arrival as if she and Molly were royalty. Only yesterday not one would help. She resisted the urge to spit on them, wondering if they'd placed bets on the odds of them making it to town, and which side had been favored.

Molly urged the horse into a high-stepping canter and sat up, straight-backed and regal. Mariah would have stopped before getting to the heart of the crush. But Molly rode right down Main Street to the thick of the mostly male throng, waving and nodding, cooing to the men, obviously enjoying the spectacle she made.

A welcoming committee greeted them, led by a rollicking young Irishman. He tipped his hat to them with a jaunty air that matched Molly's. "Phil O'Rourke at your service, ladies." He spoke in a heavy, lilting brogue, and seemed for all the world a happy-go-lucky sort, and handsome, too, with merry, dancing eyes. Mariah would have appreciated his attentions, but to her disappointment, he focused them on Molly.

"Is this all the women? Is there no one else?" A male voice punctuated the murmur of the crowd, interrupting Phil's speech. The depth of passion and pain in the timbre of his words silenced the masses. The crowd around him parted, exposing him to view. He came forward toward the horse slowly, his features laced tautly with apprehension.

"My Samille, my wife, was supposed to be with this here party. Did you happen to meet her and my baby girl on the trail?" His voice wavered. Up close, he looked much younger than Mariah had imagined, no more than twenty-one or two. He was plain-featured and thin, in want of grooming and new clothes. The breeze tossed his unkempt brown hair over his eyes. He didn't bother to brush it aside. But somewhere in his simple features, the jut of his chin, the shape of his face, Mariah saw a resemblance to little Lizzie.

Molly turned around to look at Mariah over her shoulder, her clear blue eyes filled with sympathy. "Lizzie's father?"

Mariah forced a solemn nod, at a loss as to what she should say to the anxious young man before them. Molly turned around again. Mariah peeked around her shoulder to see Molly stroke Lizzie's fine baby hair with a soft, motherly touch. "I'm sorry, sir, but we bring you only one girl. You have our deepest sympathy." Molly spoke softly, resting her hand on the child's head.

He stared at Lizzie, appearing to see her for the first time. His mouth moved, but nothing came out as he appeared to search for words. When they came, they came slowly. "She can be no other's but my Samille's. Her eyes. Her chin." His voice cracked. "Oh, Samille!"

"And you must be...?" Molly asked.

"Michael Brayhorst." In answering her question, he regained some composure, but tears stood in his eyes.

"'Tis the name her mother gave me," Mariah whispered into Molly's ear.

"I'd like to hold my daughter." Brayhorst reached for his girl.

As Mariah grabbed Lizzie's small bundle from behind her, in preparation for passing it down, her heart squeezed into a tight knot and a lump filled her throat. Poor man, poor child! She was loath to part with little Lizzie, wanting reassurance that she would be well cared for. It was only a small solace that Samille had always praised her man as being kind.

Brayhorst seemed to realize that Mariah had the information he wanted, and addressed her directly. "Her mother?"

Mariah cast her eyes down, unable to meet his, and shook her head. "Buried in Montana. A fever took her a little over a week ago."

"So close," he whispered, clutching Lizzie and her bundle to him. The child did not fight his embrace, though he must have been nearly a stranger to her.

Brayhorst nodded, seeming to suddenly remember the crowd around him. "Thank you, for Lizzie."

Then he turned and walked away with his child cradled in his arms through the aisle the crowd created for him, a solitary man taking steps heavy with grief. For just an instant before the crowd swallowed him up, the sun reflected off his brown hair, illuminating soft red highlights, silhouetting him against the others, marking his loneliness.

Molly touched Mariah's arm. "You did the right thing, lass. The child needs her father, and he her. Being the bearer of bad news is never easy or pleasant. You can't help what happened to her mother, but you saved Lizzie. You're braver than any man here. You should be proud."

The rest of the crowd, however, seemed little affected by this singular tragedy. As soon as Brayhorst departed, upstretched arms extended toward her and Molly, eager to offer assistance in dismounting. Molly simply ignored them, sat on her horse, and looked out over the town. Mariah pictured Molly with a small, self-satisfied smile toying with her lips and her gorgeous blue eyes wide as she appraised Phil O'Rourke.

Mariah admired Molly's confident, perusing manner. In her presence, Mariah felt young and inexperienced.

"And who might you be, me pretty colleen?" Phil stood his ground, but he seemed affected by her gaze. How could Molly force a man to lose his heart with just a look?

"I am Molly Burdan." Calm, seductive, unequivocal.

"Well now, for the life of me, I'd never have thought it, Molly b'Dam." He spoke loudly, clearly intent on entertaining the growing crowd. "I ask you, isn't that a terrible name for such a fine lady as yourself? Molly b'Dam."

Molly laughed and, not to be outdone, continued the jest. "What's further," she mimicked, "I'll be as Irish as ye, so don't be having ideas ye'll get the laugh at me expense without getting back better than ye give."

The crowd roared.

"And this lovely young woman," Molly continued, "is Mariah."

"Ah, now, blonde hair, blue eyes, and just as lovely as you. Might she be your sister?" Phil's look darted between the two of them.

Molly laughed again. "My friend."

"I see. And may I be so bold as to inquire what brings so fair a pair of ladies as yourselves into this den of iniquity?"

Mariah remained mute. Molly commanded all the attention now, and Mariah was happy she did. Would these rough men believe that Mariah intended to pan for gold and make a fortune for herself? Would they scoff at her dreams? If a man could do it, why not she? She was as tired of poverty as anyone. She intended to be rich.

No one back home believed her capable of it. How would she defend herself among the cutthroats and cheats that populated the gold rush states? Why not marry a local boy? She had the beauty to catch a fine one. But not, Mariah thought, one well enough off to suit her. And she had no intention of scratching out a living and bringing a babe into the world every other year.

Molly stared intently into the twinkling eyes of Phil O'Rourke. "I," she said without a moment of hesitation or embarrassment, "am moving into Cabin Number One."

Mariah felt the shock ripple through the crowd, and, in her innocence, didn't understand the sensation until she heard the mutterings of those nearest her.

"A madam? That pretty gal is a madam?"

"She must be. She wants the first cabin in the red light row, the madam's cabin."

A *madam*, Mariah thought, trying to contain her shock. No wonder Molly understood how to appeal to men so well.

"Well, I'll be!" Phil O'Rourke seemed to speak for everyone.

Molly smiled into the crowd and nodded. "Now, my friend and I are tired. Find her a good cabin, and take her some good food. Bring the bill to me."

The eyes of the crowd turned to Mariah. She nodded and smiled at the inquiring looks she received. No doubt they thought her a whore, too. Many wore salacious looks. They'd find out soon enough that tumbling around a bed with sweaty, foul-smelling gold seekers was not what she had in mind to do in gold country.

"Help me down, please." Molly directed the attention back to herself with her command. Half a dozen men vied for the pleasure, but Mr. O'Rourke beat them all out. The man was smitten.

I looked up from my reading to watch a stray hawk arc lazily above me, riding a thermal that preceded the impending storm. I was named for that whore, Molly b'Dam, as was at least one woman in every generation of my family. Few people knew it. I certainly didn't advertise it. My real name was Molly Burdan McKenzie.

I smiled to myself. I guess I was a bit like my famous ancestor, a little rebellious. Contrary to family tradition, I insisted on being called Burdan, and I'm sure my mother, at least, thought I was indeed. Gran didn't think the name fit, and nicknamed me Dani.

Having a Molly in each generation would have led to some confusion, if not for my family's clever convention. Molly's original name, as Gran had told me, was Maggie Hall. Later she married Mr. Burdan, who thought Maggie an undignified name and insisted on calling her Molly. So although we were all given the name Molly, one generation was called Molly and the next Maggie. I should have been called Maggie, like Gran. My mother went by Molly. I sighed, wistful and hopeless. The legacy stopped with barren me. I wasn't likely to have a daughter.

I wanted to keep reading, but a wave of tiredness washed over me. I had no desire to fight it. I put the pages back in the manuscript box and stood, intent on going upstairs to nap. When I woke up, I'd have to plan my strategy for dealing with the mess I called my life.

In my room, I cautiously checked my phone before I napped. I had a text from Sean.

Do you really want a divorce?

CHAPTER THREE

I stared at my phone screen, shaking with raw emotion. The truth was, that "really" stunned me more than all the rest of Sean's simple, blunt statement. Why? Because it was so Sean. It was so us. My mind drifted back to the first months and years of our marriage, back when we were very much in love.

We married Labor Day Weekend at the start of our senior year in college and started classes the following week. Both of us were electrical engineering majors. We had all but one class together. We spent twenty-three hours a day with each other. *Twenty-three.* Any decent marriage counselor, any good friend or old sage would have advised us against so much togetherness. Every couple needs a little time apart. I felt stifled, smothered.

I loved Sean madly, which made my feelings traitor-ous. It's why, when I think back, I never took his last name. I wanted to retain something of Dani, some sepa-rate identity. Sean was never happy with my choice.

The realization startled me, all these years later. I had let a unique set of circumstances settle us into a pattern that separated us for our entire marriage. Keeping a maiden name serves many women well. I just didn't do it for the right reasons.

But back then, with so many shared experiences, we had nothing to talk about, no new anecdotes to relate, nothing. Living in a microscopic apartment with no personal space and spending so much time together, it was not surprising we got on each other's nerves. Our first fight was horrendous. Funny that I couldn't re-member what it was about now. Probably over some-thing silly and insignificant. What I do remember is running out of our apartment into the pouring rain without so much as a coat.

Sean followed me. I ignored him as he came up be-hind me and flung my coat over my shoulders. My tears mingled with the rain.

"I want a divorce," I said. And in that unhappy mo-ment, I meant it.

"Oh, baby, no. I love you."

I nodded and slowed my pace. I turned to face him. He'd jammed his hands into the pockets of his jeans and stood there with his hands balled, feeling impotent, I imagine now, and hurting. Rain soaked his shirt. He hadn't grabbed his own coat. Rain beaded in his hair and clumped in his lashes. He stood there trembling, his face reflecting fear. I could see it all now as if it were yesterday, feeling the poignancy of that moment wash over me.

"Do you really?" Sean asked.

I threw myself into his arms, suddenly repentant. "No, no, no!" I sobbed into his already wet shirt as he hugged me close. "I *love* you."

We had many more fights over things big and small those first years. To my shame, I threatened divorce another time or two and Sean always asked the same question: "Really?"

Over time we settled into domestic complacency, and though we still fought on occasion, I didn't threaten anymore. Our married life appeared more stable, but had it been? Maybe the passion was just gone, replaced by a sinister apathy, a tenuous calm, a restlessness I couldn't overcome. Some lucky people settle happily into the security of a strong and stable love, but had we? Or had we merely settled?

I couldn't help yearning for those days when the pendulum of emotion swung high and wide. In retrospect, the peaks seemed worth all the valleys life threw at us.

At that moment, I wished I could have seen how Sean looked when he'd typed that message. Had he hunched over the phone, defeated and worried? Had tears stood in his eyes as they had all those years ago? Was he reaching out, remembering the young us? Did he realize how serious I was this time?

Or was he the cold, unfeeling bastard he'd become in recent years? Impenetrable. Withdrawn. Unfeeling.

A man I could no longer hurt or comfort? A man who only needed an answer so he could plan his future and organize his life?

I wished, how I wished, I knew what that "really" staring back at me from the screen meant. Maybe then I'd know how to answer. But for now, I couldn't. I just couldn't.

I put my phone away and curled up to sleep. I napped restlessly until Lucy called me to dinner.

We ate a casual supper in the kitchen. Outside, thunderclouds oppressed the sky, continuing to build for their imminent attack on us. The air sat still, heavy and hot, and too calm. I felt sticky and moist. Even perpetually cold Gran used her linen napkin to wipe away tiny beads of perspiration dotting her forehead.

We dined on cold chicken salad and slices of cantaloupe. I found myself picking at my food. Something gnawed at my stomach, but whether it was hunger or nausea, fear or despair, I couldn't tell.

The heat exaggerated my PMS symptoms. My stomach rebelled at the sight of the mayonnaise-rich salad. I ate the melon and picked at a dry roll, no butter, and felt somewhat better.

Gran shook her finger at the sky out the window. "Oh, these nasty thunderstorms. I wish nature would just get to her business, do her damage. It'll be much cooler when the rain comes."

Lucy nodded in agreement.

Yeah, I'd be much more comfortable if nature would get to her business with me, too.

I thought of my parents sitting down to dinner in the mansion on the north side of town. "I don't imagine Dad agrees with you, Gran."

Dad was chief executive officer of East State Water Power, the predominant power company in the area. When I was a child, when he'd been manager of line office operations, a storm meant he'd be called out to supervise power line repairs and direct crews. Now it only meant losing from his bottom line. Too many big storms and his bonus would be cut.

"Oh, your dad doesn't have to go out in these blasted storms anymore, Dani," Gran said. "So I don't worry. We'll have to call your mother tomorrow. The storm gives us an excuse for not calling sooner." Gran set her napkin down.

"And Dad. I'll have to call him and Reed tomorrow."

"No damage done in spending an idle day with your gran. How do you like our book so far, Dani?" She sounded casual enough, but she perched birdlike on her chair, eager for my appreciation and compliments.

"Very engrossing." I wrapped my hands around my cool water glass, wishing I could splash it over my face.

Gran's smile spread quickly across her face, and the flush of heat already coloring her cheeks grew deeper with pleasure.

"But I have a question—why tell the story from Mariah's perspective? Isn't the real story we want Molly's? As our ancestor, shouldn't she be the focus?"

Gran's initial surprise turned quickly to amusement. "Didn't you listen to the stories I told you when you were young? Molly was a prostitute. She died childless.

We aren't related to her!" A trace of indignation laced Gran's voice.

Now I was confused. "But we *are* named for her?"

"Oh, certainly. But we're Mariah's descendants."

That explained Gran's manuscript, but it opened another book of questions in my mind. And though it hadn't been Gran's direct intent, it further piqued my interest in her little story. "Mariah's?"

Lucy got up to clear the dishes and serve dessert.

Gran nodded. "How far have you gotten?"

"They've just arrived in Murray."

"Oh dear." She looked crestfallen. "You haven't gotten far."

"I'm sorry. I napped most of the afternoon. I don't know why I'm so tired."

Gran frowned. I wasn't usually the type to nap at all. "I hope it's not depression," she said mildly. I shrugged and she changed the subject. "You aren't anywhere near the part that's got us stumped."

As Lucy served strawberry pie piled high with freshly whipped cream, I promised to read more immediately after dinner. The first thunderclap sounded as I helped Lucy with the last of the dishes. Gran handed me a flashlight as I headed upstairs.

"We'll probably lose power before this storm is done with us. We usually do." She sighed. "You may need this to read by. It's got fresh batteries. They should be good for several hours. One of these days I'm going to talk to your dad about getting a backup generator."

Though the sun still hung in the sky, the storm reduced the light to twilight. I had to turn on the lamp in my bedroom to read. By the time I settled in, the storm had turned into a real banger. I picked up a page of the manuscript and stared blindly at it. My thoughts kept returning to Sean. What I wouldn't give to return to those early days when passion ran high.

And Rand, the bastard. What was I going to do about him? He'd been so seductive, so attractive. And I'd been so lonely. He'd put the moves on me and pushed so hard that, thinking of it now, I saw how intentional it had been. The power of hindsight. I felt my anger rising again and turned to Gran's book for diversion.

As the crowd began to disperse, Mariah, assisted by Phil O'Rourke, slid from the horse and surveyed the town. Murray was new and hastily built in the middle of a white pine forest, a collection of a few wooden buildings, mostly saloons and stores, surrounded by a sea of tents housing thousands of men. The streets were rutted mud; the boardwalks dirty. The women populating it few. The men rough, mostly unshaven, wearing flannel and denim in abundance and fur coats and pelts of all sorts. A little creek ran right down the middle of town separating the barely respectable from a row of small cabins off to themselves on the other side.

"I think we can settle Miss Mariah into a fine little cabin just across Placer Creek from Gold Street. You'll be well enough able to keep an eye on her there," Phil said to Molly, who'd already set him straight that Mariah was not in the profession. He pointed to the small row of cabins on the opposite side of the creek. "There's your kingdom, Miss b'Dam. Gold Street."

An entourage of men followed them, hauling the ladies' bags. They deposited Mariah in a one-room cabin exactly where Phil promised. She stood in the middle of it, assessing her new home. She saw no sunlight peeking through the roof or evidence of water damage to the floor. She assumed the roof must be reliable. Though dirty, the windows held real glass. A wood stove stood in one corner, a bed against another wall. A table, two chairs, a wardrobe, a cupboard, and a nightstand completed the furnishings.

One of the men was already working on starting a fire.

"A miner lived here up till a month ago. Then he just gave up and left," Phil said.

"Rest assured that I won't be quitting, Mr. O'Rourke. I don't mean to leave this valley until I'm rich." Mariah gave him her best smile.

He laughed. "Don't be making promises you can't likely keep. This is rough country, lass. But all the same, I'll be wishing you success."

Molly bid her goodbye. "I'll be back to see you when we've both settled in."

Phil promised to send over food and cleaning supplies and then they left her alone. It wasn't much later that a knock on the door interrupted Mariah's unpacking and tidying up. Eager for her supplies, she threw the door open. To her great surprise, Lizzie's father, Michael, stood outside, with Lizzie in his arms.

"Might I come in, ma'am?" Although he spoke calmly, an overtone of desperation tinged his voice. Dark circles rimmed his red eyes. Could have been from drinking, but Mariah smelled no alcohol on his breath and had the sense that he'd been crying.

"Please." She stood aside to let him pass. "Have a seat. I can't offer you anything yet. My supplies haven't come."

He didn't sit, but stood with little Lizzie clinging to him.

"I expected you'd come sooner or later." Mariah felt uncomfortable in his silence. "You want to know about Samille, of course. I can't tell you much. But put your mind at ease. Samille didn't suffer long. The fever took her quick.

"She's buried in Montana. I drew a map to her grave." A lump swelled in Mariah's throat. "She made me promise to give it to you when I brought Lizzie to her papa. It's in the bundle I gave you. Did you find it?"

He nodded mutely, looking as forlorn and beaten as a man could. She touched his arm and said in a bare whisper, "I'm sorry."

He still didn't speak. She dropped her hand.

"I come on other business," he said at last. "To thank you."

He seemed extremely uncomfortable, though Mariah couldn't say why.

"No need."

"No, there is. And, well, this is hard, but..." He looked at the floor. His words tumbled out in rapid succession. "I've come to ask you something. Lizzie needs a ma. I can't watch her while I'm working the claim. She knows you and you seem to care about her. I guess I'm asking you to marry me."

Stunned, Mariah stared at the young man before her. Compassion for them all tore at her, but it didn't compel her to marry a stranger. Still, she felt selfish for the refusal she had to give. "I'm sorry, but I can't."

He blushed and nodded. "It was worth a shot. Guess now I'll have to up and sell the claim and take Lizzie to my ma in Oregon Territory." He grabbed Mariah's hand and dropped a small leather pouch into it. "For your trouble." He turned and left without another word.

When Mariah peeked in, she found a stash of gold nuggets. She couldn't take this man's fortune, but his sense of honor and the worth of his daughter touched her. She caught him as he turned onto the street. As she grabbed his hand and forced the pouch back into it, she said, "Keep this"—her voice broke—"as my gift for Lizzie. Treat her well."

He nodded and walked away with Lizzie. The picture they made broke Mariah's heart. She pushed it away with golden dreams, vowing to get herself a claim straight away.

First thing the next morning, she made good on the promise she'd made herself and went to the land clerk's office.

"Sorry, miss," the clerk said. "Ain't no claims anywhere close enough by to be safe for a lady. Ain't hardly no claims left at all. You might buy yourself a claim from someone. But lately, they ain't been going cheap."

She left the office dejected. She hadn't expected such a setback. The newspapers back home had been so full of stories of the Idaho gold rush that she'd been certain of success. She remembered Lizzie's father then. She didn't have much cash, but if he meant to sell, maybe she could buy him out, or suggest a partnership, work something out to make both their dreams come true. But she was too late. He'd already sold out and gone. Mariah never saw him or Lizzie again.

Mariah cataloged her first few days in Murray in a journal. Saturday she went to Molly's for a visit and advice, then took a walk, and ran some errands, arriving home in the late afternoon to find a line of men forming at her front door. Righteousness anger girding her, she lashed out: "What's the meaning of this? Gold Street is across Placer Creek. I've none of it."

To a man, they blushed, and stared at their feet mumbling. Finally, one brave soul spoke up: "Oh, no, ma'am, we didn't think... It's just we're here courting, hoping you might choose one of us to dine with, have some conversation."

She frowned. What good would it do to alienate these men? "I won't be seeing any suitors until I'm properly settled in. Please excuse me." She pushed past them into her cabin.

"Ma'am," one called after her, "you'll let us know when that is?"

She slammed the door and threw herself on her bed in disgust.

On Sunday, a loud knock on the door woke her early.

"I know you're in there, Mariah. Get up and get yourself dressed. We're going to church, you and me." Molly's voice carried through the door. She had a soft way of speaking, but she was always heard.

Mariah slid out of bed. What did Molly mean? They were going to church? The last week had taught Mariah that Molly, though kind and gentle, was eccentric, but this? What church let prostitutes worship? To silence the knocking, Mariah unlatched the door and let Molly in.

Molly wore a modest high-necked dress, a hat, and gloves, and, excepting her bewitching beauty and the devilish twinkle in her eyes, looked entirely respectable. She went immediately to the small, knotty wardrobe in the corner and swung the doors wide open. "Let's see what you have that will be suitable." She tossed Mariah her corset. "I'll lace you in. Oh, dear," Molly said, fingering Mariah's few worn gowns. "You haven't much to choose from, have you? First up the coming week, we'll get you a suitable Sunday dress." Molly picked the least worn gown from the hook, and, shaking her head, tossed it to Mariah. "We'll see if we can find a dressmaker tomorrow. There must be one in town. Next Sunday I want you in nothing so shabby."

"I can't afford a dressmaker."

Molly laughed. "Fortunately, I can. You must show more optimism, my future rich friend. 'I can't afford one *yet*,' you should say. You've got to pick yourself up, lass. Are you giving up already? I guess your bold words to Phil our first day here meant nothing."

Mariah grumbled. "I'm not giving up. Molly. You sure about going to church?" She paused, uncertain how to put what she had to say without offending Molly. "No one will be expecting us to go."

Molly's response caught Mariah short. "No one but God." For the first time, Molly's smile looked sad. "You don't go to please people, or let them scare you away from your duty to God." She laughed self-deprecatingly. "I know there's those who believe differently, given what I do for a living, Mariah, but I still have a soul and it needs feeding. You do, too. Now turn around and let me lace you."

Mariah did as commanded. "But people can be mighty harsh." Mariah dreaded facing the righteous indignation of the churchgoers.

Molly shrugged. "The Lord Jesus walked among the prostitutes of his day—what can people say to turn us away? We have as much right to worship as anyone."

Mariah gasped as Molly gave an extra-hard tug on the corset strings, suspecting Molly did it to prevent Mariah from asking the question on her lips. Just how had Molly, who seemed educated and certainly had class, come to this?

"When properly cinched, you've got a nice, tiny waist, Mariah. It's a fine asset."

Mariah turned around.

Molly was still smiling. "You don't have to fear church people."

Mariah couldn't hide her skepticism.

"For all have sinned and come short of the glory of God." Molly nodded to herself. "They've nothing on us."

A scripture-quoting madam bent on going to church—if that wasn't the last thing Mariah, in her limited life experience, thought she'd meet. As soon as she finished dressing, Molly herded Mariah outside to the street, where a double-file line of the Gold Street girls waited.

It surprised Mariah how easily the prostitutes all accepted Molly's leadership. Molly had explained that the whore business in town had been in disarray. The girls were at the mercy of the miners and, with no leadership, resorted to bickering among themselves. The women were grateful that someone had come along to organize things. And, Molly added, everyone likes a little mothering now and again, someone to take care of them. The ladies were no exception.

Once Mariah got in line, Molly marched them straight past the stares of the previous night's customers to the tiny Methodist church. Minutes later Molly, her girls, and Mariah sat quietly on a bench in the back of the church.

The Catholic Mariah squirmed, uncomfortable in the Protestant domain, surrounded by whores. Mariah had seen Molly cross herself the night Molly rescued her, a certain sign of a Catholic upbringing. Why hadn't Molly taken them to the Catholic mission? They'd turned into the tiny chapel so quickly that Mariah hadn't had time to protest or question Molly about it.

Once inside, the ladies attracted more than their share of stares, but Molly sat head high, apparently unaware of the commotion she caused. She turned, and, merriment dancing in her eyes, spoke softly into Mariah's ear. "This ought to set you up respectably in town. And think of it—that line of suitors filling your front yard will certainly know now to behave themselves around you, a woman with morals."

When the collection plate came past, Molly slipped a twenty-dollar gold piece in. Mariah gawked and passed the plate on without tossing in even two bits of her own. Ten percent of nothing was exactly that—nothing. Until God saw fit to bless her with some earnings, she saw no reason to give back to him. Molly frowned at her.

When the service ended, the minister came directly to them. He spoke in a clear voice that carried nicely and obviously through the silent room. "We are pleased that you are with us. You are always welcome in this house of worship." Then he left to stand at the door and wish his congregation a good and fruitful week.

Molly paused as she stopped to shake the pastor's hand. "Very nice sermon, reverend."

He thanked her, seemingly pleased by her compliment.

"You've picked quite a flock to shepherd." Molly's smile was always stunning. She spoke in a soft voice, her burr barely evident. "Nothing like living in Gomorrah."

The pastor took no apparent affront at her statement, seeming amused instead. "Where else would a good man choose? Didn't the Lord himself pick just such men as these to reach? What use have the righteous of my services?" His words were not barbed; rather, the two of them sparred.

"You think redemption possible for anyone, then?" Molly turned suddenly serious.

Mariah watched, mute. She heard the trace of melancholy in Molly's voice.

The pastor considered a moment. Evidently, he wasn't a man with a pat answer or scripture for everything. "I do, indeed. The Lord knows a person's circumstance and heart and the reasons they do what they do. He knows when they're trapped."

Mariah watched him give Molly's hand a little squeeze and release it.

"You, Miss Molly, are the one who must believe. If you believe in a God who is creator of everything, with infinite wisdom and power, how could you not believe that he has the power to forgive?"

He made a good point. Judging from the look on her face, Molly thought he did, too.

"A further thought," he said. "God gave man the power to forgive. Don't forget to exercise that power, Miss Molly."

She nodded, but Mariah could see that she doubted. Mariah had lost track of what he meant anyway. Who had Molly to forgive? Maybe someone who had wounded her in the past?

"I hope you will come back and visit us again," he said.

Molly started to move on. "We will, sir."

And she kept her promise. As long as Molly reigned as madam, she insisted they attend church every Sunday. Though Mariah protested, the next week Molly bought her several elegant dresses for Sundays. Molly, her girls, and Mariah made a spectacle week after week, turned out for church in the height of respectable fashion.

They visited each Protestant church in town in turn and were welcomed in every one and encouraged to return, which they did on a rotating basis. It got so that Mariah needed a calendar to know which church they would visit any given Lord's Day. But they never went to the Catholic mission.

When Mariah finally got the nerve to ask Molly about it, she replied, "They excommunicated me years ago. There's nothing for me there."

CHAPTER FOUR

Mariah had very little cash left from her trip west. She realized now that she'd been foolish to believe making a fortune would be easy. Molly had been generous, stocking Mariah's cupboards with enough supplies for weeks, but she couldn't continue living on Molly's charity. She needed a job, but dreaded the options open to her—take in washing or cooking. She could have done that and lived in poverty back home. She went to Molly for advice.

"You're too late to make your fortune mining gold," Molly said.

They sat in Molly's comfortable cabin. Molly wore a robe of the palest pink satin. Mariah had never seen such fine quality before. Molly wasn't an early riser, but she welcomed Mariah's intrusion cordially enough.

"My being here should be your first clue. I follow when the wealth flows, not before. By the time I arrive, there's very little gold still to be found. But there's other ways to get a share of the money. Lonely men can always use the services of a clever woman."

Mariah snorted. "Like cooking and cleaning? I've thought of that already. But what's the good of it? I'd work myself to death and still be poor as ever."

Molly nodded her approval. "Yes, exactly so. Smart girl. I wasn't talking about anything so mundane. My girls make good money. Had you the inclination, you could make your fortune like they do."

Mariah shook her head.

Molly laughed. "I've never led a woman down the path to prostitution, and I don't intend to now. But I'm not going to let you harbor false hopes. Every foot of this country for miles around in every direction has been thoroughly prospected. Even if you should lay your hands on a claim, it'd be worthless. And you've already rejected a woman's most respectable means of surviving."

"But I want to be rich, Molly," Mariah protested.

"Then catch yourself a rich man, dear." Molly winked at her. "A patron or a husband, whichever suits you best. In the end, either may be the same."

Mariah frowned at Molly's cynical view of men and marriage. "I don't want either one! First, I want my own money, freedom. Then I can marry by choice, purely for love, or not marry at all." Mariah sighed. "Besides, there isn't a man I've met that I'd consider marrying."

"Then you've got to find one. If I were you, and this is only the advice of a friend, I would ask Jacob Goetz for a job in his saloon. It's plush. It's busy. And it's where all the men go to spend their pokes of gold and gamble. A clever girl could watch, figure out who had the real cash, and make her move." Molly nodded.

"I don't want just any man, Molly. I want to be in love."

Molly's laugh sounded harsh. "Don't we all! But we usually don't get both love *and* wealth. In the end, wealth might be the greater comfort. Love too often carries a bite. Wealth, properly managed, can see you set for life." Molly sounded wistful.

Mariah felt inexplicably sorry for her. What had wealth done for Molly? She had plenty of money and yet still wasn't happy. Some fellow had tied a lock around Molly's heart, hardened her until no man's attentions could penetrate it. Phil O'Rourke tried hard enough, flirting with Molly at every opportunity. Molly seemed to enjoy it, but anyone could see that while Phil could easily give his heart, Molly held herself aloof. Poor Molly. Poor Phil.

"Anyway," Molly continued, "working at Jake's would keep you in shoe leather. A resourceful hurdy can make good money. I've known my share who have done quite well. Jake needs himself a hurdy-girl, someone to dance with the men, have a drink with them, offer them a little attention and conversation between card games. You ought to be able to get fifty cents per dance."

"Just for dancing?" *There has to be more to it*, Mariah thought.

"My! You are suspicious. Yes, just for dancing." Molly shrugged. "Of course, if you wanted to add to your income, you could take them upstairs for a little more personal fun. But it's not required."

"Don't bait me, Molly. It sounds too easy. Why, five or six dances and a girl would make as much as a man back home made in a whole day of laboring in the fields or mines!"

"Indeed! And now, my little lassie, you're learning all about business, supply and demand. And how to be clever. Women out here are in short supply. Men are lonely. Shortage of supply makes for a high price. You've got a commodity that they want, and beauty on top. Don't waste it."

"Doesn't sound respectable."

"Oh, it's respectable enough. Hurdy-girls stand a good chance of marrying well and living happily in the community. I've seen it happen many a time, or I wouldn't have suggested it. That's what you want, isn't it? All you have to do is dance with those lonely men. That's all." Molly's eyes sparkled. Mariah could tell that she thought she'd come up with the perfect solution to Mariah's troubles.

Mariah frowned. "I don't dance well."

Molly waved down her protests. "Oh, that's nothing. I'll teach you to dance. The girls will help." Molly smiled and nodded to herself. "This is the perfect thing, believe me. I've known girls up and down the circuits I've traveled that make a good living being hurdies. You won't get rich, but if you don't get greedy, you'll never have to go to the back room with a man—unless you want to." Molly paused, lost in thought. "You'll need some dancing dresses. Maybe Jake will go in half on those."

Molly—and thoughts of chapped hands, a back stiff from bending over a washboard, being used up and looking old and haggard from too much hard work, or going hungry or moving on—convinced her. Within a week, Mariah found herself dressed in indecent ankle-length dresses, firmly established as Jake's hurdy-girl in his plush saloon and gambling hall.

She danced for free, but the men had to buy her a drink afterward. Jake charged them a dollar a drink and split it down the middle with Mariah. She made fifty cents, just like Molly predicted. The men got real alcohol. Mariah got cold tea, which she quickly learned to hate.

Mariah became an expert at small talk and banter. She mastered a few other things, too—how to clean perspiration stains out of the sash of her dress where the miners rested their sweaty palms during a dance, how to soothe sore feet, how to fend off advances and turn down marriage proposals. Fortunately, Jake employed a hefty bouncer to keep the peace. Mariah never had any real trouble. Also, as Molly had said, Mariah made decent money, enough so that she could be extremely particular about choosing a man. On a good night she could net twenty-five dollars. As her bank account grew, she became increasingly finicky.

Mariah saw too many men with all their faults exposed. Drunkenness turned some men mean, others foolish. She wanted a temperate man, one moderate in all his undertakings, except pulling gold out of the mountain. On that score she wanted heaps of hard work, enthusiasm, and skill.

Placer mining wasn't what Mariah had pictured. When she'd set out from the Midwest for the gold country, she imagined men kneeling by placid streams, swirling water in pans, gold nuggets glinting in the sun. That may have been how a few found their gold, but not the majority. Placer mining used the most modern technology available—pumps and water pressure. Sophisticated and well-equipped miners rigged pumps to push ground and stream water with terrific force through hoses. Then they took aim and literally washed the mountains down. The eroded dirt and rocks were washed into a sluice box and dredged for gold. They dumped the tailings, the dirt and rocks left after the gold had been removed, outside of town.

The landscape surrounding the town had changed dramatically since the gold rush began. The valley below quickly filled with unstable tailings. The hiss of rushing water and the hum of hardworking pumps filled the air daily. The sounds provided a reassuring background noise—as long as it existed, Murray and her people prospered.

Phil O'Rourke frequented Dutch Jake's on a regular basis. Phil wasn't a miner. He preferred cards and gaming to working a claim, often boasting loudly that the odds of becoming rich doing either seemed about

the same. He'd rather have fun and face off against Lady Luck than meet the mountain. He was gaming one
day while Mariah worked. In a worthless win, he took a
claim as his prize. Mariah, knowing Phil as she did, saw
the opportunity she'd been waiting for. She approached
him and offered to buy it.

"Why'd you want it, lass?" Phil said. "It's nothing
but an eroded, overworked patch of land. It isn't good
for farming or planting, or homesteading."

"I don't care." Mariah wanted that claim. But she
couldn't let Phil see how much. "If it's so worthless
you'll part with it cheap."

"I'll part with it for the price of a good shot of whiskey and a trot around the dance floor with you, lass."
His always-merry eyes twinkled as he spoke.

"Done." Mariah met his look with an elated one of
her own. "Pour the man a drink, Jake." She looked toward the pianist. "Play us a good tune, professor—
whatever Mr. O'Rourke here desires."

"I'm telling you, lass. I'm getting the best end of this
deal, and I'll be having no regrets like you will."

Phil, who loved to show off and tease, picked a fast
Irish jig for his dance. He nearly danced Mariah to exhaustion, but her prize was worth every lively step.

The gloved lady—Mariah earned the nickname
shortly after dancing that claim away from Phil. She
forgot all about hard work making her haggard and
stooped before her time, about chapped hands and fatigue lines. The pursuit of gold seemed worth any fate.

She bought herself a sturdy pair of work gloves over
at Jim Wardner's store, along with a good set of sup-

plies for doing her own mining. She learned about techniques for gold mining from the lonely miners she danced with at Jake's. She found that what she didn't know, she could easily get an answer for with a few well-placed questions put to her dance partners. She couldn't give up her paying job, so she stayed on at Jake's.

But even wearing gloves, digging and sluicing took its toll on her hands. She hadn't the means to rig a pump and use water pressure to do her digging. Mariah used the few gold nuggets she found to buy another couple of pairs of gloves—elegant, elbow-length ones fit to wear with dancing dresses. The men grumbled at first. They liked touching a lady's bare hand when they danced. They had so few opportunities to hold the delicate, frail hand of a lady. They enjoyed the titillation of feeling her soft little one nestled in theirs. How surprised they'd be to see her hands now! They differed little from the men's own callused, chapped hands.

Mariah was glad enough for the excuse to not have to touch the men. Long ago she'd tired of the feel of rough skin, fingernails stuffed with dirt, bodies stinking of cigarette smoke and camp life. How Molly's girls did what they did for their living, Mariah couldn't fathom. She'd have long ago started hating men. As it was, she enjoyed them well enough, at least the polite, attractive ones. But she never came across one who took her fancy, not even one who came close, nor had she met one rich enough to tempt her to overcome the lack of physical attraction.

Phil teased her about her claim. "Well, Mariah, I see that claim has helped you earn a worker's set of hands and a nickname to boot. But where's the gold, lass?"

Mariah sighed. "No regrets on my part, Phil. None at all. I'm going to be a rich woman. I know I am." Did she sound as desperate as she was beginning to feel?

"I suppose you've had a vision, one of those recurring dreams like the Reverend Davis had." Phil laughed.

"No, no visions, just a very clear feeling inside." Mariah thumped her chest with her fist.

"A feeling, aye? Well, I don't suppose that's as good as a dream telling you exactly where to look for your gold. Still, I've never discounted lucky feelings." Phil cocked a crooked grin. "Without them lucky feelings I'd be an even poorer man than I am now. Still, it's a bit of a shame that Reverend Davis had to blow into town with his gold dust dream and get everyone's hopes up."

Phil spoke the truth. Gold was becoming scarce in Murray. The boom had passed. Some of the men were talking about moving on. Then Floyd Davis appeared.

Reverend Davis was an odd specimen. Dressed in a dark ministerial frock, he came to Murray in the spring, shortly after Molly and Mariah arrived. Somewhere in his early thirties, tall and imposing, he looked like a very stern man of the cloth. Mariah had groaned inwardly on meeting him. *He'll probably set up another church for Molly to drag me to. Or, at the very least, hold a revival meeting,* she thought.

To her surprise, and everyone else's, he did no such thing. In fact, he told Mariah one afternoon when he came by Jake's for a drink that he had no intention of preaching. Instead, he spent his time watching operations up and down Placer Creek, asking questions about mining. Some of her dancing clients told Mariah that, knowing preachers never had a cent to their names, they'd offered him money. And, go figure, he'd politely turned them down, saying he had enough for his simple needs. Then one day he bought himself some supplies and an old jackass and headed out of town. No one heard from him again until October, when he rode back into town with his saddlebags filled with gold.

The newspapers were full of his story. Back when he was farming a small tract and riding the circuit preaching, he had a recurring dream. The third night in a row he had it, he heard a voice clear and strong, as if it came from someone standing in the very room where he slept. It told him to follow the landmarks and he would find great riches. And that's what he did.

His story, however implausible, fueled Mariah's hopes. She would be a rich woman. She knew it. But as Phil said, she had no visions, only confidence in herself and a feeling of destiny.

I knew that feeling of destiny. I had been so certain of my own success.

A flash of light, a boom of thunder on its heels, lit the room. I set the manuscript pages down and watched the light show.

Mariah never made her fortune with gold. I knew that much. There'd never been gold in the family. I wanted to shout back over time at Mariah to stop using

herself up, wasting her beauty and time on vain pur-
suits. A hundred years into the future, would someone
feel the same way about me?

The night seemed sadly lacking in answers. I turned
back to Gran's book.

Mariah avoided becoming friends with Molly's girls.
Most of them were hard, foul-mouthed, dishonest
wenches—they'd just as soon steal a client's poke of
gold as not. Those who'd originally had any softness
had long ago lost it. Desperation and hopelessness
clung too heavily to most of them to make their company sweet. Mariah had a hard enough time fighting off
despair without being reminded of it at every turn. But
without female companionship, she felt lonely.

Molly had become almost a mother or an older sister
to her. Mariah admired her and stood too much in awe
of her to share silly, girlish dreams with her.

Molly had a maternal nature that ran deep. She kept
her girls in line, prevented them from stealing more
than nominally from their clients, and made sure they
didn't drink too hard. And she did it all while shower-
ing them with affection and attention. All in all, she
had a kind heart, a heart that seemed to long for redemption not of this life.

Molly gave tirelessly to others, helping out anyone
in need or trouble. She brought food to those women
and children whose men had gambled away their pokes
or fallen on hard times. She nursed the sick. The local
journalists filled the columns of the newspaper with her
acts of kindness. She did it all, and Mariah was right

there beside her, helping and taking it in, wondering at Molly and her ways. At twice Mariah's age, Molly made her a good mentor and friend, but Mariah needed someone young to run with.

Unfortunately, around Murray, Mariah was a paradox. The decent families appreciated her circumstances, admired her for handling herself as she did, and socialized with her at church and around town. But there seemed to be a limit to their tolerance. None of them wanted to see their own daughters develop too close a friendship with Mariah, who was, after all, under the influence of a madam, no matter how kindhearted.

So when pretty Edith Bergoine moved to town with her parents, she and Mariah quickly struck up a friendship. Edith's parents owned a saloon on Main Street directly across Prichard Creek from Gold Street, where the row of red lantern cabins stood. The Bergoines ran a simple establishment. They didn't allow gaming, didn't have any dancing girls or any professor to play piano. They served drink. Good, honest folk, they didn't allow Edith to work there—too many men to give her the eye.

Edith's older sister married respectably shortly after the family arrived. Edith, the prettier of the sisters, was round and nicely shaped to catch the male eye. More dangerously, she knew it, and liked the attention she generated. But unlike her sister, Edith turned down the numerous offers of marriage that came her way.

She and Mariah had the same dream—to be rich. Only, as Mariah came to find out, Edith had a different plan for attaining it.

"You must like Joe Warner very much," Mariah said to her one day as they walked down the shady lane outside of town in search of wild huckleberries. Each girl had a berry basket draped over her arm.

"No, on the contrary. I don't like him at all." Edith sounded breezy and light, almost teasing.

"Funny. That's not what I heard. I hear you were caught coming out of the woods with him outside of town just the other side of the creek." Mariah paused and considered her friend. Edith was a slippery one. How best to catch her? "And you looked slightly askew."

"Askew?" Edith's laugh boomed. "What in the world does that mean?"

"You know what I'm hinting at, Edith."

"Your source must have been mistaken."

"I know you when I see you."

Edith stopped and turned to stare at her. "You are a card, Mariah." Then she laughed again and shrugged. "Well, I guess there's no use hiding it from you. Guilty as charged. I was askew, but like you said, only slightly." Edith pulled a gold necklace out of her bodice. A deep ruby garnet pendant swung from the end. "Joe isn't rich enough for my tastes, not at all. You know that, Mariah. But he does part easily enough with what he has. It's pretty, isn't it?"

Mariah stepped close and looped the necklace over her palm to inspect it. "Very nice. What did you have to do to get it?"

"Don't sound so condemning, Mariah. Joe and I had a little fun in the woods. We kissed and touched, that's all. Now I suppose he thinks he's my beau, so he gave me a gift."

Oh, that Edith! Mariah felt like strangling her. She walked in dangerous territory. "You'd better make it clear to Joe that you aren't serious and don't intend to go farther."

Edith shrugged. "He'll know soon enough—when I've got a new fellow on my arm."

Mariah released the necklace and Edith slid it back under her bodice. "Why do you hide the necklace?"

"Pa wouldn't approve. He'd get all the wrong ideas and think I'd better be marrying Joe." Edith grimaced.

Mariah wanted to believe her. But losing her family and living in Murray had swept the rose-colored glasses from her eyes. Edith seemed a little too easy and noncommittal to be pure of motive. Mariah hated herself for the thought. Maybe she'd been around Molly's girls too often lately.

Edith laughed again. "You should see the scowl you're wearing. How can you be so judgmental? I merely accepted a gift from a gentleman—"

"An expensive one."

"—you take money."

"Oh, heavens, Edith! How can you make any comparison? You have two parents with a tidy little business to support you. If I don't dance, I don't eat.

Simple. Anyway, at least I'm straightforward in my tactics. I dance with a fellow, he buys me a drink—no subterfuge or hurt feelings."

"Yes, but you're looking for the same thing I am—a wealthy man to latch on to. Working at Jake's you've got the upper hand on me. You'll get the wealthiest fellow in town first."

That Edith! Mariah laughed. "Is that what's bothering you? Tell you what—I'll send the second-wealthiest fellow your way."

Edith smiled and they started walking again.

"In fact, if I can't fall in love with him, I'll let you have the first-wealthiest fellow." Mariah turned suddenly serious. "Just be careful who you go into the woods with. Promise me. Not all the men in this town are gentlemen. You don't have a bouncer like I do at Jake's. Don't take any chances, Edith."

Edith gave Mariah a hug. "Oh, dear, concerned friend, don't worry about me. I can take care of myself. Just promise to send the rich men my way."

CHAPTER FIVE

Molly and Mariah were having a quiet conversation in Molly's cabin one afternoon when Rebecca, one of Molly's girls, burst in.

"Moll, there's been a big strike on the Stewart claim." She spoke hurriedly between gasps of breath, sounding like she'd been running. "Word is they're coming to town, and they're ready to celebrate." Rebecca looked significantly from Molly to Mariah. "They want a real party, Molly."

Molly and Mariah had been discussing going across the creek into town to see if Miss Gustaf might make them some new gowns. Mariah needed a dancing dress, something new and startling. With gold getting harder to find, business had been slow lately. Molly just liked to get a new gown now and then. Mariah saw the gleam

63

in Molly's eye. The shopping would have to be postponed.

Molly stepped to the door and eyed the weather. A warm day beckoned. The air smelled of pine and dust— the scents of summer heat. Molly brushed a piece of lint from her skirt, gave herself a little shake and smiled coyly. "Hmmm, the weather's been hot. I feel a mite dusty, in need of a bath."

Mariah's heart raced. Payday! "Moll, you have one scheduled in two days. The Rutledge boys and their men promised to be in town then. They'll be mad if they miss the fun, and they're a troublesome, mean lot. You don't want to miss their gold. The sight of a shapely calf always parts them with their money." She tried to temper her enthusiasm.

Molly shrugged as she walked to the bureau and pulled a stack of handbills from a drawer. "Oh, I can work up a sweat again, lassie. I sure can." She handed the fliers to Rebecca. "Post these around town. Get the other girls to help you."

Rebecca turned to leave. Molly caught her by the sleeve. "Tell the girls to prepare for a busy night. Let's make us a fortune today."

Rebecca flew off. Molly turned to Mariah. "Get the tub ready." Molly was already pulling the hairpins out of her chignon and reaching for her brush. "Oh, and change into one of your dancing outfits, the shortest one you've got. On this short notice I'll need all the advertising I can get. Run off now and do as I say. After you've dressed, take a stroll through town and see who follows you back here."

An hour later, Mariah peeked from the door of Molly's cabin out back over Paradise Alley at a full crowd of men, who catcalled and hooted and begged Molly to come on out.

"Go warm up the crowd, darling. I've got to finish my last-minute preparations." Molly pushed Mariah out the door, and the act began.

Mariah strode out and curtsied toward the crowd, eyeing them and trying to get a feel for their mood. "Gentlemen," she cooed. She stood, smiled, and flipped the edge of her skirt to expose her leg almost to the knee. The men hooted in reply. "I, myself, never bathe on any day except Saturday. I'm willing to wager that you gents don't either." She was willing to wager most of them didn't bathe at all. "What day is today?" She knew full well, but Mariah knew how to play the game.

A chorus of male voices replied, "Wednesday!"

"Ah shucks!" Mariah snapped her fingers in a disappointed gesture and pouted. "Guess it's not my day to get cleaned up."

The men all moaned. Mariah held up her hands to silence them. "But now, my friend Molly, she took an awful spill, fell right into a patch of mud this morning."

The men shouted their condolences.

"She simply *must* get bathed."

The boys nodded and shouted their agreement.

"Problem is, she likes to bathe outside in the fresh air. It's good for her constitution, you know."

Agreement.

"But, alas, you all are standing out here in her bathing spot. Now I'm going to have to ask you all to turn around and behave like gentleman so a lady can come on out and take her bath."

She enjoyed this part of the act, bossing the men around. Mariah motioned them all to turn around. Some balked, and she came right up to them, grabbed them by the shoulders, and turned them herself, flirting in the process. When every last man faced away, she turned back and yelled toward the cabin. "Molly, come on out. The coast is clear."

Molly emerged from the cabin, dragging a washtub filled with water behind her. Her blonde hair sat in golden, curled piles on her head, and draperies flowed around her, showing off curves and other enticing attributes of the female figure.

"Isn't this a sight?" Molly dropped the tub. "Mariah's got you all cowed with her sense of decency, and here I am left to drag my own tub while a pile of sturdy, strong men do nothing to help a lady out."

The crowd roared and turned with the precision of a military drill team. Molly faced them, eyes twinkling, laughing softly. Men fought to be first to drag that tub on out.

"I do declare, boys, it's a fine day for a bath—a great day for a big cleanup!"

Cheers. The code word had been spoken. The boys had cleaned up in the mines; Molly would clean up in town.

Molly flipped back the hem of her robe to reveal her bare leg all the way up to the knee. She pointed her toe like a dancer en pointe and dipped it into the water. "Mmmm," she murmured, head back, looking enraptured. She had the crowd now. "Just right." Then she kicked her foot and splashed the front row of fellows, who laughed and looked downright honored to be touched by water that had touched Molly's bare foot.

With a sudden movement, Molly flipped her robe back into place and peered disappointedly into the water. "Oh, no, I'm missing something."

On cue, Mariah spoke up. "Your bath salts?"

"No, much worse." Molly looked lovely when she pouted, truly feminine and vulnerable, though she was anything but vulnerable.

Mariah looked back at the crowd. Every man was ready to defend Molly, to do whatever it took to please her.

"I can't take a bath on that—the plain metal of a washtub!" Molly peered anxiously around at the men, then she turned sideways, stuck out her nice, rounded fanny, and rubbed it gingerly. "I'm very delicate. Why, I can't bathe on anything but gold! Dig into those pockets of yours, boys, and cover my tub before the water cools off. You wouldn't want to see me get cold now, would you?"

Deep, rich laughter filled the air. She didn't have to ask twice. Gold flowed from pockets to tub quickly.

Mariah watched from the crowd's edge, awestruck, as always, by the sight of so much wealth thrown away so casually for nothing more than a peep show. The men fought to come forward and add their dust as Molly told ribald stories and jokes to keep the rest occupied. In the excitement, someone bumped Mariah.

"Pardon me." The voice was deep and cultured.

Mariah looked up into a stranger's eyes, dark and snapping, so intense she couldn't look away. Her heart fluttered. Broad shoulders, expensive, well-tailored clothes, hair so dark it was nearly black, a carelessly handsome face. He strode past her, tossed a few nuggets into the bath, and disappeared back to the edge of the crowd. Long after, Mariah's heart still danced and thumped in her chest. What an odd reaction, like the infatuation she'd had with Harry, the neighbor boy back home. The stranger drew her gaze like Molly drew gold dust to her bath. And, even more flustering, he stared blatantly back at her. A heated flush pinkened Mariah's cheeks. Molly's happy chatter drew her attention back around.

"Oh, my, look at this! The tub's covered. How thoughtful of you boys!" She dropped her robe and folded her curvaceous body into the tub. She sat there on her gold, telling stories, drops of water sparkling on her body in the morning light. "Mariah, hand me my soap."

Every male in that crowd stared intently at Molly—all but one. He was fixed on Mariah. She saw it as she handed the soap to Molly. She was so flustered that it slipped from her fingers before Molly could grab it. But Molly never let anything bother her. She scooped up that soap, smooth as glass, held up her scrub brush, and called out, "Anyone want to help a lady scrub her back?"

The crowd rushed forward.

"My, so many volunteers! How will I ever choose?"

Gold once again flowed from pockets to Molly. The action momentarily diverted Mariah's attention. When she turned back to look for the stranger, he'd disappeared. Not a man who liked a peep show? No trace of the voyeur—she liked that.

Molly had her bath for pulling gold from the miners. She gave back a piece of it to Mariah for her part in the show, but it wasn't Mariah's primary way of getting her share of the payoff. Mariah hurried out ahead of the crowd, back to Dutch Jake's. Her feet would ache tonight. The men were ripe for drinking, dancing, and gambling.

Jake stood behind the bar, polishing and humming.

"Hey, Jake," she said. He looked happy. No doubt thoughts of big profits filled his head.

"Mariah. You got your dancing shoes on?"

"I sure do, Jake. You and me ought to rake it in tonight. I'm up for it as long as my feet hold out."

"Hey, if it isn't my favorite hurdy-girl," Phil O'Rourke called out from a table in the back of the room.

"What, Phil? You weren't at Molly's bath? I can't believe you'd miss it!"

Phil scowled. Oh, he was sweet on Molly for sure. Mariah guessed he wasn't happy about other men getting an eyeful of what he desired. If only he'd realize he didn't have a chance of ever winning her—no man did.

"I was there a time. But I had to leave early to get set up, just like you. Come over and meet an old friend of mine." Phil waved her over.

In that instant, Mariah saw the stranger, the one who'd bumped her earlier at the bath. He sat with a deck of cards in hand, flipping them, shuffling them. He gave her a lazy smile as she approached the table. She frowned. A friend of Phil's meant one thing—a gambling man. The one fellow to stir any interest in her all the time she'd been here, a gambler. Of all the rotten luck.

Her heart raced as she approached the table.

"Mariah, the gloved lady," Phil said with drama, "I'd like you to meet Dallas Baldwin."

Dallas stood. He took the hand she extended and shook it robustly. "Miss Mariah." He drawled her name slow and lazily, with the barest Southern accent.

Through the cotton of her glove, she felt the heat of his touch. Dangerous—that's what this one was to her. She felt giddy and weak and embarrassed and flushed and young—not a winning combination. Dallas had the same merry eyes as Phil, the same good-humored nature. His smile dazzled her. *He* dazzled her.

"The gloved lady?" He arched a brow.

"The lassie's crazy as a coot," Phil said affectionately. "She bought a used-up gold claim from me. Ignoring my warnings, she works like a mule on that worthless piece of dirt. She's ruined her hands—which explains the gloves. The gloved lady."

"Most of us here have little claim to sanity, Phil." Mariah hadn't pulled her gaze away from Dallas. *Dallas*. She liked the name. Strong, masculine.

Dallas appraised her calmly, openly. "So why *do* you work that claim, Miss Mariah?"

"Because it is my destiny to be rich, Mr. Baldwin."

"And is striking gold the way to get there?"

"As I haven't met a man yet to fill the need, it must be."

Dallas laughed as he turned to Phil. "I like her. She's honest."

"And one of the prettiest little lasses in town." Phil winked at her. "If she only weren't so stubborn and finicky, she'd be a fine match for some brave man. Now, as is, she's turned down the offers of just about every fellow around. No one rich enough for her, I'm guessing."

"Empty, hollow proposals, all! I haven't turned you down, Phil, darling. Why is it that *you* haven't asked me?" She liked sparring with Phil. He was a friend, nothing more, and easy to joke with.

Phil shook his head solemnly. "I'll not be tossing my heart out to be stomped on, lass. I haven't the money to keep you in the style you're seeking."

"Phil makes me sound mercenary. Forgive him, Mr. Baldwin. I do have my good side."

Phil nodded in agreement. "Aye, she does, Dal, she does. She's a virtuous woman, a woman of impeccable standards, and has a kind heart to match." He gave Mariah a crooked grin. "Though why I'm explaining, I don't know. Dal here knows when I'm teasing."

Just then the doors swung open and a crowd of men swarmed in. Jake yelled to the professor to fire up the piano. Over the tinkling, vibrant strains of the music, Mariah excused herself to go to work. If she expected Dallas to ask her for the first dance, she was disappointed. Seconds later, she danced in the arms of a sweaty miner whose name she didn't know, but her attention kept drifting back to Dallas.

By two in the morning Mariah had had enough. Her feet swelled in her shoes, so puffy she could barely stand. The party would continue all night, but by this late hour the men were pretty well drunk. Jake's bouncers regularly tossed out ruffians. Toss one out, go back for another. Time for a lady to bow out for the night. Mariah felt limp, waterlogged. With the last three customers she hadn't even made a pretense of sipping her drink.

Mariah had been pawed and propositioned, and now she was talked out, tired of making small flirtations. All the iced tea she'd drunk jittered her nerves. Worse, she felt let down, a shade depressed. Dallas Baldwin had not once asked her out on the floor. It piqued her. She wasn't pretty enough, interesting enough? Then why did he watch her continually, never smiling, just looking between poker hands? No matter now. She was calling it quits for the night.

"Hey, Jake, I'm going home." Mariah pulled her shawl off a peg behind the bar.

"Off with you, then. You had a good night. I'd say you've earned yourself close to forty dollars."

Mariah laughed. "Have I run you out of cold tea?"

"Not quite, but I'd say you've had enough."

As he always did, halfway through the evening Jake started serving her the same glass of tea, always topped off, each time she came back with a new customer.

"You want me to send Whitey to walk you home? We've tossed a few drunks out tonight, a few who were fresh with you. I don't like the thought of you walking home alone."

Bless Jake for his protectiveness. Mariah lived just blocks away, but Jake generally sent one of his men to see her safely home. The first time she'd commented that she preferred the solitude of a quiet walk home, Jake had permanently assigned Whitey the duty. Whitey didn't make much noise, ever. Mariah was cut off before she could answer.

"Your boys have their hands full tonight, Jake." Dallas Baldwin folded and tossed his cards onto the table. Mariah hadn't even been aware that he'd been listening to their conversation. "I've lost the luck. I'll walk Miss Mariah home."

Why this sudden interest in her? She must have looked about to refuse his offer, because he cut her off again.

"I insist." His tone left no room for argument.

Jake looked relieved. Dallas stood and offered her his arm. There wasn't much she could do but go with him.

Outside Jake's, the air was still and cool. The pines refused to whisper tonight. Drunks littered the town. Across the way over on Gold Street, a line of men still waited for their turn with one of Molly's girls. Molly was making a fortune tonight. Mariah couldn't complain. She'd gotten a fair share.

"Which way?" Dallas asked.

Mariah pointed toward home. "There, at the end of the block."

"You live across from Gold Street?" His question raised her hackles.

"Across the creek. Yes, I do. Molly got me the cabin when we first arrived in town. She wanted me close by so she could watch out for me. She's got a protective streak in her." Mariah turned to look at him as they strolled along. He stared straight ahead. She couldn't guess what he was thinking. "Molly rescued me, saved me from a blizzard."

"Yes, I know."

"You know?"

"Phil told me."

Thank goodness for the cover of darkness. Mariah felt her cheeks flush. He'd asked about her. She shouldn't be so pleased. "Then you know I'm not one of her girls." Mariah nodded toward the cabins in the distance. It was best to dispel any notions he might have about joining her once she got home. "Not like them."

His hearty laugh boomed out. "Don't worry. That's not what I had in mind when I offered to walk you home."

She bit back her tongue, suddenly offended by his lack of interest, wanting to ask what he did have in mind. "You're a puzzle to me, Mr. Baldwin."

"Call me Dallas. I am? How so?"

"You didn't ask me to dance all evening. I'm a working girl. A gentleman might have helped me out by asking for a dance. You seemed to be winning your share tonight, from what I could see as I whirled by.

You don't like me? Or you don't like dancing?" They'd reached the walkway to her cabin.

"I love dancing. And I can't think of a woman I've ever met more fascinating than you, Mariah."

His words danced right through the still air into her heart. She was much too easily charmed. *Remember, Mariah,* she warned herself, *charm is how he makes his living, or stays alive doing what he does. Don't believe him.* "Then I'm even more confused." They walked to her front porch and up the stairs.

"Don't be. The explanation is simple enough—I knew from the first moment I saw you that you'd be mine."

His words stunned her. He was either the most arrogant man she'd ever met, or the most romantic. Which was it?

"I don't want to buy your favors. That makes me just another customer. I want you to give me your affection, freely. I want to dance with you ungloved."

"My first impression of you was correct: you are an arrogant man." Mariah's heart beat out of control. "But I have to warn you, Phil wasn't all tease earlier today. You're just another gambling man, a drifter, a dandy. There's nothing you can offer a girl that I want. I have ambitions, and I have standards."

"You underestimate me, Mariah. We have the same goals, you and I. We're gamblers in different mediums, is all. You look for your luck in the land. I find mine at the card table."

Mariah shook her head, fighting her impulses regarding him. She had liked him too much on sight.

That kind of instant attraction could only lead to trouble, especially when directed toward a shiftless man. Ma and Pa, looking down from heaven, would surely frown at the idea of her and a gambler. It wasn't respectable, and it wasn't smart. She refused to end up in a gutter. "Like you said earlier, I have another choice— wait for a rich fellow. One's bound to come along, and Murray's as likely a place to find a recently rich man as anywhere. So a lady has an option." She turned to go into the cabin. His nearness rattled her.

He covered her hand on the knob with his own. "Just a warning—I always get what I want." He lifted her hand from the knob, stripped it of its glove, and solemnly kissed it. Just as suddenly, he dropped her hand and opened the door for her like a true gentleman. "Lock the door, darling, and sleep tight." He receded into the darkness, nothing but an intriguing silhouette against the night.

I woke from a strange dream to find the room light, the storm passed. Morning, so suddenly? I barely remembered turning off the flashlight and settling into bed. That stupid menstrual flow had better start soon so that I could get my energy back. Back to the dream—something about Rand, yes, Rand dancing with me in a period saloon. In his arms I felt light and free until the storm started and he turned into a raging monster. I shuddered at the memory.

Gran's manuscript blended roughly into my dreams, convoluted with reality. Oh, beware, Mariah, your Dallas sounds like your downfall. Funny how he and Rand sparked comparison in my mind—maybe it was only the association of trouble.

Speaking of trouble—Mom and Dad were sure to stop by Gran's today. Before I went down to breakfast, I grabbed my phone. Another message from Sean.

All right, so you aren't speaking to me. What does your silence mean? You're hurt, angry? You don't know how to answer? You're punishing me? You're serious this time? It's tearing me up imagining what's going through your mind.

I know you—when you're hurt, you retreat inside yourself. I was hoping you understood the same about me. Maybe I've withdrawn too far these last years. I'm not the unfeeling bastard you think I am.

Dani, I'm dying here. I keep remembering the last time we made love. It was right after you came home from Vegas, right after the incident. I can't even say the word. I want to explode, damage something when I think of it. Was that a pity boink?

I hate that SOB, but I've never stopped loving you. Just thought I should clarify my position—I'm willing to try and work things out. It won't be easy and I don't promise success. I don't know if I'm a big enough man to forgive it all. But can we just give up?

A common theme in my life and Mariah's—familiar sentiments expressed by trying men. Maybe history really did repeat itself, in small, personal ways as well as large. I was shaking as I put the phone away without answering.

CHAPTER SIX

We were halfway through breakfast when Mom breezed in. I spotted her through the window as she parked her white Lexus in the driveway. Breakfast had already been trying enough as I fought to hide the impact of Sean's texts from Gran and Lucy. Now I was going to have to deal with my mother. I pushed my plate away, the rest of my meager appetite vanished. I was in for it now. Mom never restrained her blows.

Gran gave me an arch look. "What is *she* doing here?"

"ESP?" I shrugged. "Don't look at me. I didn't call her."

Moments later Mom stood before us in the kitchen, her arms wide open, expecting a hug from her baby girl.

"Dani!" Mom sounded happy to see me, looked delighted by my presence, but, by definition, she was the queen of charades and phoniness.

I stood reluctantly to receive my motherly affection, the only dose I'd be likely to get until Christmas. Molly McKenzie had never been known for her maternal instincts. As I expected, her hug felt stiff, impersonal, forced. But Mom looked good. She always did. Backlit by the door, her blunt-cut, chin-length hair shone blonde and beautiful, though its natural color had long ago gone gray. She kept trim and fit by working out four times a week, so much so that at first glance a stranger would have thought her years younger than her true age of fifty-seven.

Mom was an accomplished artist, one whose own face was her blank canvas. She used only the priciest cosmetics and sable hairbrushes fit for a master painter. Personally, I found her supply of cosmetics overwhelming. Long ago she tried to teach me her techniques for creating perfection and illusion. But I could never match her skill.

Mom looked me over critically. Did she ever look at me any other way? "You look pale. Try using a bit more blush, here on the cheekbones." She gestured where I should apply it.

"Molly, we were just finishing our breakfast. Would you like some?" Gran rose from her chair and gave Mom a hug of genuine delight. Hard to believe the two women came from the same bloodline, were mother and daughter. Poor Gran, to have given birth to a bitch such as my mother.

"No thanks, Mom. Just coffee."

While Lucy poured Mom her coffee, we all pulled up chairs and sat.

"It's terribly naughty of you, Mom," my mother said to Gran, "to squirrel my daughter away here and not let me know she was in town."

Gran chuckled. "Oh, Molly, where did you get that dramatic streak? Must have been your father. You know how Dani has always liked to hide out here, where I can spoil her. That's what grandmas do. So I kept her to myself for a day? Where's the crime in that? We were going to call you after we ate."

Mom didn't look as if she believed Gran. "Spoil her! Exactly. She knows that if she comes to visit her parents, she'll have to act like an adult."

I stifled a retaliatory response and kept my mouth shut for Gran's sake. I tried a sip of Gran's homegrown peppermint tea to calm my nervous stomach. Mom's presence always upset me.

"Shouldn't you be at work? What are you doing here?" Mom stirred a bit of artificial sweetener into her coffee. Wasn't everything about her artificial? Just once I wished for a little motherly concern.

"I'm taking a few days off to help Gran with her book."

Mom rolled her eyes at the mention of the book, and her face clouded. She suspected there was something I wasn't telling her. "You're not in trouble, are you?"

"Mom! Please."

"Serious career women can't afford too much time off." Mom kept stirring her coffee, slowly and mindlessly. "Where's Sean?"

"Home. He couldn't get away."

Gran and Lucy sat mute during our exchange. Gran gave me a measured look. I knew she wouldn't betray my confidence to my mother, who would only make me feel worse.

"Dani's already been a big help with our book," Gran said to change the subject.

"Oh, heavens!" Mom laughed. "I can't believe you've dragged my baby in on that project."

A day ago I agreed with her chagrin. But Gran looked defiant and defensive. And, after starting to read it, I'd changed my mind. The history, if not Gran's writing, was fascinating. Mariah's story had begun to take over my thoughts. "I haven't done that much."

"Oh, Dani, darling, be careful," Mom teased. "Your gran will have you completely caught up in her hundred-year-old mystery. I've warned her not to drag this up, but she won't listen to reason." Mom gave Gran an affectionate look. "We should let old Mariah rest in whatever peace her murderous soul is allowed."

"Murderous?" Gran hadn't said a thing about murder. I flashed her an incredulous look. Mariah, a woman who risked her life to save a child in a blizzard, a murderess?

Mom looked at Gran and back to me, then she smiled and laughed softly at the pot she'd stirred up. "Ah, the joke's on me. Gran hasn't gotten you hook, line, and sinker yet. I've inadvertently piqued your interest." Mom made a cluck of disapproval, but her eyes sparkled mischievously as she spoke. "Mariah killed her lover."

"Gran? Is this true?" I asked. "I thought we were just piecing together the missing pieces of Mariah's life. Now you're playing Miss Marple and trying to solve a sleeping murder? Why didn't you tell me?"

"Sleeping murder!" Gran laughed like she liked the idea of playing Miss Marple.

"Well?" I said.

Gran tilted her head, birdlike, as she regarded me, looking like an innocent little old lady who'd watched too many episodes of *Masterpiece Mystery* on public TV and knew exactly how to play Miss Marple. "I thought an element of surprise would be good. I didn't want you biased against Mariah from the start. How far have you gotten?"

Gran sounded too casual. The old schemer. I wondered what she was up to.

"Dallas Baldwin just arrived in town and met Mariah during Molly's big cleanup bath."

Gran nodded. "I don't want to prejudice you, then, Dani. You aren't far enough along in Mariah's tale to make a judgment. All I can say is that a man died under suspicious circumstances. Nothing was ever proven, one way or the other."

Mom laughed. "Gran doesn't want to admit that our grandmother of generations past murdered someone. But it seems clear enough. That's why I told her to let it rest, Dani. Why drag our family's skeletons out of the closet and record them for posterity?" Mom turned to Gran. "Have you shown her Mariah's picture, Mom?"

"You have a picture, Gran?"

Gran started to rise slowly from her chair, but Lucy jumped up. "I'll get it, Maggie. You sit and visit."

"I have one, taken when she was a young woman in her prime."

Lucy returned with the framed photo and handed it to Gran. Gran stared at it a moment. "She looks forlorn and serious. But don't let that influence you, Dani. No one smiled in photos back then. I didn't want you to see this until you'd formed some impression of her for yourself."

I took the frame from Gran. When I looked into the old photograph, I gasped. The woman who stared back at me, in time-worn and black and white, looked like a reflection of myself—a picture of soul searching.

"When was this taken?" I asked. "I mean, in relation to the incident?"

"Just after," Gran said.

I nodded.

Mom gently took the picture from me and stared at it herself. "I could tell from your reaction—you saw the family resemblance. It's uncanny. Mariah's looks have stood the test of generations."

I looked over Mom's shoulder at the full-length figure in the picture. Blonde hair swept up in an elegant chignon. Luminous, light-colored eyes, whether green or blue, I couldn't tell. A pert nose, slightly upturned to give her a saucy appearance. A curvy figure, hourglass enhanced by the aid of a corset. She stood to the side of an old-fashioned chair, slender arms bare, delicate fingers resting lightly on the back. Mariah wore a gown of obvious style and quality. She looked perfectly respectable, except for those sorrowful eyes that made the onlooker suspicious of the cause.

I wondered that our fathers' genes were so weak. Had we inherited nothing from them? People always said that I looked like my mother. Evidently it went further back than that. When they met Gran they never seemed surprised. Sean had always said he knew exactly how I would age. How I would look in thirty years and fifty.

"She was beautiful, no denying that." Mom spoke reverently, seemingly unaware that in complimenting Mariah, she flattered herself.

"Do you have any more pictures, Gran?" I asked.

Gran shook her head. "No, just the one. It's amazing really, that we have it at all, considering how old it is. You've seen everything else I have—the letters and part of Mariah's diary. I've also collected old newspaper clippings and stories from the time. I got many of them from over at the Cowles historical library. There wasn't much handed down to us directly. Nothing more than gossip and this photograph."

"Small wonder," my mother said. "Our ancestors buried it well enough. I'm sure they thought no stranger would care about the tale. And certainly, none of their own would turn on them."

Gran laughed at Mom's ribbing. "I'm no traitor. I just want to pass the truth along for posterity." Gran turned to look at me. "Remember, Dani, I hinted at this mystery when you first arrived. But, as I said, I didn't want to influence you until you had made some kind of impartial impression of your own of Mariah. Scandal and gossip are powerful forces. They can destroy or, in rare cases, even make a person's life. That's really all we have on Mariah—gossip and theories and circumstantial evidence.

"I think it's time I gave the rest of the research I have to you, but I'd like you to read to the end of my story first. I think I've been fair and impartial up to where I've ended. There's little room to be biased. I've based my narrative purely on the facts. It's where the death occurs that things get muddy. Mariah never writes of it in her journals. It makes me think she suffered greatly over the whole incident. She hints vaguely at the gossip, but that's it."

"Very puzzling," I said. "Gran, she could have had another reason for never writing about it? Nothing is so damning as a written confession."

Gran nodded slowly. "Maybe."

I thought a minute before asking Gran a question. "Speaking of research, I'd like to pop by the Cowles myself and do a little research. Have you checked their collection for information on Dallas and Phil and any others involved or in town at the time?"

Gran's eyes lit up. "I must be getting tunnel vision as I age," she said. "I hadn't thought of them. I have everything they have on Molly and Mariah."

"Okay, then. After lunch I'll stop over and see what I can dig up."

Gran nodded her approval. "I'll give you a list of some of the other players before you go."

We chatted just a few minutes longer. Then Mom became fidgety. Obviously, her obligatory visit was drawing to a close.

"Well, I've got to be off. I'm on my way to a garden club meeting," Mom said. "I'll expect you all for dinner tomorrow night."

I smiled to myself. Could I read my mother or not?

After Mom departed, I left Gran and Lucy and headed two doors down to the Cowles Museum. The Cowles Museum was a modern structure, relative to Helen Campbell's house, anyway. For a modest fee you could tour the house and the museum. The Cowles Museum housed a collection of Native American and settler artifacts, as well as the obligatory gift shop and an archival library.

It was Sunday afternoon and the museum had just opened for business. Gran was a lifetime historical society member. I nodded to the docent, flashed Gran's membership card at the door, and headed straight to the library counter. You need an appointment to access the stacks. But I had the advantage of knowing the librarian, Ann Wilson, since I was a little girl. She recognized me and waved a friendly hello. We exchanged pleasantries and chitchat before getting down to business.

"I'm assuming Maggie's sent you over on an errand for her book," Ann said. "She's been so excited about your visit. She's talked about practically nothing else for the last week." Ann paused to give me a bright smile. She was about Mom's age, only, unlike Mom, she looked like a woman in her late fifties. Stout and gray. But she was kind and interested in history. A much better combination than Mom's beauty and scorn. "Has Maggie had another idea? What is it she wants?"

I handed Ann the list of characters Gran had written out for me in her spidery hand. "She's interested in anything you can find on any of these people."

I could barely read Gran's list, but Ann had no problem with it. She immediately headed to her computer and scanned the archives for anything she could find.

"I'm sorry," she said at last. "Your gran has everything we have. There is an obscure old book with a mention of the Baldwin brothers in it. It was published in the mid-fifties. Come take a look." She waved me back behind the counter to the computer. "It's not in our collection and it's out of print and not in digital. But I can contact the collection and see if they'll make me a copy of anything pertinent." She turned to look at me. "I doubt they'll let the book out of their possession or I'd ask for an inter-collection loan. But I'm guessing with a book that age, they won't mind making a few copies."

"That's fine. Sounds great, Ann."

"I'll put in the request right away. I'll let you know when I get a response. It will probably take a few days." She flashed me a smile.

We chatted a bit more about nothing, really. I eventually left and returned to Gran's to continue my reading. It must be said that Gran's manuscript was not written in scintillating prose. Gran was an educated, but amateur, writer. She had the tendency to write passively and blandly. But more and more I found the history fascinating and let my imagination fill in the gaps and overcome the lapses and dry style of the text.

As I sat down to read, I couldn't escape the morose mood that overcame me. I kept thinking about Dallas and his certainty that Mariah was the woman for him. How could he be so certain? I'd been certain once, too, that Sean was the man for me. Forever and all eternity. Until death do us part. Until divorce looked like a cleaner option. And now I was having my doubts about that, too.

And Mariah—honorable, selfless Mariah—could she really have killed him? There were times when I hated Sean. But kill him? What would it take to reach that point where you snuff out another person's life? A person who loved you?

How did the incident happen? Why? Morbid curiosity drove me as I began to read again. I found myself mentally pleading with Mariah not to do it.

Run from that place before you become trapped and ruined, Mariah. Run!

A loud rap on the door startled Mariah awake.

"Mariah!" Becca's voice was urgent. "Are you there? Wake up and answer the door. We have a problem."

Mariah sat up groggily, trying to shake the night off. Dreams of Dallas had caressed her through her slumber. She wasn't ready to wake from his ethereal dream embraces. The sun slanted into the room from the east in long, lean shadows. Becca? What was she doing up and around this early? Mariah slipped out of bed to let her in.

"Molly's gone." Becca spat the words out before Mariah could utter a sound. "She headed out at dawn to nurse a sick old recluse, a miner name Lightning. He's a nasty, name-calling coot. But you know Molly—when someone's in trouble, she's there to help." Becca bounced on the balls of her feet, all energy and anxiety.

"Molly can handle herself, I'm sure." A chill breeze blew in, fresh and light and smelling of dew and dust and morning. Mariah wrapped her robe closer around herself and looked longingly at her warm bed.

"It's not Molly who's got the trouble. It's us. The Rutledge boys just hauled into town. They're lined up in front of the cabins, making a ruckus that won't quit."

"What! They're a day early."

Becca nodded. "Don't I know it! Molly might not have left if she'd known they was coming. They're expecting a gold dust bath. They won't leave without one."

The matter seemed simple enough. "So call the sheriff and get him to shoo them off."

"Tried that. The sheriff's got no balls, you know that. He said it's our problem. And if we don't handle it, he'll drag our pretty butts off to jail." Becca's eyes snapped with anger. "His words, not mine."

"I guess you have to give them a show, then. What other choice do you have?" Mariah sat back on the bed.

"You've all watched Molly do the bath dozens of times. Someone ought to be able to do it."

Becca shook her head. "The girls are afraid. No one wants to do it."

"Afraid of what? Whoever does the show will make a tub of cash—enough to go out on her own or quit. Fear can't overcome that?"

"We're afraid of upsetting Molly. It's her show. We don't barge in on her business. It'd be like stealing from her."

Becca was being irrational. Molly was astute enough to see the necessity of one of the gals stepping in. The fear ran deep in those girls. Their madam acted like their mother, their protector. They'd be lost without Molly. Hard as they seemed on the outside, inside they were weak and vulnerable. Tragic. Mariah's silence prompted Becca to continue with her excuses.

"Besides, no one wants to take their clothes off in broad daylight." Becca lifted her chin in a gesture of superiority. "We aren't strippers."

Ludicrous! Whores afraid of showing skin! What a time for modesty! "The men have seen it all before." Or so Mariah assumed. Their profession surely required a certain amount of getting naked.

"The girls have stage fright. No one wants to flop. Think of the humiliation! We aren't actresses."

Mariah sighed heavily. Becca's reasoning floundered all over the place. "What is it you want with me?"

"Do the show."

"What!"

"Molly treats you special. She won't get half so mad at you as anyone else. Everyone knows you want to be rich. So do something about getting your dream. You've opened for Molly before. You know the routine. You do it, and we'll back you up. Jake promised to lend us his bouncers. They'll handle anyone who gets out of line."

Take her clothes off in front of hundreds of men! The thought repulsed her, and yet the money enticed. Becca scrutinized her closely, probably looking for her weakness, that chink she could breach and get Mariah to consent.

"You aren't afraid, are you, Mariah?" Becca's tone taunted and hit its intended target.

Mariah was afraid—of failure, of exposing herself, of what the act would do to her reputation. Yet reputation seemed a tenuous and ethereal thing. Reputation among whom? Neither side of town respected her—not the girls on Gold Street or the folks on the right side of the water. If she did this, the girls would never question her again, never slight her. One thing about whores: once you had their respect, losing it wasn't an easy thing to do.

Thoughts of dancing at Jake's came to mind. If she did this one thing, showed off her body to a group of men, no touching, no fondling, no propositioning, likely she'd never have to dance again. So what was worse, one strip show or nights of dancing? The bath could buy her freedom for at least as long as the money lasted.

"I'll do it." Mariah's heart pounded heavily, driven by a mixture of fear and anticipation. "Grab my brush. Help me put my hair up and get ready." Mariah pointed toward her dressing table.

Becca smiled.

She's enjoying this victory, Mariah thought.

Less than fifteen minutes later, Mariah stood just inside the door of Molly's cabin, bending to get a handle on Molly's washtub with Becca at her side.

"Showtime," she mumbled more to herself than to Becca. Mariah took a bracing breath and stepped outside to confront a crowd of men, some of them drunk, all of them rowdy. Becca followed her out, a large white towel in hand.

"Howdy, boys." Water sloshed as Mariah pulled the washtub over the stoop. The blasted thing was heavy. Maneuvering it gracefully took more art than Mariah could manage. *Lug the basin. Try not to sound out of breath. Banter, Mariah, banter!* Her heart thumped, uncontrollably wild.

She reached the center of the clearing and dropped the basin to stare out over the crowd.

"Where's Molly? Send her out!"

Regal, appear regal. Don't let the impatient fool rattle you. Mariah tried to picture Molly; pretended that she *was* Molly. Dressed in a robe loosely belted at her waist, with her golden hair piled high on her head in a mass of curls, she almost imagined she could pass for the grand madam.

"My, oh, my, what a fine day for a bath." She stood to her full height and stretched luxuriously so that the hem of her robe lifted, making sure to show a little ankle. Then she leaned down and skimmed her fingers across the bath water. "The water's just right." Mariah sighed. "Seems a shame to waste it. I'll answer the gentleman's question right away. Molly's been called away."

The crowd moaned collectively. Cussing pierced the air. Mariah held up her hands to stop the barrage. "Now, you boys know that Molly wouldn't miss a big cleanup bath for no good reason. No, she wouldn't. Nothing pleases her more than sitting on a pile of gold for a good scrub. But all of you boys know that Molly's real treasure is her heart. It's solid gold, not dust."

The boys quieted a bit.

"When there's someone in trouble, as many of you can attest, who's the first gal on the scene?"

"Molly," someone yelled.

Mariah smiled. "You're exactly right, sir. And we wouldn't have it any other way, would we?"

The crowd mumbled its agreement.

"If one of you were sick, you'd want her mopping *your* brow and feeding *you* broth. That's where she is right now, tending to a sick one of our own, a recluse outside town." Mariah scanned the crowd and nodded, trying to assess the mood of the men.

"Back to my point, we drew her up a nice bath, heated the water ourselves. Seems a shame to waste it, especially when I could use a good soak myself. I had a late night of dancing. Why, a bath would be a luxury."

A chorus of "Take it off!" rose from the crowd.

Finally a tall, bearded young man stepped forward, swept the hat from his head, and bowed politely. "Miss Mariah, it would please us greatly if you would take Molly's bath for yourself."

Mariah smiled and winked. "Why, thank you, boys! I was hoping someone would make the offer."

The crowd whooped.

Mariah paused for effect and stared into the tub as she wrinkled her nose. "You know, boys, something's missing. I can't get started. I just can't bear the thought of sitting on bare metal." She rubbed her bottom just the way Molly did. "I've got a delicate bottom, too, just like my friend Molly."

"You got curves like hers, too?" someone yelled. Laughter erupted.

Mariah winked as she slid the robe down off her shoulders and clutched it just above her breasts. At the same time, she pulled one leg out from the robe, exposing ankle, calf, thigh, and one fine butt cheek. Working her claim had kept her nice and firm. She watched the eyes of the crowd follow her progress.

The men applauded.

"Dig deep, boys, before the bath gets cold."

Hundreds of hands reached for their gold in unison. One man stepped suddenly from the crowd.

"This ought to cover your tub completely, Miss Mariah." Dallas Baldwin held out a large poke of gold and a handful of double eagles.

The blasted man, what was he up to? Now she supposed he'd want to be the one to get to scrub her back.

The crowd roared its approval.

"Do I have to dump it out, or do you trust me? It'd be easier to just take the poke than to have to scoop wet gold from the tub later." Though he smiled broadly, and spoke lightly, Mariah had the distinct impression he wasn't pleased by the spectacle before him.

Mariah reached out and snatched the gold. Keeping her gaze leveled on Dallas, she hefted the poke. Heavy. Weighed about right.

The crowd stood silent, watching the couple. Awe for Dallas, for one man buying out the bath, seemed to ripple through the men like the breeze through the pines. They leaned forward, just waiting for that robe to drop. Why did Mariah feel as if Dallas accused her of unfaithfulness?

She'd show him. Dallas could buy the bath, but he didn't own the woman. She set the poke at her feet. Mariah untied the sash of her robe, slid it off her waist and around her shoulders like a boa, then held it at arm's length and tossed it toward the crowd, ignoring the catcalls and lewd comments that followed.

"A gal can't take a bath wearing her robe." She tried to sound flirtatious. This was what Dallas wanted, wasn't it? An up-close view to the peep show? In a smooth motion, Mariah peeled back the robe to discard it.

Dallas moved like a mountain lion on the pounce. He whisked the towel away from Becca so quickly she didn't have time to struggle, just stood staring at her empty hands. He swung the piece of bath linen like a cape in front of Mariah just as the robe fell away. An instant later he had her wrapped in it, and spun her into his arms. He kissed her, as she stood with her robe at her feet, naked in his arms except for that towel.

Dallas Baldwin kissed like no man she knew. In his arms the world closed in to include only the two of them. He smelled good, tasted better, and felt like heaven itself. Only the sound of applause brought her back to reality. How come the men didn't mutiny?

To her surprise, the faces she saw looked amused, pleased by the show. Some seemed almost embarrassed.

"They can't complain. They didn't lose a nickel," Dallas said.

Mariah wondered if he could read minds. Respect for him welled up inside her. He read human nature well. But what a chance he'd taken.

The show was over. The crowed dispersed.

Dallas retrieved her robe from the ground, shook it off, and handed it to her. "You'd better get dressed."

Of course she should, but she had a bone to pick with him. She scooped up her gold and hurried into Molly's cabin, holding the towel tight against her. Irrational, that's what she was being. Dallas Baldwin had just saved her reputation, saved her the embarrassment of baring all, but somehow that didn't dim her fury with him. She banged the cabin door shut, pulled the robe on, and threw the door back open so quickly it might never have been shut.

Dallas was walking away.

"Mr. Baldwin! Dallas!"

He paused to let her catch up.

"I thought you'd never buy my favors." She sounded breathless as she caught up to him.

"As far as I know, I didn't."

"You ruined my show."

"Did I?"

"Of course you did." Mariah grabbed his arm, pulled his hand forward, and thrust his bag of gold in it. "That bath would have made me rich. Flattered as I should be, I can't take this. It's one thing to take a little from each man in a mob, but I don't want one man's entire fortune."

Dallas looked stunned, and pleased. His expression confused Mariah. She blushed.

"You're foolish with your money, Dallas. You treat it too lightly," she said.

"It was easily won."

"That's no reason to part with it easily. I couldn't ever fall in love with a man who's got no sense." She picked up the skirt of her robe and ran back to the cabin barefoot before he could shove the gold back at her. The dust felt good between her toes, real, not like the dream she'd lived the last hours. At the cabin stoop, she looked back over her shoulder to see Dallas still standing in place, looking after her.

"Blast you, Dallas. Now I'll have go back to dancing at Jake's. I won't easily forgive you that." She turned into the cabin and slammed the door. She stood leaning against it, heart hammering away in a jagged rhythm for a long time.

CHAPTER SEVEN

Several days later, Molly sat across the table from Mariah, sipping tea. Molly looked peaked and worn down physically, but her spirits seemed high.

"You were gone three days, Molly. You should rest. Heaven knows how much trouble you had on your hands with Lightning and the mountain fever." Mariah sipped her own tea and regarded her friend. Molly had come directly to Mariah's as soon as she'd gotten back to town. Mariah had known the minute Molly arrived. Gossip and news flew quickly. Mariah wondered about Molly's motives for coming so soon. No doubt Molly knew about the gold dust bath.

Sunlight slanted in the cabin window, casting long shadows where it would, giving a picturesque balance of light to the room. Backlit, Molly's hair shone like a halo. And truly, she must have an angelic streak to have ministered to an old coot like Lightning.

"Lightning wasn't in any shape to cause trouble. I poured quinine and whiskey down him until the fever passed, then I came home."

"You're too modest, Molly. I heard about the scene his partner made at Jake's when you went to find him and get him to take you to the cabin. Those two had no right to blame you for Lightning being foolish enough to get his poke stolen by one of the girls. Any man with enough sense to get up in the morning knows not to take more gold to the row than he needs for the night's pleasures." Mariah made small talk, all the while feeling nervous and edgy, wishing Molly would get to the point of her visit.

Molly sighed. "You're right, of course, but the fool lost a whole year's worth of work that night."

Mariah nodded. "A rumor has it that the girls returned the gold and you brought it back to him."

Molly laughed. "So they trust you now, do they?" She paused and her mood turned solemn. "I heard about the gold dust bath."

Mariah set her teacup down so that Molly couldn't see her shake, fearing Molly's disapproval.

"Gold dust baths, big cleanup baths, are not for you, Mariah," Molly said.

Having braced for a tongue-lashing, Mariah had no good reply. "No, I suppose not. I made a mess of the job."

Molly shook her head, perched on the edge of her seat, and leaned forward toward Mariah. "That's not what I mean, Mariah, not what I mean at all." Molly pushed her teacup out of the way. "I know why you did it. The girls explained. They admire you, you know that?"

Mariah nodded, happy that someone did.

"No, I meant the bath is not what you should be doing. Thank goodness Mr. Baldwin saved you from yourself." Molly grabbed Mariah's hand and squeezed it. "You remind me of myself." Molly laughed again. "Now don't look shocked, I meant myself long ago, before I became what I am." Her tone shifted and she seemed sad. "I wasn't always Molly b'Dam. In fact, I wasn't always Molly. That was *his* idea. I used to be Maggie, Maggie Hall."

Molly chuckled, but it sounded hollow, regretful. "Maggie wasn't dignified enough for the wife of a man of his family's stature." Molly paused. "You look shocked, my friend. I don't have to be a mind reader to know what you're thinking. You're wondering what happened? Am I a widow?"

Molly stared blankly out the window. "Truthfully, I may be married still. I don't know if he ever divorced me. I only know my own actions. And I never tried to get one." Then Molly looked directly into Mariah's eyes. Molly's shone startlingly blue and clear, but in the depths, torment danced. "So you see, I live up to my name. I truly am damned, both whore and adulteress. A lethal combination to one's soul, unforgivable. Not even a thousand rosaries are penance enough for an admission to heaven."

"Oh, Molly." Mariah could think of nothing better to say.

"I didn't come here for pity. My life is what it is. I've come to give you the only warning I'm likely to give, though I'm thinking it's going to fall on deaf ears. Just don't disregard the source, because of who I am and what I do."

"Oh, Moll, I admire you too much to ignore your advice."

Molly shook her head ruefully. "So you say. Time will tell. I've never known lecturing to work one whit, so I'm going to share my own experience with you. But you must promise never to repeat what I say."

"Promise, Molly. Never." What else could Mariah do, eager as she was to hear the tale? Her own fears over why Molly spoke evaporated, driven away by curiosity.

"Well, then." Molly patted Mariah's hand, then pulled away to sit erect in her chair. "I've always played up my Irish half. My mother is an Irish Catholic. She raised me in the church. But my father is a Protestant Englishman. Proper, conservative people both. But broad enough minded to allow me a good deal of education. I've studied Shakespeare, Milton, Shelley." Molly grinned. "You've heard me quote scripture. No, they never neglected my education, but they never nurtured my spirit. I've been restless since I was born." She laughed. "Why else would I end up in gold country?" She shook her head, amused at her own nature.

"Near as I could to turning twenty, I headed out of Dublin straight for America, chasing adventure. Mother, Father, my priest, they all begged me to stay. But

I'd have none of it. They never approved of my friends, always accused me of taking in the wrong sort. Maybe I should have listened to them. In the end I took in the wrong sort of man altogether. But I'm getting ahead of myself.

"When I got to New York, I found a job as a barmaid. It was beneath my position in society back home, but it suited me fine for that first year. I became the pet of all the boys at the bar, but they respected me. I guess my parents' training ran deep in me. I didn't put up with any nonsense, didn't let a single fellow court me. A bit like you, Mariah." Her voice held the lilt of a tease in it. "I was a prim sort of girl. That is—until *he* came."

A prim girl? Molly?

Molly smiled. "Funny how the thought of that night is still so pleasant. Seeing him in my mind's eye, I feel the passion of that moment, the strike of lightning that jolted my heart into action over him, the feeling of youth, the world spinning crazily, the poignancy of his presence.

"I've never, not any day since, seen a man as handsome as he. He dressed faultlessly, always. But that night he looked splendid in a pearl-gray vest, tweed jacket, silk topper, and cane. He stared at me all through the night. His gaze followed every move I made. He drank far more than he should have and stayed late.

"After he left, the barkeeper warned me against him, much like I've come here to warn you."

"Warn me?" Mariah frowned. "About what, a man, men?"

"I'm getting to that. The barkeeper said, 'Maggie, stay away from him. He's nothing more than the wastrel son of a prominent family who's got nothing better to do than to drink up the allowance they give him and eye the ladies. In the end, he won't be worth more than a stray dog, nor any better company.'"

Molly eyed Mariah directly. "You see, I didn't listen. Youth and optimism overrode his warnings. That's why I'm afraid you'll hear, but not heed me."

"Molly, you speak in riddles. Who are you warning me about?"

Molly shook her head and continued. "Burdan, that was his name, came three nights in a row. That last night, he proposed. I'll tell you frankly, I was never so pleasantly shocked, or have been again in my life, as I was that night. I demurely put him off, saying I'd be pleased to think about it. But he wouldn't be deterred.

"'I'll give you until my next highball in about three minutes,' he said.

"What could I do? I wanted to marry him, but my sense of responsibility interfered. 'I can't leave during business hours,' I said.

"'To hell with it', he said. 'You're through working.'

"I protested further: 'We can't wake the father at this time of night.'

"'Father? We aren't going to any priest. We're going to a justice of the peace I know.'

"I should have been wary right then. Burdan held no respect for my beliefs. Later I learned he had no religious beliefs at all, and fewer scruples. When I protested, saying that I wouldn't feel married, he laughed.

"'Oh, my friend will tie us up tighter than any black robe.'

"So we married, but not before he warned me that it must remain secret. His father, so he said, believed that a Burdan reigned on a sub-throne right below God. His old man was a stubborn, arrogant damned bastard, but he'd work him down. Once he got a chance to show me off to the old coot, things would be fine.

"Then as soon as the justice pronounced us man and wife, Burdan whooped. He looked me straight in the eye. I should have seen his own arrogance then, for he said, 'No one hangs the name Maggie onto the Burdan name. From now on, you'll be Molly Burdan. Nothing else suits you.'

"We went to live in a luxurious apartment he maintained. I worked hard preparing myself to meet his parents. I lost me brogue, I did." Molly laughed at herself.

"I learned to wear the most fashionable clothes, dresses made of Chinese and Indian silks, glace, taffetas, Venetian lace, satin and velvet. Burdan bought me a wardrobe full, with hats to match. Oh, we had so much fun in those few golden days." She looked wistful. "But little did I know how fast Burdan was going through his remittance. Weeks turned into months. I didn't meet his parents, but they found out about me." Her expression hardened along with the tone of her voice. "One day they cut the money off. Burdan pleaded with them, but they would not relent. No more money.

"I offered to go back to the bar, but Burdan wouldn't hear of it. He started drinking again, on whose money I can only guess. We moved to a cheaper flat, and then another to dodge our bills."

A faraway look filled Molly's eyes. "Burdan claimed he was looking for work, but nothing came up. Then one day he arrived home acting different. Strange. Oh, Mariah, if you could have seen him. He was always immaculate in appearance. That day, because of our financial difficulties, he needed a shave and a haircut. Locks of hair fell wildly over his eyes. But it was the emptiness of his expression, the hollow, desperate look I saw in his eyes that broke my heart." She shook her head. "Pathetic. Beaten. Desperate. He surely would have melted your heart, too. I near to cried just looking at him. Maybe that's why I did what he asked, though it went against every grain of my being. I was such a fool for that man.

"'Molly,' he said, 'I've found something. Listen carefully and let me finish. There's a friend of mine downstairs. He's loaned me one hundred dollars. He'll give me another hundred and forget the loan if—if—Molly, we're desperate—if he can spend one hour with you alone and—you submit to him.'"

Mariah gasped.

Molly laughed bitterly and nodded. "I protested. 'Burdan, please, I love you. I've never been with another man. What you ask is an unpardonable sin. The church will never forgive me.'

"'The church! The church!' Most likely a person could hear his yelling down to the end of the hall. 'Have you ever read the Old Testament? Every great religious leader had a harem of concubines. Besides, you don't really feel married. You said so yourself.'"

Mariah couldn't say a thing. Outrage choked her. She simply sat and stared at Molly.

"I can see what you think," Molly said. "Had I not loved him beyond reason, I wouldn't have looked past his insults, his perversion of my feelings, and what the Holy Bible says. But I was blinded back then. So instead, I slipped my arms around his neck and kissed him. Then I simply said, 'I'll be waiting.'"

Molly's face hardened. "I went to church the next day and confessed my sin. I did penance and was forgiven. I kept hoping that would be the last of it. But a few days later, Burdan brought another fellow over. So easy for him." Molly sounded like bitterness perfected. "The church forgave me again. But the third time the church would not, and I wouldn't forgive Burdan. My wild, tumultuous love died as quickly and irrevocably as it had come.

"I could deny the truth no longer. My husband was pimping for me. As that was the case, why should I do all the work and turn the money over to him?

"So the church excommunicated me. And I left Burdan."

"Oh, Molly." Mariah spoke past the lump in throat. "So you think the bath would have led me down a similar path? Where's the betrayal there?"

"No. I'm warning you about men. Dallas Baldwin bought the bath out, so I heard. That's exactly the kind of act that can turn a girl's head.

"No, Mariah, I'm warning you to stay away from men you meet in bars, from gambling, charming sorts who drink too hard and don't know a thing about earning a living or loving a woman. I'm warning you, Mariah, about Dallas Baldwin. Watch out for him."

Mariah laughed off the warning. Dallas Baldwin might be handsome and sophisticated, but she knew better than to throw her lot in with his. "You have nothing to worry about. I know Dallas will never be anything more than a two-bit gambler."

Molly shook her head and slapped the table. "I wish I believed you, Mariah. But your sense of reason may betray you once your heart gets involved. You should see how soft you look when you speak of him. A bad sign. A *very* bad sign.

"I have to get back to the girls now." Molly rose to leave. "Glad my story entertained you. Maybe someday I'll tell you how I scared Calamity Jane off of coming out here to be my competition. That was right before I met you." Molly gave Mariah a hug and left.

Sweat trickled down Mariah's forehead as she bent digging in the dirt. The air sat still, allowing the sun to beat down with full intensity. She straightened and swept the floppy, broad-brimmed felt hat off her head and wiped beads of moisture away with the back of her shirtsleeve.

Nothing glinted back at her from the sluice box. No gold. A morning's digging turned no profit. Doubtless a good wash of water would uncover nothing more. Gold lived in these hills. Men dragged it into town by the bagful. Why couldn't she unearth any? Why did the hills fight her?

"Cough it up!" Mariah yelled into the stand of trees on her hillside, shaking her fist for emphasis. "Just give me enough to leave this place behind and I promise I won't ever sell this claim. I'll stop picking at you and make sure no one else ever gets the chance."

The whinny of a horse coming down the road above her claim caught her attention. An instant later, Dallas rode into view down the hill, perched in the saddle with an amused grin cocked on his face. "Hello there, darling."

"Dallas." She nodded, looking him up and down. Dressed in denim pants and a white work shirt, he looked out of character. What was this? His attempt at dressing for a day at the digs? It didn't really matter. He looked especially fine. She chided herself for the thought.

Dallas reined to a stop and looked around pointedly before dismounting, as if to confirm she was alone. "Reasoning with the hills ever get them to cooperate?"

"No more than reasoning with a man ever did."

His good humor couldn't be chased away, nor, apparently, could his male instincts. He gave her a blatant perusal, an up-and-down scan that left her feeling flushed and naked. What could he possibly see in her today?

She wore men's pants with an old oversized shirt tucked in them. It was clinging to her sticky body where it could. Her boots were made for wading. Her old hat kept her hair tucked out of sight. It was probably a fright by now anyway. Dirt streaked her face and arms where it clung to her moist skin. Perspiration ran in rivulets between her breasts, exposed by the buttons she'd left open on the shirt. Yet Dallas wore an expression of absolute appreciation. She didn't see any mocking behind it, either.

"You still mad at me about the bath?" he said over his shoulder as he tied his horse to a nearby tree.

"Is that why you came out here, to check my mood?"

"No, that's just a side benefit. I came to see for myself this place that absorbs so much of you."

Absorbed described her relationship with the claim fairly well. It drained her strength. It stole her hopes. It sopped up the very water from her body. Right now Mariah felt so dry and parched that given a breeze of any sort, she would blow away. Dallas handed her a canteen.

When she hesitated, he said, "Just water. You don't trust me a bit, do you?"

"Should I?" Mariah peeled off her work gloves before reaching for the canteen. That was a mistake. Dirt had seeped into the gloves, stained her fingers, and embedded under her fingernails. Dallas surely noticed. She looked like a common field hand. Too late now. She took a deep swig of water.

Dallas looked around, examining the claim. "I take it the morning hasn't yielded much gold."

Mariah sighed. "Didn't have to think far to determine that." She plopped down on the hillside.

Dallas walked to the sluice box and peered in. "You haven't answered my question. What draws you here?

Why do you gamble on this"—he spread his arms—"to fulfill your dreams of wealth?"

"Gambling's what you do. I just work hard."

He laughed and shook his head. "Ah, Mariah, we're both gamblers. You're banking on this land having gold just beneath the surface. It may. Or it may not. How's that different from me betting that I hold a better hand than the next fellow?"

"I'm not taking anybody else's fortune. Whatever I find doesn't take away from another person. If I'm foolish enough to believe I'll find gold, I'm the only one affected."

"I've never twisted a man's arm to get him to play poker."

"No, I suppose not. And you'll probably argue that your foe got some entertainment for his money, but that doesn't alter fact. Your gain is his loss, and vice versa." She set the canteen down. "Another difference between you and me, Dallas—I have a regular job. This dreaming business is strictly on the side. I pay my bills first. If I choose to work twice as hard so I can chase a dream, who's to find fault with me?"

Dallas didn't answer. Instead he picked up the shovel she'd discarded and finished filling the sluice box. She watched his easy, fluid motions as he dug and shoveled. He swung the pick with equal ease. Clearly, for all his gaming, he hadn't gone soft. His boot thumped on the shovel and penetrated the ground with no apparent effort. Being a man, she considered, would make this job twice as easy. Looking at the size of him, Mariah guessed Dallas, though lean and muscular, weighed twice as much as she did. Mariah had always been slightly built and slender. Think of having an extra hundred pounds to drive that shovel. What would it be like to have his kind of muscles? What would it be like to have him holding her close?

She stopped herself short. No good would ever came of daydreaming about a man like him.

Dallas started sifting the diggings. Mariah jumped up and grabbed the other end of the box to help him glide it back and forth. Two people could sift without using water. When she worked alone the box was too heavy to lift, so she washed it out a bucket of water at a time. When the dust settled, they peered into it together. Nothing. Wordlessly, Dallas went back to his digging. Mariah went back to her sitting. Mariah lost track of time, but they repeated the process half a dozen times before a nugget stared them back in the face.

Dallas held it out to her. "It's a good-sized rock. Half an ounce or better, I'd say."

Mariah took it and polished it up against her shirtsleeve. As always, finding gold sent a shiver of pleasure through her. Who said the search was half the fun? Finding was all. "Big enough to share," she pronounced. "What will you do with your half?"

Dallas wore an expression of astonishment. "It's yours."

"Only half." She slipped it into her pocket. "I'd have been three days finding it. You did most of the work. I always pay my debts. When we get back to town I'll take it to the assayer and pay you out in cash for half its value." She picked up the canteen and handed it to him.

He looked as dust-streaked and filthy as she imagined she did. Too bad the dirt didn't dim his appeal.

"Freedom," she said, and looked him in the eye, wondering if she'd have to explain herself.

He nodded. "Is that why you work the claim or is that what you're hoping to get?"

Mariah laughed. "You're sharp, Dallas. Maybe too smart. You understand me, think like me, and that scares me. Despite that, I like you."

His laugh boomed out and echoed off the hill. She liked the sound and the pleased expression in his eyes.

"Good," he said. "I mean, for you to like me."

"So what do you think I mean?"

"I think both, but you tell me."

She nodded. "Obviously, I could strike it rich and that would certainly mean freedom. But even now, I'm freer here than anywhere. Look at me." She tugged at her pants. "Dressed like a fellow, far away from the confines of a corset and stays."

"I can see that."

From where his gaze rested, she knew certainly that he did. "Don't get me wrong, I like dressing up and showing off a tiny waist and all, but it is confining. We live in a man's world. I don't think men understand the full impact of that.

"A man can be single and still thought respectable, make his way quite comfortably in any manner of methods. But a woman has so few choices, and most of them revolve around satisfying a man's needs." She tried to gauge his reaction. She didn't mean to sound condemning, but the truth stood where it did.

"My best choice for security is to marry—wisely and well, that is. But without anything of my own, I'll always be at my husband's mercy, tied to his purse strings. You don't know how that scares me, how angry that makes me."

"Angry? Why?" He sounded sincere.

"Because nothing else I may do, as a woman of humble background, short of striking it rich here, stands me any chance of making a fortune. Nothing, that is, except pursuing Molly's profession. Flat on my back at a man's beck and call, cooing and moaning sentiments I don't feel and feigning indifference to the degrading nature of it all—no thank you."

"Is that what the girls on Gold Street do, pretend?" Dallas laughed. "Don't tell my friends. They'll be sorely disappointed."

Though he teased, Mariah frowned. Men and their egos. She snorted. "They'd be fools to think their prowess could affect women as jaded as Molly's girls." Mariah paused. "We're all jaded to some extent, even me. I won't go as far as Molly's girls, so I compromise. I earn my living tantalizing men with a little civility, a little flirtation, letting them feel a woman in their arms. I'm criticized for the innocent diversion I provide. My reputation suffers, but I'll wager no one thinks less of my partners. Most sympathize with them, poor, lonely souls. Well, what of me?"

"Are you lonely, Mariah?" He spoke without innuendo.

"In a place as vast as this, how could I help it? There's no one else like me, not that I've found. The few women in town sit in two separate camps that I can only straddle—Molly's girls and decent folks.

"In town, when I'm dressed like a woman, I'm expected to act a certain way, speak a certain way, and criticized for any manner that I do it. Out here, none of that applies. I like to imagine what it would be like to be a man, to be free. Here, the work is mindless. I can think and dream and go places in my mind I'll never actually visit."

"Yes, I see how you can. But you don't have to be lonely any more, Mariah. I'm here." He took a step into her as she moved into him. In a swift action, he pulled the felt hat from her head and tossed it to the ground.

Her hair felt moist and plastered to her head. Free, she wanted everything free and cool. She pulled out the pins that bound her hair to her head, ran her fingers through it, and shook it loose to fall nearly to her waist.

"Mariah, you are the most beautiful woman I've ever met." Before she could protest such a ludicrous remark, he pulled her into an embrace and kissed her.

Dallas neither smelled, nor kissed like a gentleman. He kissed her full force, open-mouthed and so wantonly, it left her nearly breathless.

He smelled of hard work, of sun-scorched labor, and he tasted earthy, elemental, of dirt and sweat. Gritty described the man, the kiss, the embrace, and her own desperate desire. Why should the taste of earth on his lips be such a potent charm?

What a clever man, to get himself into a state of dishevelment to match her own, to make her feel at ease, to not fear the dust he tasted on her lips. She kissed him back with a vigor to match his, free here to be on equal footing with him. Unfettered by a voluminous skirt, she pressed up against him, tight between his legs.

He led her to a clump of dry grass on the hillside and pulled her down next to him as the grass crackled beneath them. They kissed. They groped. They explored each other with their hands. She let him touch and squeeze and fondle whatever he wanted, until he tried to undo her pants.

"No. I'm not a loose woman." She grabbed his hand with one hand; with the other she clutched her pants fly closed.

"Mariah, you push me to the edge." Then Dallas rolled back from her and sat up.

Mariah lay there staring up at the blue sky a moment before daring to turn her gaze on him. He leaned on one elbow next to her, staring at her with an intensity that was almost frightening.

"Marry me, Mariah."

She laughed. "Contrary to the bulge in your pants, you can't be that desperate."

"I'm serious, Mariah. Let's go back into town and find us the justice of the peace and get this thing done with."

"We don't even know each other." With Molly's warning tale ringing in her ears, the whole scene took on an eerie quality of history repeating.

"I know you well enough."

She must have snickered.

"You think I'm taking this lightly, that I don't know my own mind or what I want?" He rolled up tight against her and leaned over her. "I'm not a boy, Mariah, nor am I inexperienced. I've been with enough women to know what I'm looking for, and I'm smart enough to know when I've found it. I realized the very instant I first saw you that we were meant to be together. Today only confirms my impression. When something's right, a person knows right off. So, are you marrying me today, or are you going to prolong the inevitable?"

"However much I like you, however attractive I find you, I'm not marrying you, Dallas. I refuse to marry in haste and then spend the rest of my life regretting it." To her surprise, he didn't flinch or yell, or argue. He just sat there silently, wearing an unreadable expression.

"I won't marry you today," she said at last, just to break the silence. "But I'd like to get to know you better." She regretted the tiny concession even before it fully slid out of her mouth. What was she saying? She liked him too much already, and she knew well enough that he'd never be any good for her.

"You're throwing me a bone, Mariah. Don't think I don't realize that. Just don't wait too long to take up my offer. A person never knows what will happen tomorrow."

CHAPTER EIGHT

I confess. Gran did not write a love scene, a courting scene, or even any kissing, in her little book. Gran simply wrote, *Dallas went to the claim to check it out. He found Mariah there and proposed marriage. Of course, because of Molly's warning, Mariah turned him down.*

I just couldn't see the whole thing being that simple, so I let my own imagination take over and fill in the details. Whose interpretation was correct, Gran's or mine?

Dallas reminded me too much of Rand—a charming rogue, a seducer, a risk-taker who'd do anything, say anything to get what he wanted. Hard to resist a confident man who offered a dream. Would Dallas have stayed in the marriage if they'd gone through with it, or taken off at the first sign of boredom?

At least Mariah had the sense to keep her pants on. A glass of wine, an exotic locale, a fancy hotel room, and I let my skirt plop to the floor and tangled in a bed with a handsome man who was not mine.

Sensual images of Rand came unbidden. Moans and sweaty bodies, wild pumping, desperate exploring. The hard curve of biceps braced around me. The late night stubble of a dark beard scrubbing my neck, my cheeks, my breasts. Passion and spontaneity—powerful temptresses to a lonely girl like myself. Damn that Rand!

I sighed, feeling like Molly had about Burdan when he'd betrayed her. That spark had died. And Sean deserved an answer. Steadfast, committed Sean. Another man as unwilling to give up on me and as willing to swallow his pride wouldn't be easy to find.

I texted Sean the most truthful message I could: *Do I really want a divorce? I don't know.*

Dallas couldn't have realized how prophetic his words would turn out to be. Just days later, Dallas and his buddy Phil O'Rourke sat in Jake's plush saloon playing cards for stakes too high for respectable men, at least to Mariah's way of thinking. The shadows had just begun to grow long as evening crept in, and already Phil sat several hundred dollars deep in IOU debts. Dallas's pile looked only marginally smaller. Mariah frowned. The look on Dallas's face spoke of pure enjoyment.

The man loved gambling. He'd never give up his ways, much as he claimed he could. He'd said just the other day that he only meant to win enough to win her, and then he'd quit cold. Flattering, if she could have believed him capable of keeping the promise. As it looked now, his goal was farther away than ever.

Hard as she tried to avoid him, she couldn't keep her gaze from flitting back to Dallas. She liked the sight of his strong profile far too much. Every glance of him only served to remind her how equally well she liked the feel of his taut body next to hers, how she craved the sound of his easy laughter, his lighthearted manner. His kisses and caresses occupied her mind nearly constantly. He and Phil made a reckless, irresponsible, irrepressible pair. Mariah liked Phil immensely, mainly because of those qualities. But Phil posed no threat to her heart. Dallas represented only danger.

Mariah had spent the last several days mulling over Dallas's proposal, wondering if the idea of marrying him had any merit. She must be going weak in the head. That her body lusted for Dallas, there was no denying. One side of her argued that she, being nothing more than a poor girl, had nothing to lose by hooking up with him. He was fun and handsome and claimed to be in love with her. What more could a girl ask for?

Respectability. A stable, comfortable living. She had only one chance to make something of her life. That, in itself, was a stake too high to gamble with.

Aside from a few gamblers, the place was empty. With no one to dance with, Mariah stood idly by the bar. Phil had already done his obligation by her and given her one dance. Dallas still refused to pay for the pleasure and she wouldn't dance for free. The night held all the promise of a slow one.

The door swung open. In strode Noah Kellogg, an old, good-for-nothing, shiftless vagabond who'd been past his last nickel last time he'd been in town.

"Been a while since we've seen the likes of him," Jake said of the grizzled, gaunt prospector and panhandler. "I thought Peck and Doc Cooper grubstaked him off on a boondoggle looking for gold just to get him out of their hair. What's he doing back so soon?"

Mariah gave Noah a thoughtful look. Poor old man; no one ever gave him any respect or notice. Phil made the mistake of looking up from his card game and smiling at Noah. Noah strode toward him.

"Looks like he means to put the bee on Phil for a meal." Mariah shifted at the bar. "Wonder what he has in the sack?"

Jake shrugged. "Can't be too important. Probably fool's gold, if he was that lucky." Jake laughed.

"Hey, Phil," Noah called out. "I got something to show you. Let's go into the back room."

Phil glanced at Dallas.

"Dallas, too," Noah said.

"Sure, come on."

Mariah watched them disappear into the back.

Dallas wondered at Phil's patience in dealing with the likes of Noah. For himself, he'd been ready to hand the old man a silver dollar and be done with it. Noah looked around furtively before emptying his sack of samples on the table. He hefted one and handed it to Phil. He passed another to Dallas.

"Iron rock," Noah said.

"For the making of cannonballs, Noah?" Phil laughed. Then, as he studied the rocks, a serious look lit his eyes. "Sure, the feel of it is different from iron. More to the likes of lead, I'm thinking."

"Let's have a go at cracking it open," Dallas said. Why not humor the old man? He handed Phil Noah's pick. "Do the honors." Dallas laid out the samples on the floor.

As soon as Phil split them open, it became evident that these were no ordinary rocks. Dallas and Phil reached in unison to pick one up.

"Bejabbers, me friend." Phil sounded stunned as he studied them. His voice came out a croaking whisper. "It's for sure pure galena—solid silver and lead! The richest I ever did lay me eyes on! Where by the Holy Mary did you find it?"

In his excitement and eagerness to be listened to and tell his tale, Noah tripped over his words. "Over yonder in a gulch of the South Fork. You reckon it really is something?"

"Something?" Dallas said. "Don't you have any sense at all? This is much bigger than something! Does anybody else know about this?"

"Well, I...I put up a couple of location notices for me and Peck and Cooper, just in case. But when I showed them these samples, they just cussed me out. Didn't think they were worth a plugged nickel. Those two, they only wanted gold. They didn't want nothing to do with it. They called off the grubstake and sent me packing, which is why I came here looking for a meal."

"Wait here, old man. And don't say nothing to anyone," Phil said.

He dashed out and returned moments later with his pal Con Sullivan, Jake, and his partner Harry Baer. By the time they walked in, Dallas's heart beat out a rhythm of unbridled excitement.

The new arrivals studied the samples as Noah recounted his tale, the proportions growing right along with the proud swell of his chest.

"Sure now, and we'll waste no more time at all a getting over there." Phil spoke what weighed on everyone's mind: "We'll be clear beating those two bastards before word gets around."

Mariah watched the comings and goings from the back room with mild interest. What were the boys up to? Suddenly tending bar seemed the farthest thing from Jake and Harry's minds, and the card game had lost all its appeal for Phil and Dallas. Dallas hurried out without a backward glance toward her with Phil trailing on his heels. Jake closed the bar early, before the two a.m. hour, leaving her to walk home alone in the early morning. What a waste of an evening, Mariah thought. Why she'd barely cleared three dollars for her trouble.

As she turned into her yard, she saw six silhouettes on horseback slipping silently out of town. She recognized Dallas from the way he sat his horse. Sure enough, Phil and Noah accompanied him. From the distance, she couldn't make out the other men. What could they be up to? They'd been acting suspicious all night. Had Noah found another gold strike? If so, why would he let the others in on the deal? She didn't like being left out, but wasn't that a woman's lot?

It wasn't like Harry and Jake to just close up shop without a word to anyone. But that's exactly what they'd done. At the outset, Mariah thought certain that whatever urgent mission they'd run off to, they'd be back at Dutch's first thing the next morning.

Whatever had called them away, and she'd considered many possibilities, couldn't keep them long. Maybe they'd set off for a lynching, common enough in these parts. Or maybe they'd ventured off to try a new homebrew, though closing down for that seemed unlikely. Maybe someone just needed help, which seemed most plausible. Someone who'd been caught up to no good or dubious dealings and didn't want a big show made. Anyhow, Mariah knew enough to keep quiet about the midnight disappearance she'd witnessed.

Five days passed with no sign of them, and the town began to speculate. Mariah worried that they'd left for good, skipped town, or been killed. She particularly hated that last thought, pushed it from her mind when she could. Thinking they'd run off gave her no more comfort and piqued feelings of being badly used by Dallas. How dare he desert her? But what else explained their sudden lack of interest in Dutch Jake's? Maybe the town should send a search party out after them.

This unexpected, unforeseen circumstance muddied her plans, as well. The gold stampede had dwindled to practically nothing. Even the furor from Reverend Davies' discovery had pretty much died down when no one found additional strikes. Once again men were packing, itching to leave town and follow the next boom. Which left Mariah in a dilemma—no suitable rich men to marry, jobs becoming more and more scarce as the population shrank, and her pitiful claim refusing to cough up much gold. She couldn't linger too long hoping Jake would return.

Mariah found herself in a dejected frame of mind as she made her way to Wardner's store to check on an order she'd placed several weeks prior for lavender water and French-milled soap. If Jake ever had the decency to turn up again, she'd bill him for these extravagances of her trade. Men wanted women to smell like women—clean and perfumed.

She had to walk directly past Jake's to get to Wardner's. She found a commotion. The doors to Jake's were flung wide open, a great variety of horses were tethered in front, and men and beer flowed freely into the street. The men were back! Elation! Then sudden fury overrode her relief—why had no one told her? Why hadn't Dallas called on her directly?

She pushed her way through the excited crowd into the saloon. Jake and Harry presided over the bar like kings, pouring free drinks for any man still sober enough to sidle up. Miners could drink fast and lay on drunkenness quicker than most anyone. Dutch Jake's couldn't have been open for more than fifteen minutes and it already swarmed with rowdy men.

Standing there with arms crossed and eyes narrowed, she made no attempt to hide her displeasure. But when Jake spotted her, he laughed.

"Ah, there's our favorite hurdy-girl. Come on in, Mariah, and have a cold one to celebrate our newly found wealth." Jake sounded amazingly chipper for one who'd been out on clandestine business for close to six days.

"You know, Jake, I vowed to myself not five minutes ago that if I ever saw you again, I'd make you pay for the toilet water and soap I ordered from Jim Wardner."

Jake's happiness seemingly couldn't be stymied by any douse of reality. "And so I will, dear girl, and gladly. And pay you for the dances you missed because of us. It was abominable of me and Harry to run off like that, but when fortune calls..." He leaned across the bar and pulled Mariah close. "Look at this." He slid a heavy, gray, rather ordinary rock across to her.

"What's this?"

"Heft it."

She obeyed. "Heavy." Mariah set it back down.

"Galena."

"Galena?"

"Silver ore, girl, a mixture of lead and silver, some of the highest-grade silver ore ever discovered."

Mariah slid her hand over the rock. The chunk had jagged, irregular, sharp edges and a slight silver sheen when examined in the light. "Yours?"

"That and a hillside of others. I'm a rich man, or soon to be, Mariah."

Mariah turned to look at the silent, grinning Harry, who stood next to him. She cocked a brow in question.

"Him, too, and Phil and Con and Dallas. We've staked us a couple of claims up the South Fork."

"And Noah?" Suspicion and anger gilded her words. They'd cut her out of the deal of a lifetime!

Dallas strode into the room before Jake could answer. He headed directly to her, caught her in his arms up off the ground despite her protests, swung her around, and kissed her firmly right in front of every man there. "I've just come from the assayer's office. What Jake says is true—soon we'll all be rich men." He looked directly into her eyes with an excited, heady intensity.

She first thought he'd been drinking, but she could smell no alcohol on his breath.

"Marry me, Mariah. You've no reason to turn me down now."

She shoved him as hard as she could, resisting the urge to claw him. He hadn't been expecting her reaction, and stumbled backward against the bar. She found the look on his face priceless.

"You no-good, filthy swindler!" She stepped into him, waving her finger in his face. "I was there the night Noah came in and you and he went to the back room. You cut me out of the deal of a lifetime and now you want me to marry you?"

Suddenly struck by a misplaced humor of the situation, to her way of thinking, anyway, his face lit up. He caught Mariah by the wrists, and began to shake with laughter while she shook with rage.

"You know what they say," he said, "'all's fair in love.' Listen, honey, I have every right to use all the weapons at my disposal. Why shouldn't I have wealth and the woman I want? What's mine is yours anyway, providing you marry me."

"Skunk!" she screamed at him, but her anger was fading in light of the circumstances. "You're too much a gambler, Dallas. I may never forgive you this."

"You will, and marry me to boot."

She gave him the narrow eye, but her heart pounded traitorously at the nearness of him and the thought of his fortune. She considered how best to punish him and still get what she wanted. "I'll think about it, providing you can hang on to *our* fortune for a few days, at least. Stay away from the gaming tables, Dallas. Don't you dare be wagering my half while I calm down and consider my answer. I don't want my fortune squandered."

She didn't miss the hopeful light in his eyes as she turned suddenly playful. "I have my reputation to consider here. If I marry you now, the town will be thinking me nothing more than a gold digger."

Dallas pulled her against him playfully. "And isn't that exactly what you are, darling?"

She frowned. He suddenly grew serious. "A few days, fine. But you'll marry me, Mariah, and soon."

He kissed her once again—for good measure, she assumed, or maybe to seal the deal. Was a tacit agreement binding?

CHAPTER NINE

Before the sun slipped over the mountains to the west, signaling the end of day, a rush of stampeders streamed out of Murray on mules and horseback, whatever they could round up. They headed to the South Fork and the galena deposits, hoping to find their own silver mines and fortune. According to the recording office, Dallas and company had named their claims the Bunker Hill, after the Revolutionary War battle, and the Sullivan. Speculation flew around town as to the naming of the latter. Was it named after Con Sullivan, or the boxer John L. Sullivan?

Mariah thought the latter more likely. Con had never impressed her as a conceited man, and she couldn't see the others allowing it to be named after just one of them. For all their charm, Dallas, Harry, Jake, and

Phil, and even old Noah, especially since the discovery, were gregarious men who sought the center of attention themselves. No, not likely they'd hand over the glory to Con. Besides, she knew them all to be great boxing fans, especially Jake.

The Bunker Hill name had her wondering, though. None of the men seemed particularly enthralled with history, or that war in particular. Peculiar, but maybe they felt they'd won their own battle, one on par with the original, in beating the odds and finding that hill of galena.

For two days Mariah danced her feet sore at Jake's. An ebullient mood hummed throughout town. The men wanted to dance and drink before heading out to the isolation of the South Fork. And each day more and more streamed in, filling Jake's to capacity. If she expected tender, attentive courting out of Dallas, however, she set herself up for disappointment.

Dallas was conspicuously missing. What kept him occupied and where, Mariah didn't know. Truthfully, she felt jilted and angry. Soon Murray would be bursting with rich men, plenty of them sure to be more responsible and attentive than Dallas Baldwin. To her way of thinking, he was a fool to leave her unattended. Any right-thinking man would not simply have staked his claim, so to speak, but filed it good and proper. The more time passed, the madder Mariah grew at him.

When Dallas finally resurfaced, he wasn't alone. Mariah was working, as usual, at Jake's when Dallas strode in. Something in his manner alerted Mariah to trouble. His usual good humor and lighthearted manner seemed subdued. Next to him stood a man who could have been his brother or his reflection, and just might be for all Mariah knew. Immaculately dressed, tall, good-looking, with the same dark hair and eyes and strong physique, the new arrival made an impressive specimen. But unlike Dallas, who exuded charm and high spirit, from his stance and manner the man appeared serious and reserved. The two of them seemed like harlequin masks reflecting opposite personalities.

When Dallas spotted her, his smile turned wide. "Ah, there she is, Jerrod, my future wife."

The new arrival followed Dallas over and bowed politely as Dallas made introductions. "Mariah, this is my cousin, Jerrod Baldwin."

"Your cousin? Heavens, Dallas, I thought he was your twin." Mariah spoke lightly, intent on flirting with the newcomer and punishing Dallas for his lack of attentiveness.

"Two months separate us in age, ma'am." Jerrod's voice resonated deep and seductive, his tone polite. He had the same lazy, pleasant drawl as Dallas. "I am his elder and, therefore, the wiser of the two of us." Just a hint of humor laced his tone.

"A common mistake, darling." Dallas punched Jerrod in the arm. "Jerrod and I are double cousins. Our mothers are twin sisters, our fathers twin brothers. I suppose we're just about as near as brothers. Jerrod's the first person I wired news of my new fortune to."

Mariah's emotions tumbled over each other. They really did look like twins. "What brings you here, Mr. Baldwin? Are you here to stake your own claim?"

"No, ma'am. I'm neither miner nor gambler. The way I figure, I'm too late anyway. All the most likely land is probably claimed by now. No, I came out to keep an eye on my cousin and make sure that he doesn't squander his new fortune." He gave Dallas, who only grinned, a significant look. "My cousin is not the most responsible man, as far as money is concerned. He likes his cards too much."

Dallas shrugged lightly, but a dark look crossed his face. "Jerrod has had some legal training, and most recently has done some bank work."

"I have a good head for math and investments." Jerrod had a self-deprecating manner. "And great restraint and patience."

Mariah liked Jerrod's answers as much as the man himself. He was as handsome as Dallas, but serious-minded and responsible, with humor a subdued version of Dallas's.

Dallas looked toward the bar and the darkness swung over his expression again. "I have to speak with Jake and Harry."

"Bad news, Dallas?" She touched his sleeve as he spoke. His gaze turned to hers. Maybe she pried, but he looked both angry and worried.

Dallas shook his head. "Those bastards—"

Jerrod cut him off. "Dal, there's a lady present."

Dallas frowned. "Peck and Cooper have filed an action against us claiming they own the Bunker because of their grubstake agreement with Noah. The dirty thieves, they had nullified the agreement. They're—"

"Calm down, Dal. We'll get this straightened out. Go talk to your partners. I'll keep the lady entertained."

Dallas nodded and headed for the bar. "I'll be back directly."

Jerrod smiled at her and offered his arm. "You're a dancing girl, I see. What does it take to get a dance with such a lovely creature?"

"Oh, dancing's free. But, house rules, you have to buy the lady and yourself a drink. For that privilege, you pay a dollar."

"Seems a fair price. Shall we?"

He danced well, and she told him so. "It's a pleasure to dance with a gentleman who knows how." And it really was.

Jerrod smiled lightly. "Thank you." He nodded toward the bar. "You really going to marry my cousin?"

Mariah's gaze followed Jerrod's. Dallas stood at the bar in conference with Harry and Jake. When he caught her look, he motioned toward the back room, indicating a private meeting. She turned back to Jerrod. "I only said I'd consider his proposal."

Jerrod's smile seemed to convey more than mere friendliness.

Mariah nodded toward the back room. "What's that about? And what did Dallas mean about Mr. Peck and Dr. Cooper?"

"You don't know?"

"I wouldn't be asking if I did."

They finished their dance. Jerrod indicated a table. Both Harry and Jake had gone back with Dallas. Jerrod confidently set a dollar next to the till, poured himself a whiskey, and turned to Mariah. "What can I get you?"

"Pour me a glass from the bottle under the counter, the one with my name on it." She indicated a space near the till.

He cocked a brow. "You have your own private reserve?" He complied with her wish and brought it to her. Just before sitting down, he took a whiff of her drink. "Cold tea?"

"After the first few months I developed a strong hatred for the drink, but I tolerate it now. A girl has to stay alert. Some of the boys get a little too friendly. And I wouldn't be able to stand, let alone work all night, after more than a few real drinks."

"A true lady." He raised his glass to her.

"You were telling me a story?"

Jerrod set his glass down. "Ah, yes. You know old Noah Kellogg?"

"I know about him."

"I only know what Dal has told me," Jerrod said. "You'll know the players better than I do. From what I gather, old Noah Kellogg had been down on his luck these last months. Indeed, he never was much more than a common panhandler. About three weeks ago he went to Peck and Cooper, as they're claiming, and begged a grubstake off them.

"Noah told me himself that they gave it to him more out of pity than out of any idea he'd actually find anything. They told him specifically that they wanted gold, nothing else. So they gave him a voucher for twenty dollars' worth of provision from Wardner's store, no tobacco or whiskey included." Jerrod smiled. "Noah's still complaining about that. Anyway, he set out with an old, balky mule that had been hanging about town with no apparent owner."

Mariah nodded. "I know the one. I've seen Noah with the poor, mangy animal before. What a loud, braying, raucous beast he was, too."

"The very one. Noah rode out on him, and after several days found a hunk of galena down the South Fork near where Dallas and company staked their claims. When he came back and showed Peck and Cooper his rocks, they threw him out and tore up their agreement. So Noah came to Phil and Dallas and showed him their find. Recognizing it for galena, they set out to stake their own claims. You know the rest. Peck and Cooper voided their agreement, but later, realizing what they missed out on, they changed their minds. Now they're claiming the agreement is still valid."

Mariah frowned, remembering Dallas, Harry, Jake, Phil, and Noah sneaking out in the middle of the night. Was it just excitement, or was there a certain amount of dishonesty involved?

"So what do you think?" she asked. "Do Peck and Cooper have a solid claim?" Remembering the scene at the saloon that night, certain questions came to mind. Noah had come in and had a private conference with the boys in the back room. Immediately after that they'd sneaked out of town and been gone five days. Was it then that they discovered that the rocks Noah had were galena? When had Peck and Cooper been told the true worth of what they'd rejected?

"No, I don't think so. Noah showed them his find first, fair and square. And Noah, thinking the rocks were just iron rock, didn't stake a claim. Remembering what they said about only wanting placer gold or gold quartz, he wanted to check with his partners, Peck and Cooper, first to see what they wanted to do." Jerrod paused.

"So what's the meeting about? Do Jake and Harry know?"

The two burst from the back room. Dallas trailed them.

"Damn them bastards to hell," Jake said, and followed with a further stream of profanity.

"Look," Dallas said, "we'll get a lawyer and beat them at their own game."

Jake answered with another stream of profanity. Then he turned back over his shoulder and shouted to Mariah, "Close up, lass. We'll be too busy to be working the bar today."

Mariah nodded.

Jerrod looked solemn.

"Do Phil and Con Sullivan know?" Mariah asked.

"I expect that's where they're headed." Jerrod nodded toward Jake and the boys.

Jake grabbed his hat and stormed out the door. Harry followed silently. Dallas gave Jerrod and Mariah an apologetic shrug. "Jerrod, keep her company until I get back."

"Gladly." Jerrod gave her an earth-moving smile.

Later that day, after having spent a pleasant afternoon in Jerrod's company, Mariah plopped onto her bed to think things over. Jerrod didn't seem concerned about Dallas's problems. His calm confidence set her own worries to rest. He told her anecdotes about his and Dallas's childhood. They'd grown up next door to each other in southern Missouri, near Springfield, both of them rascals.

"Any brothers or sisters?" she'd asked.

"Me, I have two younger sisters. Dallas is any only child. His ma died having him. I don't think his pa ever got over it, or over his envy that my pa still had his wife."

"Your mothers were identical twins?"

"I don't remember Dallas's ma, of course, but that's what everyone said. Few people could tell our mothers apart."

"All those years it must have been very hard for Dallas's pa to live right next to a woman who looked so much like the woman he loved. Every day must have been a reminder of what he'd lost. I wonder why he stayed?"

Jerrod shook his head. "Because my ma wouldn't hear of any woman other than herself raising her sister's son. Ma and her sister were very close. People said they acted like one person, and that after Auntie died, Ma always felt like half herself had gone, too." Jerrod paused. "Besides, my pa and Dallas's were twins, as well, and nearly as inseparable as our mothers had been. I don't think they could have survived living apart." Jerrod laughed. "Ours is a strange and unique family."

"So did Dallas's pa ever remarry?" Dallas and Jerrod's upbringing intrigued Mariah.

"Never even considered it. It would have broken my ma's heart. Besides, his twin had my ma and that seemed to satisfy the both of them." He must have caught Mariah's shocked expression, because he quickly amended his statement: "Sorry. I'm not implying anything untoward. Dallas's pa was no saint. He had loose women in town that he consorted with. But my ma was company enough for both men. She kept both houses, with the help of a maid, and cooked meals for both families, raised all the children. You understand?"

Mariah blushed. She put her hand to her throat self-consciously. "I'm sorry. I guess I've lived too long among the girls on Gold Street. Naturally, I—"

Jerrod held up a hand to silence her. "No need to explain. But you see how Dallas turned out the way he did, don't you, considering how he was brought up? Ma did her best, but Dallas still didn't have a ma proper. And his pa indulged him something awful, Dallas being his only child. Other men might have blamed their son. But my uncle only seemed determined that Dallas enjoy life double—once for himself, and once for his ma who died so young." Jerrod chuckled. "Oh, that Dallas, he ran my poor ma ragged. She never could instill a sense of responsibility in him. And now here I am, taking over where Ma left off."

A knock on the door brought Mariah out of her reverie.

"Mariah! It's me. Dallas."

An instant later, she ushered him into the room and offered him a seat. He seemed subdued. He sat with hat resting on his knees and stared silently at her a moment before speaking. Where had his usual lightheartedness gone?

Finally, she spoke: "Did you find a lawyer?"

He nodded. "I think so. We wired to Spokane Falls for one. How much did Jerrod explain of what's going on?"

"Everything he knew. He told me all about Noah's prior agreement with Dr. Cooper and Mr. Peck."

"It was null and void. They tore the paper up."

"Jerrod told me that, too." Mariah paused. It wasn't any of her business, yet she had to ask. "I was there at Jake's the night Noah came in. I don't know what all happened in the backroom. But later, I saw the six of you riding out of town about midnight. It looks suspicious, Dallas. Did Dr. Cooper and Mr. Peck know the value of what they'd refused?"

Dallas set his jaw. "I don't know, Mariah. And personally, I don't care. We were on the up and up. Peck and Cooper—"

"I'm sorry. I'm not attacking your character."

He nodded. "Look, Mariah. I didn't come here to talk about the mining business, though it's wrapped up in what I have to say." He cleared his throat.

She perched expectantly on the edge of the bed.

"I'm afraid I'm going to have to take back my marriage proposal. I haven't kept my end of our deal—"

"You gambled away our share of the mine?" Mariah felt her anger rising.

He shook his head to still her protests. "Not the way you think, darling. It's this lawsuit. Until it's settled, none of us really own anything. Me and the partners stand a chance of losing it all." He gave her a halfhearted grin. "Your piece of mine along with it. That's where I've messed up. We all may be the paupers we've always been."

Mariah didn't know what to think. She didn't have to. Dallas leaped from his chair, sending his hat flying. He slid over on bent knee next to her and pried her hands from their prim pose to clasp them between his own. "I love you, Mariah. I always will. I expect we'll marry one day, but it won't be as soon as I hoped. It may not be soon at all."

Mariah sat quietly, unable to answer. Dallas surprised her every minute.

"I know you want a rich man." He smiled for the first time since arriving. "And I intend to be that man. But for the moment, we have to fight this court battle. Hiring a lawyer is going to be expensive, and none of us has much extra cash to spare right now. We were counting on the Bunker for our fortune.

"So in the end, I may, or I may not be, a rich man. I'm thinking that there's more silver in these hills, and others are sure to find some. One of those fortunate fellows may steal your heart while I'm off fighting my battle. I can't ask you to gamble on my future fortune, so I'm letting you go."

"Dallas Baldwin, you have the most confounded, strange sense of honor of any man I've ever known! I don't know what to make of it. First you cheat me out of a share of a promising mine. Then you take back your offer of marriage. And as I never gave you my consent in the first place, I don't guess you can let me go. There was no agreement between us." She tried to sound light and teasing, but she felt weighed down by her own surprising sadness.

He nodded and released his grip. "Right or wrong, the boys and I have decided to work the claim and get what we can out of it until the case is settled. We'll be leaving first thing." He sighed. "The claim is no place anyway for a lady or a pair of newlyweds." He looked past her out the open window. Birds chirped, unaware of her present unhappiness.

"How long will you be gone?"

"There's no telling. Our lawyer says there's a good chance the case won't get on the docket until next summer."

"Can justice move so slowly?"

"Apparently so," he said. "I'll let you know the court date as soon as we have it." He turned to leave.

"Dallas."

He stopped and turned back to look at her.

"If it's all the same to you, I'll just keep on considering your offer. At least until a better one comes along."

He didn't return her smile.

CHAPTER TEN

On Monday, Lucy and I loaded Gran in her Cadillac for the drive to Mom and Dad's house for the visit we'd promised the day before. Though the temperature had climbed to nearly ninety, Gran wore her usual sweater. Lucy rolled the windows up as we backed out of the drive. Initially, I had a vain hope she'd turn the air conditioning on, but I should have known better. Thinking back, I don't recall Gran ever using the air conditioning. Lucy's only concession to my comfort: she turned the fan on and pointed it in my direction.

I had felt hot and flushed all day, partly from the heat, and partly, I suspected, from my hormones gone crazy. My stupid period refused to flow. But the rest of my body didn't seem to realize, and proceeded with the monthly symptoms right on schedule. I suffered from the usual hot flashes, fatigue, irritability, and nausea. Premenstrual cramps were conspicuously absent.

Riding along in the car, I felt thoroughly disheartened. The day had produced nothing but Lucy's surprise at my request that she buy green grapes while at the store. She commented that she'd never realized I had a fondness for green grapes. And I didn't, usually.

Most importantly, or disturbingly, Sean had not responded to my message.

For once I was actually looking forward to seeing my father. Dad was politically savvy and extremely sharp. He'd have insight and some wisdom to offer on how to squelch the office rumors about Rand and me that were probably raging in my absence. I would need to do damage control when I got back. So I'd decided to swallow my pride and confess my situation to him.

Gran, who rode next to Lucy in the front seat, turned and smiled at me. "You'll be fine, dear," she said. "Telling Bill is the right thing to do. He's sensible. He'll know what to do about work. And he can hardly be condemning." Gran's voice dripped censure and disdain.

Gran hinted at a long-ago incident. Mom caught Dad in bed with a lovely young assistant. From her tone, I could have finished her unspoken thought: *Look what he's shown his daughter. Look what an example he set.*

One might think the affair would have ruined my parents' marriage. But quite the contrary—it seemed to strengthen it. Somehow my parents worked things out. As far as I knew, Dad never strayed again. I think, in the end, the whole sordid thing gave Mom a new sort of emotional power over him that balanced out the previous tip of the scales in favor of Dad and his financial strength, community prestige, and earning potential. But Gran, as the mother of the injured party, never fully forgave Dad, nor did she completely trust him again.

I nodded to her, trying to keep my stomach under control in the stifling heat of the car.

"You look pale, dear. Are you feeling well?"

"Fine, Gran," I lied.

Mom and Dad lived in a pretentious house on the north side of town. Their home hugged a steep ridge on the top of a bluff and commanded a dramatic view. My parents enjoyed looking down on people.

I had always had the distinct impression, or maybe fear is more accurate, that I would fall right off the property. The east-facing backyard dropped off steeply down the slope just beyond the fence. To the north, a rock wall separated them from their elevated neighbor. To the south, another rock wall pronounced their elevated position. Only the street side blended smoothly with the property. *Edges on all sides, just like life*, I thought ruefully.

Their house was a rambling monstrosity with a view of Mount Spokane. As Lucy pulled into their circular drive, Dad emerged from the house wearing a barbecue apron.

"Looks like Dad's playing chef tonight," I said to Gran.

She only shrugged as Dad pulled open the car door and helped her out. Just turned sixty, Dad still looked trim and handsome. He'd given up jogging years ago for bicycling, and that obviously served him well. He sported a close-cropped auburn beard sprinkled with gray that he'd never had all the years of my youth. He claimed his chin had gone soft, a family defect. The beard disguised it. I could hardly wait for that affliction to hit me. Without a beard to turn to, what would I do?

Dad had only recently gotten prescription reading glasses. I inherited my good vision from him. His green eyes, always intelligent and alert, still shone clear and observant.

"Ladies," Dad said as he took Gran's arm. His gaze turned to me. "Dani, my little girl!" His first reaction of delight turned to a frown as he took in my pallor. "You look pale. Are you feeling all right?"

Dad the observant.

"Fine, Dad. It's good to see you."

Mom stepped from the door and waved to us as she came over. "Here, let me get Mom, Bill," she said as she reached us. She led Gran and Lucy to the house. Lucy went with Gran wherever she went. That included visits to Mom and Dad's. I thought Gran needed the emotional fortification that Lucy provided. Mom seemed to think of Lucy as a necessary fixture. It was a strange, yet amicable arrangement. Mom, for all her social climbing, treated Lucy warmly. Maybe Mom did have a heart somewhere deep inside her.

With Mom, Lucy, and Gran safely off to the house, I turned to Dad and gave his apron a tug. "Free promotional giveaway?" I cocked a speculative brow. "What's this, big guy? Don't tell me the barbecue's already hot? What about appetizers and before-dinner drinks?"

He laughed. "Upset your mother's entertaining order? Never." He pointed to the logo emblazoned in a circle on his chest. "Read it, Dani."

"Cookie baking champ, first annual leadership bake-off?" I gave him a sidelong glance. "Don't tell me you bake cookies now, Dad."

"Leadership building exercise, Dani. Whomped up some of the best chocolate chip cookies this side of the Rockies. Shot those others bastards' efforts to hell. I guess that showed them why I'm the boss."

Dad had a competitive side that wouldn't quit.

"Yeah, and who judged? The savvy subordinate is going to vote for you, Dad, even if your cookies taste like shoe leather." I shook my head. "The team who bakes together stays together? What is this baloney, Dad? Another one of those 'fall and you'll catch me' trust-building exercises? What consulting firm came up with this idea?" I paused, still shaking my head teasingly. "And I don't mean to sound sexist, but weren't there any girls in this competition?"

"Ah, Dani, I've raised a cynic. A sexist one at that. You should be proud of your old man. I won fair and square." He pulled me close. "The secret to a prize-winning cookie—use plenty of butter and nuts. And forget that bland vanilla flavoring. Substitute the best pure rum flavoring you can find. No one can resist rum." He nodded sagely. "Just look what bay rum has done for men over the centuries."

"I'll remember that, Dad."

We joined the others on the terrace by the pool. Mom had a plate of prosciutto and fruit set out on the wrought iron and glass patio table, along with a bowl of seasoned pecans, and another of Southern cheese swirls.

The pool sparkled enticingly, light blue and clear. What I wouldn't have given to dive in and cure this case of hot flashes.

"How's the sleuthing coming, Dani?" my mother asked. "Any closer to solving Gran's little mystery?"

The gas grill hadn't been fired up. I figured we were at least an hour away from dinner. "Slowly."

The need to unburden myself overwhelmed me—that and the desire to sit in the air-conditioned house. "Mom, do you mind if I borrow Dad for a few minutes? I have a business matter I need to discuss with him privately. We can talk about our research over dinner."

My mother's eyes narrowed, but she nodded her consent.

"Dad," I said, taking his arm. "Let's talk in your study."

Though the shaded terrace had always provided a comfortably cool evening place to entertain, Dad's air-conditioned study felt like heaven to my flushed little self.

Dad looked concerned as he studied me. "What's this about, Dani? Are you in trouble?"

I nodded mutely, taking a moment to gather my courage and think how to proceed.

"Professional?" He plopped into his aging brown leather desk chair. The spring squeaked under his weight. He sat there staring at me, waiting calmly like a therapist with a patient. His stare could have been intimidating had there not be a gleam of sympathy and concern in his eyes.

"A personal problem that spills into my professional life." I sat across his desk from him, feeling much like an employee of his who needed corrective action or career guidance.

"I need a promise from you, Dad. Otherwise I can't tell you a thing and I'll just have to deal with this on my own." My voice cracked. I leaned forward on his desk, head on hands, prostrate.

Dad reached across the desk and took my hands in his. "Name it, baby girl."

"You can't tell Mom. She wouldn't understand."

Dad came around from his side of the desk and surrounded me from behind in his strong, power-executive, fatherly arms.

"Promise."

Dad was a man of his word. I trusted him.

It was a relief to blurt it out. "I slept with a coworker and now the rumors are flying..."

I told him everything.

"So Sean knows?" he said when I finished.

I nodded.

"This Rand fellow?"

"A class-one bastard."

Dad patted my hand and stood up. I guess his own life experience gave him enough sympathy and sense not to push into dangerous territory. He shook his head, an obviously distant look in his eyes. Then he turned back to me and nodded. "You and Sean, you can work it out, assuming you want to. Get yourself the best marriage counselor you can find. Do whatever it takes. Your mother and I made it..." He trailed off, apparently remembering his own transgressions. "I have every confidence that you and Sean will do what's right for the two of you and keep it decent."

"Dad, we're thinking of divorcing. I may need a lawyer."

"I'll call Reed for you, if you like."

I nodded. "I'd appreciate it."

And Dad, who never liked discussing personal matters, immediately switched topics, giving me a lesson on office politics and how to deal with rumors and innuendo.

"Bill." Mom's voice drifted in from the direction of the patio as Dad's lecture wound down. "Will you be ready to grill soon? The steaks are ready."

"Coming, Molly."

He came over and squeezed my shoulder, nodding toward the door. "Come on. We've kept your mother waiting long enough." He chuckled. "She's probably dying from curiosity."

The old man enjoyed this.

"You won't tell her?"

"I promised I wouldn't." He chuckled again. "But I may have to tell a few lies. Back me up if I need it."

"Naturally." It was like old times, Dad and me keeping secrets from Mom.

Somehow I made it through dinner, though my stomach rolled like a coaster at the sight of Dad's thick tenderloin steaks cooked just until warm. I picked at my potato salad. Anything with fat or grease seemed hideously repulsive. Maybe I was growing up, just naturally coming into my own as a healthy eater. Such optimism for one who felt overwhelmed with nausea.

I managed dinner by snagging carrots and celery from the relish tray and picking the melon balls and grapes from the fruit salad. We discussed everything and nothing.

"No, Mom, I haven't gotten to the murder part of Gran's story yet. I plan to read more later tonight." I smiled at Gran. "It's really an engrossing tale."

"Well, when you've got it figured out, let's all get together for a party." Mom nodded. "Yes, a summer party with murder and mystery as the theme. We can all present our theories and solve this thing once and for all. Then Gran can go home and write it down for posterity and have it made into a lovely book. If she insists on digging up family skeletons, she may as well present them in style."

"Molly," Gran said. She knew when she was being patronized.

Mom slid her chair back from the table and rose. "Let me clear these dishes now and whip some cream for dessert."

Just then, with no warning, my stomach lurched. No building pain like the stomach flu, no bloating like food poisoning, just a sudden, undeniable urge to throw up.

I stood and pushed past Mom to the powder room just off the kitchen. I didn't pause long enough to turn on the light or the fan or close the door. I made it to the toilet just in time and retched horribly.

The aftereffects felt just like any other time I'd vomited. I shook and trembled with cold. My skin felt clammy, but overall I felt better. I was just congratulating myself on being fleet of foot when the light and fan came on. Four worried faces stared at me through the door as I wiped my mouth clean with toilet paper.

"Bill, what on earth did you do to the steaks to make Dani sick?" My mother, always the blamer. "Anyone else feel ill?"

Three heads shook in unison. Gran looked worried, and I could almost read her thoughts. But she had to be crazy to even consider that I was pregnant.

"It's just stress, Mom. That's all." My voice sounded strong enough, considering.

Mom looked at Dad and scowled. "You must have said something to upset her." She pursed her lips so thin they looked like a penciled line.

Poor Dad. Poor me. She would press him now until he told her something of what went on in our private meeting. I prayed Dad was as good a liar as he thought he was.

"It's work stress. That's all, Mom. Not Dad's fault. He was helping me with a work problem."

She didn't appear convinced.

Suddenly, it all seemed too much. "Hey, can't a girl have a little privacy?"

They nodded mutely. As they shuffled away, I thought, *This has gone on long enough. Tomorrow you're buying a pregnancy test to scare away these premenstrual demons for good.*

CHAPTER ELEVEN

One rich autumn day as wood smoke hung lightly in the air against the long blue of the sky, Edith Bergoine stormed across Prichard Creek, gaze fixed on Gold Street. A sight to behold with her hat perched rakishly, precariously on her fine French-braided hair and her hips swinging in an exaggerated motion, she sashayed directly to Cabin Number One. Molly and Mariah watched her progress through Molly's front window as they sipped tea.

"Looks like she's heading here." Molly went to the door and threw it open suddenly, leaving Edith standing with her fist hanging midair, poised to knock.

Edith was muttering under her breath, "'Terrible girl.' I'll show him," or something to that effect. Mariah couldn't make out all of it. Edith looked surprised to find the door open without warning.

"Good. Glad you're home. It adds to the drama." Edith carried a satchel in one hand, hastily packed with dresses and petticoats hanging out, fluttering in the breeze along with the bangs framing Edith's flushed face.

"Is he watching?" Edith's words seemed to explode out of her mouth. They reverberated against the plank wood walls, echoing bitterly back at her.

"Who?" Molly said in a matter-of-fact tone as she tried to peer around Edith.

Edith sidestepped to block her. "No! Don't! I don't want the old man to know we know he's watching us."

"You want to come in?"

"Not particularly." Edith brushed a stray tendril of hair out of her face. "I want him to see me conducting my business, contracting with a madam to get a job."

"Edith, no!" Mariah cried out. "Have you gone mad? You could have any man in camp."

Edith frowned at her. "Innocent!" She shook her head and returned her gaze to Molly. "I've been working a while now, Molly. I cater only to high-class men. I've got my own man, an older fellow named Jack. He screens clients for me and makes sure there's no trouble." She set her satchel down at her feet and rubbed her evidently stiff fingers together. "I'm asking for a cabin, that's all."

Molly cleared her throat. "And your father?"

"That old coot."

Mariah could see Edith actually trembling.

"He told me I'm a terrible girl to bring this shame on them—him and Ma. Then I told him that he's no better than me. He makes money selling booze that men want. I make more money than him selling something they want more." Her laugh sounded brittle. "Then he threw me out. Told me never to come through the door again." A smile broke across her face and a wicked light played in her eyes. "So I came here. I want to be where he can look out his window and see me plying my trade, and remember who and where his daughter is."

"I don't care what kind of men you take in or who scares up your customers, I get my share off the top," Molly said, sounding cool and unimpressed by this interruption to her teatime.

How Molly could discuss such matters in a business-like tone, Mariah would never know. Mariah sat, stuck to the chair, with her tongue frozen in her mouth. She shouldn't have been so surprised. She remembered the walk they took last summer and Edith's garnet necklace. Edith was on the path then, but Mariah had been foolish enough to ignore the signs.

"You won't be getting any special favors from me," Molly was saying.

Edith nodded her agreement. "I don't expect any."

"Camp's been growing with news of the silver strike. We could use another girl. And I've got an empty cabin or two."

"That's the only consideration I want—a cabin directly across from Pa's saloon."

Molly frowned. "Have it your way." She stepped out onto the stoop and appeared to be giving Edith directions. Mariah confronted her when she came back in.

"Why'd you let her do it, Molly?" Mariah just couldn't understand. Edith came from a good family. Molly should have sent her directly back across the creek.

Molly looked confused by her question, like any fool should know why. Finally, she shook her head. "Mariah, you're not a good judge of character. That girl's a bad seed."

"No, I disagree, Molly. Can anyone really be a bad seed? That implies they can't change, that they're born that way. Edith could walk away from this."

A small look of pity lit Molly's eyes, pity intended for Mariah, who squirmed under her gaze. "Edith's in too deep. She's been whoring all summer. Me sending her away wouldn't change that. She'd still find a way to fill her bed with men willing to pay. I may as well make some money off her efforts."

Molly walked over to stand directly above Mariah. "I told you once that I never brought a girl into the business, not by cajoling or force or any means. I've seen all sorts of girls, some hurting, some running, some just down on their luck. I know a woman with a whore's soul when I see one, and that girl is it. She does it because she likes to, because she wants to fly in the face of convention, throw it up to her family, live what she thinks is an exciting life. And it will be for a while.

"Being desired by so many men, especially rich and powerful ones, can be heady, Mariah. I know you don't believe me, but it's true. Eventually, though, a girl wears out and the adoration and the money don't mean a thing. All the girls blow out one way or another. Let's just hope Edith has some soul left when she reaches that point, or enough savvy to start her own business. But I fear she is, as her father said, 'a terrible girl...'" Molly stared into space. She looked suddenly worn and tired. Mariah excused herself, patting Molly on the shoulder as she left.

So Mariah lost her last "respectable" friend to the business, I thought, reading as I had been since we'd come home from Mom and Dad's. That must have shattered any respectability she had left. To whom could she turn now? Prostitutes for friends, dancing at Jake's, her man gone—her reputation had more tatters than the old towel I used for wiping down the boat.

How far would she fall? Evidently to murder, if I were to believe my mother.

I'd finally coaxed Gran's source material from her. For comparison purposes.

She'd done a fair job of sticking to the facts as outlined in the old newspaper clippings she'd collected, but they spoke to the general news of the valley, not to Mariah's specific story. Mariah's own journal gave only marginally more insight. She wrote like many people who aren't born writers. She recorded the facts of the weather, whom she'd seen in town, maybe whom she danced with, but little of what occupied her heart and thoughts.

I imagined that what she felt was too deep for words. A simple girl with meager education may not have had the means to capture it. More and more I found myself imagining the story for myself, picturing the scenes and conversations, putting emotion into Mariah's life.

So Molly's words, my own creations, echoed through my mind, taunting me. I worried about Mariah; with so much corruption and licentious behavior around her, how could she stand apart from it?

Mariah, stay away from it all, from them all, I wanted to warn. *They'll only hurt you.* I knew she couldn't hear me through the fog of time separating us, but inwardly I screamed to her all the same. *Don't let their scandal taint you. Walk above it all. Get out while you can.*

I felt her weariness, the loss of innocence. I'd seen too many people betray their principles and ideals, fall one by one into a downward spiral. I hadn't avoided it myself. *Oh, damn this life that doesn't give us what we want.*

I resumed my reading.

No more than a few days later, Edith bounced into Mariah's cabin, all flounces, feathers, and bows, done up in the latest creation her new beau and her ill-gotten gains afforded her. Mariah might have more easily been able to fend off envy had Edith looked cheap, but she looked fashionable and elegant, if a touch hard. Too much rouge stained her cheeks, giving Edith a flushed, high-spirited look. But genuine emotion seemed to heighten her color.

"You're a fool, Mariah, a simple fool to miss out on fortune because of your ideals." Edith took a seat without being offered one. "Men create wealth their way, and we women use our charms to drain theirs off our way."

"You don't give us much credit, Edith." Mariah set out a plate of cookies she'd gotten in town. "Sweets?"

"On the contrary, I give most more credit than they deserve." Edith ran her gaze up and down Mariah. "You could make close to as much money as me, you know. I might even make Jack scare you up a few fine men. I've more clients than I can handle most nights."

"You must be exhausted. It's got to be awfully hard work pleasing that many men."

Edith's laugh sounded more like a muted warble. "Sore, more like." She winked. "In my dainty places. Most of that's Jack's fault, though. Don't I love him!" Edith sighed. "And I'm happy. I've got a man and money and adoration. Half the valley's at my feet."

Mariah cleared her throat. "Or other places."

Edith bit into a cookie and spoke through the crumbs. "You've got the wrong idea, Mariah. Sometimes the work can be downright enjoyable."

"You came here to brag?"

"I might, if you'll listen. You're an innocent. You don't know what you're missing."

Edith and her superior tone!

"I can imagine, but I'd rather not. I've danced with enough dirty old men to have an idea."

"Well, then, I won't tell you about the handsome man who bought out half my night last night. He was something else."

"I thought Jack occupied your thoughts."

"Indeed he does, which is why I can't talk to him about my clients, not the ones who'd make him jealous. If he believed I enjoyed my time with another man, he'd kill me."

"And do you?"

"You caught me. Not mostly. Most of the time a girl has to be a good actress. Just moan and try to look ecstatic. The price I charge, men expect something more than most of the girls give." Edith affected the look. "Oh, oh." She panted, her eyes half closed. "Uh, ooh."

"Stop, please." Mariah turned away, embarrassed.

Edith laughed. "Last night I was panting for real. The client was quite a looker, and he knew how to use the equipment God gave him."

When Mariah looked at her friend again, Edith's expression glowed malevolently. "You want to know his name?"

"No."

"But I came to tell you directly, so you won't be missing out any longer than you have to. Mariah, Dallas Baldwin spent the night with me." Edith's smile turned coy and vile. She tossed her head and laughed. "Just think, he could be yours."

I gasped right along with Mariah. My heart pounded so loudly I thought it might break right out of my chest. The bitch! I would have clawed her eyes out.

What Mariah did at that moment is not a matter of record. Gran said only that Edith told Mariah that Dallas had been her client for the night. Mariah's journal states much the same, but the handwriting looks flat, small, insecure, and, if I imagined right, angry.

I might have pictured the scene all wrong. Edith may have come with the best of intentions to warn Mariah off Dallas. But from what I knew of female nature, I doubted it. I'd heard too many office cats brag of bedding this man or that, with full intention of hurting innocent parties. The chance seemed slim Edith was any better. If she had been, there had to be a more genteel way of getting her message across. A true friend would seek one. From all appearances, Edith was full of herself. She had the superior position to Mariah, or so she thought.

I sighed, thinking of Sean, regret and guilt piercing me. Had I at least been his friend, I might have thought of a better way of telling him the truth of Rand and me. Or maybe not. Maybe there was no better way. But that's not what I believed about Edith. There was no reason for Mariah to have ever known of Dallas's visit, whereas Sean would have found out one way or another.

Mariah was still fuming over Edith's revelation as she arrived for work at Jake's.

"How do you know it was Dallas?" she'd asked Edith. "It may have been Jerrod. They look practically the same. Hardly anyone can tell them apart."

Edith had laughed in her know-it-all way. "He told me his name, honey. That's how I know!"

Mariah didn't like the smugness that encompassed Edith's declaration. Mariah conceded to herself that love could blind a girl to a man's faults. Maybe it was only feminine vanity, but she couldn't believe Dallas would seek out Edith. Edith, who'd been her best friend. He wouldn't even pay for a dance with Mariah! On the other hand, why would Jerrod lie to Edith and claim to be Dallas?

Mariah slowed her pace, delaying her inevitable arrival. Physicists know that if you keep taking steps half the remaining distance to your destination, you'll never arrive. Unfortunately, life doesn't offer such precision. Mariah was doomed to arrive and face those despicable, cheating creatures—men.

The happy tinkle of music floated out to the boardwalk, but the usual bubbly effect music had on her feet fell flat. Why should she care what Dallas did with his time, if he had been the man with Edith? Why expect him to be celibate when the men in town considered sleeping with a whore no different than downing a shot of whiskey? Still, the accusation that he had sneaked into town and bedded Edith, Edith of all the girls—

She couldn't finish the thought. She slid through Jake's door, hoping to make it to a dark corner where her scowl wouldn't turn away potential dancing partners. As her eyes adjusted to the dimly lit establishment, she saw him behind the bar instead of Jake, head bent, wiping a shot glass clean with a bar towel.

"Dallas!" His name fell like paralyzing poison off her lips, silencing the music, turning heads her way, freezing expressions on faces.

He looked up from his business. She saw immediately the subtle differences in him and realized her mistake. "Oh, Mr. Jerrod Baldwin." She made her voice as sugary as she knew how. "Have you turned barkeeper? That awful Jake." She tossed her head and laughed.

The music picked up again. Jerrod smiled. Thank goodness she'd been spared further embarrassment.

"Only until Jake can get up enough cash to hire some boys to do his share of the mining."

Damn him for looking so much like Dallas, and yet being so charming.

"Does that make you my boss, then?" She sidled up to the counter.

"Just your protector, honey." His laugh sounded rich and warm. He winked at her. "And don't you worry, I brewed you up a fine batch of your private reserve." He lifted her bottle from beneath the counter.

"You're a thoughtful man." She sighed. "Too bad others of your sex aren't as considerate." She tried to act casual, but she wanted information that Jerrod most likely possessed. She wanted to know if Edith had been telling a tale. She half turned to survey the room and leaned on the counter with one elbow.

"Poor Jake and the others," she said. "I imagine that claim keeps them too busy to make it to town at all. It's a wonder he found time to hire you."

Jerrod's shrug gave nothing away.

"I wonder at Dallas being able to come into town last night. Maybe he's not pulling his share."

Jerrod covered his surprise with an awkward smile. "He was in town? He came to see you?" He seemed confused.

Her turn to shrug. "Not exactly. A little bird on Gold Street mentioned she'd seen him."

Jerrod turned nonchalant. He spoke in a low voice. "I wouldn't go believing everything you hear. Trusting hearsay has led to many a good woman's downfall." He pushed a glass of tea toward her and smiled. "On the house."

If Jerrod had been the one to see Edith and was playing a joke on Dallas by using his name, why didn't he own up to it? There certainly wasn't any shame in visiting a whore around this town. Mariah might have asked him outright, except that it seemed too forward, and none of her business. She raised her glass to her mouth with a trembling hand, more confused than ever.

I had resolved to do something about that pesky PMS plaguing me. The toilet incident last night was the final straw. Promptly after breakfast, on the pretense that I needed exercise, I donned my running clothes and headed out for the local Safeway. Lucy might be amenable to buying me green grapes, but asking her to pick up a home pregnancy kit was probably over the top. Besides, I didn't feel like explaining.

The morning air felt cool as I breezed past Coeur d'Alene Park and its historic gazebo. I pictured my ancestors, the Mollys and Maggies of generations past, dining in the park in the garb of their day. Coeur d'Alene Park was the first park established in Spokane. A Molly, or a Maggie, I couldn't remember which now, had been there on its christening day. There would be no more Mollys and Maggies after me. I was out to prove that very fact today. Maybe I'd insist that Gran and Lucy and I take a picnic to the park, for tradition's sake.

I was sweating by the time I reached Safeway. Although my feet moved like Dallas's low-grade galena— more lead than treasure—I felt good, more like myself than I had in days. I found the kit, made the purchase, and was out of the store and jogging home in minutes.

Back at the house, I passed Gran and Lucy at work on the book in the study.

"Will you be helping us with the story today, Dani?" Gran called out.

"Later, Gran." I sniffed my pits and wrinkled my nose. "First I need a shower, then I've got a little work to do."

Gran nodded. I raced up the steps.

In the bathroom, I stripped off the oversize T-shirt covering my spandex-clad body and strutted before the mirror, posing and admiring. Flat abs, almost hollow stomach despite the bloating. Firm biceps. Good overall toning. Short of Hollywood, not many thirty-five-year-old women looked this good. Or so I told myself to build my confidence.

I tore open the pregnancy kit, took my place on the toilet, let it flow, and stuck that little stick in the stream. For the small cost of this home test, relief within hours. I sighed. Then, still smiling, knowing absolutely the result, I pulled the stick out. The effect seeing that little negative sign had on my body always amazed me. How fickle the mind! How delicate the balance between nature and psyche!

But when I looked down, the world spun out of control. A little pink positive sign showed in the stick's window.

CHAPTER TWELVE

I felt faint. My ears rang. I couldn't breathe. The world became narrower and narrower, closing down around me. Static clouded my vision and filled my ears. The only rational thought I had—I couldn't let Gran find me passed out on the toilet. I slumped forward, pressing my head between my knees, trying hard not to hyperventilate.

Somehow I managed to pull my spandex shorts up and get off the toilet before I slumped back to the floor.

Dear God, why? Why?

The bathroom door burst open. Invading my privacy was becoming a habit with my family.

"Dani!" Gran stood above me.

"Oh, dear heavens!" Lucy repeated over and over again.

Gran knelt beside me slowly on stiff, aged knees. The torture I put my sweet gran through. Suddenly her arms encircled me. "There, there, girlie, there." She pried the test stick from my hand. I wasn't even aware that I still clutched it. Gran gasped.

"Rand!" she spat. "Damn, damn, damn!"

She must have held the stick out for Lucy to get a look. I don't know for sure, because I didn't look up and I couldn't have seen through my veil of tears anyway. Lucy gasped, too.

"Why must history repeat itself?" Gran's voice shook with rage. "Help me get her to bed, Lucy. The poor girl's in shock."

I lay in the bed with the quilt pulled over me and tucked beneath my chin, trembling. Gran sat next to me gently stroking my hair like she had when I was a girl. Lucy scurried off to make tea. I finally got up the strength to speak.

"I had sex with Sean, too. Right after." My voice sounded weak, raw, young. "It may be his." I didn't sound convinced.

Gran nodded and kept stroking, but her face clouded. What was there to say?

"That dumb test," I said. "How accurate can it be? What if it's wrong? Tomorrow I'll take another one. All this fuss for nothing."

"Denial always follows quickly on the heels of shock," Gran said. "You have all the symptoms, Dani girl." Gran's tone was gentle, soft as her touch in my hair. "And that plus sign looks very dark and certain."

She paused. "I had Lucy read the box. The test is ninety-nine percent accurate. I hate to say so, honey, but we have to face this. You're going to have a baby." She hugged me. "You've had a shock. Get some rest now. You need the strength. We'll talk later."

I lay there in bed only until Gran closed the door behind her and I heard her footsteps retreat down the stairs. I couldn't stand the quiet. The pounding of my own heart drove me crazy. I eased out of bed, trying to silence the telltale squeak of the springs as they gave up my weight. I didn't want Gran flying back up to check on me. I tiptoed to the footed mirror and eyed my sideways reflection.

My stomach looked perfectly flat, the same as always. A baby couldn't be growing in there. No, of course not. This whole morning had been a ridiculous caper, an escapade of jokes put on by nature. As soon as I got home, if indeed I ever did, I'd call Dr. Boswell and she'd put a stop to this silly notion of me being pregnant. I was infertile. I couldn't conceive. I just couldn't.

"I'm not pregnant," I said to the woman who stared back at me from the mirror. "Do you hear me? I'm not pregnant. I just can't be. I'm infertile!"

But thoughts like demons swirled around my mind, evil and sinister and ready to ruin what remained of my life. What if I really was pregnant? How did I tell Sean? It could be his, but more likely it was Rand's.

I remembered my night of passion with Rand, but now disgust, rather than pleasure, colored my view of it. We'd used a condom, but we'd been careless, wild.

When Rand pulled out, we'd noticed a tiny rip high up in the latex away from the tip. Rand inspected it.

"It doesn't look like we lost any," he'd said gravely.

"It doesn't matter," I replied lightly, full of the pleasure of the moment. "I'm infertile."

Rand shook his head. "Dani, you're really a novice at this, aren't you?"

I gave him a puzzled look.

He sighed and eyed me pointedly. "I'm clean. I swear it," he said. "No HIV, no sexual diseases. I was just test-ed last month. I've got the report. I can show it to you back in Seattle. A single man can't be too careful."

"Oh." I felt myself color. "Good. Me too. I'm clean, I mean. And I've only been with..." I was unable to finish.

"Good, then we don't need to worry." Rand looked relieved. He reached for the bottle of wine on the nightstand and poured two more glasses, though nei-ther of us needed more. Then he smiled at me, and we both broke out laughing. The awkward moment had passed.

I recoiled at my own thoughts and returned to the present.

When Sean found out, would he retract his offer and file for divorce?

I could abort this child. Neither man would ever have to know.

The thought came from nowhere, a solution, but a hideous one. Even as it crossed my mind, my arms in-stinctively reached to cover and protect my abdomen.

I couldn't! I'd wanted a baby for too long. If I was really pregnant, and Sean rejected me, I would raise the baby alone and love it madly. Even if the baby was Rand's.

I stumbled back and fell on the bed. The thought of really, truly, irrevocably losing Sean sent a new wave of unexpected terror over me. I'd thought I could leave him, toss away our years like so much garbage on trash day, but maybe the truth was that we were too intertwined to separate. Maybe, sick or not, if you cut us apart I'd wither and die. There seemed to be no constant in this suddenly nightmarish world I lived in— not even Sean.

I didn't want to dwell on it anymore. In a Scarlett O'Hara moment, I vowed to think about it tomorrow when I felt stronger.

Even as I denied, simply refused to believe that I was pregnant, I never considered telling Rand about the baby. It simply wasn't his business, not yet. Maybe it never would be. I pushed thoughts of Rand aside and settled in on the bed, nestled between two deep pillows.

A wave of tiredness crested over me, the effects of the exercise and the morning's emotional trauma. I'd just rest a few minutes, like Gran said. I drifted off to sleep almost the moment my head fell to the pillow.

Mariah felt like a stage actress that night—all painted-on smiles and feigned emotion. She laughed and flirted and played up to the men and made a record profit. But inside, she boiled with confusion over the Baldwins and disillusionment over Edith. Jerrod Baldwin's encouraging smiles got her through the hours.

His gaze seemed to follow her every move. He was there to pry a drunk off her. There with a kind word and a wink. There with a nod when she thought she just might collapse. And just when it seemed like the night would never end, he threw the last few stragglers out with good-natured aplomb. She went for her coat.

"Don't leave yet, Miss Mariah. Wait just a minute and I'll walk you home," Jerrod called out.

"No need, Mr. Baldwin. But I thank you for the offer."

"I insist." He came over and assisted her into her coat, then took her elbow and escorted her to the bar. "I just have to wipe down the bar and I'll be ready." His gaze met hers. "I know you've been upset. You look like you could use a friend with a talent for listening. You want to say what's on your mind?"

She leaned with both arms on the bar, head in hands. "Disillusionment." She caught her own reflection in the bar mirror.

"That's a mite vague. Care to elaborate?" Jerrod set his bar rag down.

"Look at me! I'm all flounces, ruffles, and frippery. Short skirts, low-cut bodice, too much ankle showing. And now my last friend just became a whore!"

"Not your last, I'd say." Jerrod came around and pulled up a stool next to her. "So far as I know, I'm not one yet."

She laughed through tears of frustration. "You barely know me."

"Didn't know that time made friends. I always thought a likeness of spirit did the trick. True friends are made in an instant. They only prove out over time." He took her hand and squeezed it. "Look, I could use a friend myself. I'm not an outgoing man like my cousin. Not many people understand a quiet man, a man who runs deep, or such a woman either." He wore an intense expression.

She gave his hand a return squeeze and let it drop as she stepped back from the bar. "Look at me—a common dance hall girl. What decent man would ever take me home to meet his mama? No wonder Dallas—"

"Leave Dallas out of this. My cousin has always been an odd duck. He makes his own rules, plays his own game. If I had my way, I'd knock some sense into him, but that's never worked in the past." He smiled. "You can't keep score by him." Jerrod spoke in a low, intense tone. "Any man, *any* man, in this town would be happy to take you home, Miss Mariah. You have only to snap your fingers. I'd be happy to take you home to Mama"—he cleared his throat and grinned—"if we weren't but friends."

"You're nothing but a two-bit flatterer, Mr. Baldwin."

He laughed. "Maybe. But if we're going to be friends, you'd better stop insulting me and start calling me Jerrod."

She nodded. "And I'm Mariah."

"On occasion, but I think 'Miss Mariah' suits you best. You deserve the respect. Let's get home now." He went for his coat.

He walked her home in the starry moonlight. The late September air sat lightly, freshly scented with heavy dew. There didn't seem to be any need for talking. He waited while she unlatched the door. Their eyes met. For a brief instant, it seemed to Mariah that something passed between them, a small spark, a bit of intimacy, a tiny trill of the heart. Her lips trembled. He bowed his head. She thought he might kiss her, but instead he gave her a hug and left her standing alone in the doorway. He tipped his hat to her as he turned onto the street and disappeared into the darkness.

I sat up, wide awake, startled from sleep by an overwhelming sense of panic and guilt. I'd been dreaming about Mariah and Jerrod Baldwin. But now, as the hazy veil of sleep lifted and my heart settled into a quiet rhythm, I remembered the dream. Rand played Jerrod's part in the stage play of my mind. Why? If dreams were metaphors for life, if they symbolized the deep fears and thoughts of life, what was I telling myself?

I went down to Gran's study, hoping a little companionship would wash away the panic. I found Gran and Lucy working on the book.

Gran sat at her desk, her glasses perched on her nose, face inches from the computer screen. Lucy sat beside her, peering just as intently. Gran pounded lightly, full-fisted on the desk. "We just can't go any farther until we know why, Lucy. Why did she do it?"

"Why, what?"

Both Gran and Lucy swiveled to face me.

"Oh, Dani, you've startled us." Concern and uncertainty wavered on Gran's face. "Are you all right, girlie? You shouldn't be up. You've had such a shock."

"Let's not talk about it, Gran. I can't face it right now."

Gran shrugged. "Just like her mother."

No compliment, I was sure. "You were saying?"

"We're still wondering if Mariah really killed Jerrod, Dani." Gran's voice trembled with passion, frustration, and a touch of old age. "I've wondered my whole life."

"Jerrod!"

They nodded in unison.

"I thought...Dallas."

They shook their heads. "Jerrod."

"Wait a minute. Wait just a minute—Jerrod?" Would there be no end to the surprises of the day?

"Well," Lucy said, "that's what some townspeople of the day claimed. We do know that Jerrod died that day out on the tailings and Mariah was there when it happened."

"And she was covered with blood," Gran added.

"And his head was bashed in," Lucy said.

"With a rock that was found next to the body." Gran clucked her tongue. "Sad business. Sad business."

I pulled up a chair next to them. "Had she dumped Dallas for good then?"

"I really wish you'd finish the story, Dani. We need your help so badly." Gran touched my arm.

"Why do you want to write this, Gran?" I couldn't believe I was suddenly siding with my mother. "It can only make the family look bad. I've grown rather fond of old Mariah. Why not let her rest in peace?" Though as deep in as I was now, I wondered if I could do the same.

"Mariah deserves to have the facts recorded so that people can draw their own conclusions." Gran gave me a squeeze. "We need your help, and time is running short. Don't you see, Dani? You'll have to go back to Seattle soon. Fate is rolling in that direction."

"Gran—"

"You're having a baby, Dani. You'll have to tell Sean. He called again this morning to check on you. You were resting, and you'd had such a shock, so I didn't bother waking you."

"He did? Gran—"

"No, listen, Dani. We have to finish this story first. Believe me. Trust me." Gran pulled my face around to direct my gaze to hers.

"All right," I said.

Gran nodded in her trembling, old-lady way, satisfied with herself. "Good, because we'll have to get you to a doctor. My first great-granddaughter needs the right start. And I'll need some pink yarn. My eyes aren't so good, especially for fine work. I've got plenty of baby things to be knitting. And the baby needs the proper nutrients while it grows inside you. Maybe I'll send Lucy to the store for some vitamins—"

"There's not going to be a baby." I was still in denial.

They looked shocked.

"I mean, I'm not pregnant." I softened my tone. "But if I were, what makes you certain it's a girl?"

"The first one always is, Dani. There hasn't been a firstborn boy in the family since before Mariah's generation. No, it will be a girl, another Molly, especially a child conceived like this. Pray God lets us raise her right."

CHAPTER THIRTEEN

Mariah liked the way Jerrod noticed the little things about her—the new way she'd pinned her hair up, her new gloves, when she switched to using rose water instead of lavender. He walked her home every night, and was always gentlemanly, always polite. He quickly became the best friend she had in town or anywhere. His friendship and concern got her through the long winter of 1885-6.

Locals said it was the worst winter they'd seen in those parts, not that history extended back much more than thirty years. The first snow flew in late October, and from then on the dirt didn't show. Snow made its own mountains around town and anywhere a person tried to shovel it out of the way. Mariah gave up working the claim. The ground froze solid. And since the blizzard the previous March, she'd had a fear of being lost in the white world. At those times she thought of Lizzie and her father and wondered if they'd made it to Oregon and a better life. As far as Mariah knew, the claim he'd owned had never paid out. She hoped he'd found something better.

Murray soon became not so much a town as a maze of ice. Mariah felt like a mole maneuvering through tunnels as she made her way about. Supplies ran low. People got sick. Everyone prayed for spring to come, but it seemed to take its time. Through it all, Jerrod took care of her. He brought her wood when her supply ran low. He gave her tiny trinkets to keep her spirits up. He brought her game he'd snared in the woods—white-tailed deer, mostly.

Deer weren't hard to get, but as the winter progressed not much meat shielded their bones. The winter took its toll on every living creature. Deer came down from the woods to the edges of the camp. No longer able to paw through the snow to get food, the deer soon stripped clean every vine and edible plant within the stretch of their necks. When they'd finished, they stayed at the edges of town, wide-eyed, hollow-ribbed, and starving to death by the dozens each day. They made convenient hunting, if meager eating.

Saloons and Molly's girls provided the only entertainment in town, but though idle men are wont to cause trouble, things stayed fairly quiet. Sheriff Johnson went about his days peacefully. The cold drained men of the energy to raise much hell.

Mariah worried about Dallas out at the Bunker Hill, mining away at frozen earth. Why her thoughts should keep returning to him, she couldn't say, but from the first moment she'd met him, she'd felt drawn to him, compelled to think of him. His absence hadn't changed that, even when he sent her no word and no encouragement.

Throughout the winter, Jerrod kept the books for the Bunker partners and handled affairs with their lawyers. Jerrod expressed confidence that they'd win. If the talk in Jake's was any indication, Mariah would have been a wise woman to lay bets to that effect. One day Mariah found him bent over a ledger back in Jake's office.

"You ever resent working so hard for them?" she asked. "Ever envious of what they have?"

As Jerrod looked up, a surprised expression overtook his face. But beneath it all, a dark humor glinted in his eyes. "Miss Mariah, darling, I haven't a jealous bone in me. Don't you know that whatever belongs to Dallas also belongs to me?" His gaze perused her, traveling over her gaudy, tight-fitting gown, lingering a moment too long on her bosom.

Mariah didn't understand Jerrod. His friendship never overstepped the bounds of a gentleman, but at times like this she knew he wanted her. He intentionally let her know, that much was certain. Did he truly feel that she belonged to both men? Coming from another man the insinuation would have angered her, but she'd grown used to forgiving Jerrod his shortcomings.

"Dal has already offered me a piece of his share."

"Did you take it?" Mariah pulled a chair across the desk from him.

He shook his head. "Taking things from Dal has always been too easy. I have enough money to get by. I don't need his." He stretched his arms out and wiggled his fingers, tight from writing. "No, I'm just here to make sure no one swindles him out of what's his and to keep an eye on Dal. He's as likely as not to gamble his good luck away, and I don't mean to let that happen."

Mariah couldn't help baiting Jerrod. "So you'd never take anything from Dallas, nothing of value?"

He leaned forward across the desk. "She would have to be a powerful temptation."

He spoke in riddles. Mariah didn't know whether he meant a woman, or a generic she, like a ship. So it went through that winter. They parried and sparred, feeling out how they felt about one another, but neither one crossed the line.

Being cooped up so long led to unpredictable behavior. Molly made it her goal to liven up the town. She took to riding her arch-necked pure white Arabian down the streets of town, stepping high. When her parading grew mundane, and she got thirsty, she'd ride right through the swinging doors of the nearest saloon and order a shot of whiskey straight up. When the bartender handed it up to her, she drank it in a single gulp. No pretenses.

Mariah thought no one acted more jittery with anticipation and eagerness for spring than Jerrod. He seemed perpetually perched for flight. He talked of leaving, of an errand he had, of personal matters back home that need tending. As March slid toward April, he only got worse.

Spring finally broke free mid-April. Stories floated up and down the mining country of destruction wrought by the sudden warming and flooding. Hungry men streamed into town from the hills where they'd somehow managed to last through winter. Mariah was having a drink with Molly in a saloon down the street from Jake's when one of these unfortunates wandered in.

He looked half-starved, probably hadn't eaten in days. The picture of him tore at Mariah's heart. She kept imagining Dallas. The stranger staggered to the bar and asked for something to eat. Quantities of food were always available to customers, but the man was broke. The owner ordered him thrown out. Mariah was only halfway to her feet, ready to stop the man and bring him home to feed him, when Molly exploded beside her.

In an instant, Molly climbed on top of the table and drew a bead on the owner with the small pistol she kept in her pocket. "Don't move, you cheap skunk!" For a petite woman she had a powerful voice, especially when angered. "You do and you'll have three eyes where now you have two." She looked around the bar, smiling at anyone who caught her eye. "Folks, for the next thirty minutes everything in the house is free, due to the kindness of the rattlesnake over there. Eat and drink everything you can hold, but don't carry anything away."

That was Molly for you—quick to anger, quick to kindness, never slow to react. Once the men got on their way to cleaning the saloon out, eating and drinking to contentment, Molly climbed down off the table and picked up their conversation like there hadn't been any interruption.

"Now that spring's come, I suppose Mr. Dallas Baldwin might be coming back to town."

"I guess he might," Mariah said.

Molly looked sympathetic. "You don't know?"

"I haven't heard."

"The swine hasn't kept up a correspondence with you?" Molly reached over and patted her hand. "Ah, lassie, don't look so depressed. Lovesickness doesn't enhance a woman's beauty any. I've heard the judge is going to schedule a trial date now that the snow has cleared. That will draw Mr. Baldwin back, surely."

Mariah shrugged and tried to feign indifference, but she couldn't fool Molly.

"If I were you, I'd be thanking providence this instant that trouble and weather have kept that man away long enough to cool his intemperate, spontaneous passion," Molly said. "Love of that sort most always passes just as easily as it forms. I take it by his silence his love has gone the general way. There's no use wasting away after him now. A marriage to him would only lead to trouble.

"Anyway, you go after him again now and people will only brand you a gold digger, though isn't that what we all are here?" She laughed.

A week later, that saloon owner sold out and moved on. A person didn't want to get on Molly's bad side, not in this town.

Several days later, Jerrod came to call on Mariah at her cabin.

"Just stopped by to let you know that the judge has set a trial date for May," he said.

"That's good, then, assuming you're prepared. Soon it will all be over."

He stood with his hat in his hand. She offered him a seat, and he took it while she put a pot of coffee on to brew. The hour was late, the evening chill.

"I think we are, though who knows what might come up."

Something about his posture led her to believe he had more to say. "You're holding something back."

"You read me well, Miss Mariah." He smiled. "I've come to say goodbye. I'll be leaving early tomorrow."

She gasped. "But with the trial—"

"I hope to be back before it starts, though I can't make any promises." He leaned toward her, his eyes filled with emotion. "Believe me, only the most urgent business could call me away now."

She looked down at the tips of her boots peeking out from beneath her skirts. "I guess I knew this was coming. You've been ready to jump the fence since the first sign of spring." Her voice failed her. "I sure am going to miss your company."

"Mariah"—he rarely called her that—"I came tonight because I have something that needs saying." He patted the chair next to him. "Here, come sit beside me and let me speak my mind."

She sat obediently, eager to hear, yet dreading the words to come.

"I know how Dallas felt about you last fall, and it's kept me silent all these months. I have to say that I don't know what he's feeling now." A look of anger shaded his face. "Meaning no disregard, I tell you that Dallas is quick to latch on to an idea, a dream, or a scheme. He's equally fast at losing his heart." Jerrod hesitated. He took her hands and held them between his. "I've seen him do it many times over the years. In the past, his feelings have cooled just as abruptly. I can't say for certain that is the case now. And not knowing, I feel disloyal for even speaking."

She held her breath, waiting for the words that followed.

He continued, his voice clear and smooth. "We started out as friends, and I hope we always will be that, but I've come to feel something deeper than friendship for you, Miss Mariah."

"Jerrod—"

He spoke over her. "The truth is, Dal asked me to look after you during the winter, and I started out doing it for him, but I ended up doing it for you...and me. I like your company, Miss Mariah." His voice broke. "Damn, Dallas! He's always put his word in first. He always gets what he wants. If things were different I would have declared myself long ago." He looked directly into her eyes.

Mariah's hands trembled in Jerrod's broad, warm ones. What could she say? She hardly knew her own mind. Finally, she found her voice: "Dallas took back his marriage proposal."

"But that doesn't mean he doesn't still think he has a claim on you."

"I'm confused. Why are you telling me this, Jerrod? What do you expect from me? And what is it between you and Dallas? I can't figure it out. A deep love of kin?"

Dejection encompassed his expression. He hung his head over her lap, where he squeezed her hands. "I'm sorry. I don't mean to be trifling with you. I...I just couldn't hold in my feelings any longer. I had to let you know how I felt before I left."

Mariah slipped a hand free to run her fingers first through his hair and then over the dark stubble on his cheeks. He pulled her hand around and kissed her palm.

"Of course, you wouldn't understand about Dal and me. We're like twin sons of different mothers. We've always looked out for each other, never backhanded the other one." He took her palm and began drawing circles on it with his finger, seemingly absorbed in his thoughts. "Well, I'll tell you a story about us so you'll understand—something no one else has ever known. It's the only way I can think of to illustrate what Dal and I are to each other, how close we are."

He took a deep breath and tipped her chin up from where she watched his fingers, mesmerized by his touch, and gazed directly into her eyes. "You must promise never to tell, not even Dal."

"I promise." Her voice came out breathy.

He smiled darkly. "You're too young to remember the War Between the States. Looking at you and your lovely young face—hell, you may not even have been born. Dal and I were just kids. Our daddies had modest farms near Springfield, Missouri. Nothing fancy, certainly not plantations. But we weren't crackers, just middle-class folk. We didn't own a single slave, but both our daddies sympathized with the Confederacy.

"You have to realize that southern Missourians are an independent breed. They don't cotton to anyone telling them what to do. Our daddies simply disliked the Union's bossiness. So despite the fact that Missouri never actually seceded, they both ran off and joined the Confederate army, just like about a third of our neighbors. That proved a mistake that they'd pay for later with the scorn of those neighbors who stayed in the Union." A kind of veil came over his expression.

"Being little boys, the war passed Dal and me by. Other than the absence of our daddies, we didn't much notice it. It was an incident after the whole thing was over, while we waited for our daddies to come home, that I can't forget.

"Union soldiers straggled past on the way north. Our farm was small, mostly not worth bothering with, but it was known that we were Southern sympathizers. A few lone soldiers raided what food supplies we couldn't hide, ran off with most of the chickens and such, but mostly they left us alone. A common enough story during those times."

Suddenly he looked distant, faraway, reliving the past. "It was Dal's eighth birthday. Our daddies weren't back yet. Ma was going to try to make something special from what she had around. She went out to the chicken coop in the barn to get an egg or two, whatever she could find. Dal and I were playing in the kitchen.

"Here's where I have to preface my story by saying that Ma was a beautiful woman. Many's the man who had his eye on her. Being a boy, I didn't realize how dangerous it was for a pretty gal like Ma to be without male protection with so many hardened, cruel, lonely soldiers coming by.

"When she didn't come back from the barn right away, Dal and I went looking for her." Jerrod shuddered. "I'll never forget the scene. Standing outside the barn door, we heard Ma's stifled screams and sounds of a struggle. Being boys, we thought our mean old cock had her cornered. We didn't know how right we were.

"Dal pushed the door open. Ma lay on the ground, her skirts pushed up around her hips. A filthy old soldier lay on top of her, his pants down around his knees, grunting and riding her."

Mariah gasped, but Jerrod didn't seem to hear.

"Dal momentarily froze. I grabbed the rusty old ax that hung on the wall. It all happened so fast. I didn't think of anything but stopping the savage and saving Ma. In an instant, I swung it right into the back of that damned Yankee's head. A second later, Dal was behind me with a shovel ready to club him." Jerrod took several deep breaths.

Mariah hugged him. There were no words to say.

"Blood squirted everywhere. The bastard slumped dead. Ma didn't scream, didn't say anything. She looked so pale she scared Dal and me. We rolled him off her and each grabbed a shovel. Somehow we managed to drag him from the barn into a brush-covered ravine, where we buried him. We never told Ma where, and she never asked. I still remember raking away the trail of blood he left, erasing that bastard from Ma's memory as best we could.

"After that, Dal and I drew Ma what seemed like a hundred baths. She bathed and bathed and couldn't ever get clean enough. We took turns guarding her, too.

"We'd seen animals mate. Dal worried Ma would get with child, but she didn't. We'd gotten there in time." He lifted his head, and his thoughts seemed to return to the present. "I hope you don't think less of Dal and me for killing a man."

"Oh, no. You were just little boys protecting your mama. I'm so sorry."

"Don't be. That wasn't my point. I'm just letting you see how deep we run. We committed murder together at eight years old and never told another soul, not even our daddies when they came home. We're inseparable, Mariah. Our secrets run deep. I couldn't live with Dal hating me anymore than he could with me hating him. That's what makes this tragic, Mariah, both of us falling in love with the same woman." He sighed. "Given our similarities, it was probably inevitable. But only one of us can win. More likely all of us will lose." He gave her a weak smile and swallowed hard before standing. The coffee boiled wildly on the stove. Mariah ignored it as she stood to match Jerrod.

"I have to be going now." He took her hands in his again. "I'm not asking you to wait for me, Mariah. I'm not asking you to choose between us. I intended to get things out in the open so we can all decide where we stand."

Before she could answer, he tugged on her hands, toppling her into him as he released his grip and cupped the back of her head with one hand and her bottom with the other. His mouth came down hard on hers. There was nothing kind or gentle about his kiss. He pressed her into him so tightly she could barely breathe. His hand on her bottom squeezed too tightly, too familiarly. He thrust his tongue too deeply into her mouth. If she had expected a reticent lover from his earlier restraint, she was sorely surprised. It was over in an instant. He released her to stand dizzily next to him, gauging her own reaction, making comparisons unbidden. Thoughts of Dallas's slow, seductive kisses at the claim forced their way to mind. The smell of summer grass, the flight of her heart. Jerrod just left her stunned.

With the scream of coffee boiling in the background, she looked into Jerrod's eyes as he studied her. What she saw there forced her to grab hold of the chair back for support. Raw lust glittered back at her in the darkness. Something akin to triumph matched it, confusing her completely. She always knew that, beneath his calm exterior, Jerrod harbored a hard edge. It gleamed before her unsheathed and lethal. In the next instant, it passed. He bent over her hand and kissed it gently. Then he donned his hat and let himself out, pausing at the door to give her a nod before disappearing into the night.

CHAPTER FOURTEEN

Less than a week after Jerrod left, a stranger rode into Murray, staggered into a crowded Jake's, and ordered a pint of whiskey. He drank it straight, without stopping, before toppling from his chair and sprawling on the floor, causing a commotion that sent everyone, including Mariah, flying over to see what had happened.

Slim Wilkins bent over the man and felt his pulse. He shook his head slowly, his mouth pursed. "He's dead." Then he rolled back the man's eyelids. "It's smallpox. Seen it before in Virginia City and Leadville."

A pale silence fell over the crowd.

"For heaven's sake," Mariah said when it became evident that no one else knew what to do. "Take him out. Wrap the body in burlap and bury it as far away from town as you can. I'll help with the wrapping." She absently touched the scar on her cheek. "It can't hurt me again."

Within two weeks, a smallpox epidemic swept through town, then up along the creek into the mountains and the most remote miners' cabins. People died by the dozens daily, mostly men alone and untended. The streets, the saloons, the town looked like a ghost town as people stayed home, trying to hide from the disease. But there was no safe place.

Molly and the girls took in half a dozen men with the fever. Mariah helped nurse them until they recovered or died. And most of them died. She and Molly stepped out onto the stoop after the most recent passing.

"I'll go for the undertaker," Mariah said. "But I don't hold out much hope he'll come anytime soon. We'd be better off finding us a strong man who can help with the burial, if there is one to be found."

Molly had been growing tenser each day. "This has to stop!" Tears stood in her eyes. "We did what we could for a few, but there's men out there dying alone while people stand by and do nothing. Soon this really will be a ghost town." She turned to Mariah. "Go find Phil O'Rourke. I hear he's back in town. Tell him to set up a street meeting for me for everyone who isn't sick. We either stand together, or die together. I'm for living."

Mariah found Phil easily enough, drinking at Jake's. He most likely would have been gaming, too, if he could have scared up enough souls brave enough to venture out. Seeing him calmed her nerves. Winter had treated him well. Phil had the lean, muscular look of a man who had worked hard. The sight of a man flushed pink with health, strong and without scabs or scars, fell with pleasure on her eye. Too often lately she'd seen only pallor, disease, and bodies laid to waste by fever.

"Hello, stranger," she said to him. "You a rich man yet?"

"One would hope. Ah, Mariah, lassie, what beauty you add to the room! So good to see you. You are a brave one, lassie, to venture out."

She pointed to the scar on her cheek. "Not really, Phil. I'm in no danger. The fever had its shot at me and lost."

"What brings you here, then? You can see I'm the only dance partner in the room." Phil laughed. "Ah, it's not me you'll be wanting to see." He shot her a crooked grin. "Maybe you hoped I'd brought a mining partner or two with me, or a letter from one?" He shook his head. "Sorry to disappoint you, lass."

"Molly sent me." She covered her embarrassment by explaining to Phil what Molly wanted. He leaped to his feet immediately.

"Consider it done." He was almost to the door by the time she caught him by the sleeve.

"Phil, before you go, tell me how things are out at the Bunker. Is everyone well?"

His look turned serious. "Aye, not a touch of the fever when I left." He flexed a muscle. "And you can see we did well enough through the winter. No mere bones here."

"Thanks, Phil. Guess you'd better be off." She dropped her hand from his arm and turned to walk away.

"Mariah, you going to leave without hearing the news you came after?"

She turned back to look at him.

"Dallas works like a dog on that claim, but when he talks about anything other than mining, it's you. I shouldn't be saying a thing. I know he's kept his distance, though I can't reckon why. He has his own rules and his own code of honor."

Mariah smiled at Phil. "Phil O'Rourke, you are probably the sweetest man to walk the earth. Problem is, I can't trust a word from your mouth. You'd sweet-talk a mule to keep it from bawling. To save you trouble in the future—I don't live and breathe by what Dallas Baldwin says or does. If he wants to keep to himself on that claim, I guess it's his business."

Phil left shaking his head and laughing. He hadn't believed her protests. Trouble was, she didn't know if she did either. Dallas's inattention to her, and his apparent visit to Edith, stung. Though something about that visit to Edith still seemed suspicious. Mariah ought to forget about him altogether, but she couldn't forget their first meetings and his early enthusiasm, his passion, his smile. The only true thing she knew—Jerrod had stirred up a whirl of doubt and indecision in her. How she'd resolve it, she didn't know.

Within the hour, Mariah stood in the crowd of frightened bystanders as Molly climbed to the top of a crate in the middle of the street. Her blue eyes flashing, she faced the mob. Somber reality returned.

"You poor, miserable fools!" Her voice shook. "Weak-kneed, spineless fools! You don't lick anything by running away from it, or hiding your heads under your pillows! You hole up in your homes thinking maybe this won't find you while your friends and neighbors are dying off alone, unattended. And you haven't done a damned thing about it because you were afraid to go near them.

"Well, I'm not afraid. There are half a dozen sick men up there in my part of town, and me and my girls are doing what we can for them. Now everyone who isn't sick is going to help. You're going to clear out the hotels and turn them into hospitals. Or me and my girls will do it ourselves. Then you'll stay with the sick as long as they need help."

Murmurs of protest and fear rose from the crowd.

"Sure, you'll be taking a chance of coming down with the fever," Molly continued. "But no more chance than standing here in the street. I see our mayor over there. Hey! Mr. Mayor, order the hotels cleared or I'll organize a committee to run you out of town. I've plenty of friends right here willing to do it."

Phil leaped up on the box to support Molly. "I'm sure you all understood the lady," he said. "I'm the first volunteer. There'd better be plenty more of you, or there's going to be worse hell than this sickness bust loose!"

Within the afternoon, makeshift hospitals were established and Mariah went to work nursing in one of them. The sickness followed so quickly on the heels of Jerrod's departure that she'd barely had time to think about his declaration or determine her feelings.

During the days that followed, the world seemed shrouded in the darkness of the fever. For Mariah, it was the return of a childhood nightmare. She often fought to overcome the fears that surfaced, the memories of her ma and pa and brothers catching the fever, their moans, their deaths, all seen from the eyes of the small girl she'd been. Powerless, she watched the terror play out again and again. Though she had no worry for herself, she spent most days with a heavy heart and the burden of fear that the disease would take someone she truly loved from her again.

Molly worked herself ragged, and no amount of pleading by Mariah could get her to slow down. All Mariah could do was match her labor for labor, ministration for ministration, and worry for worry.

The disease took only days to germinate, and ran its course quickly. Victims in the hospital were grouped in rooms according to which symptoms they exhibited. Men in the early stages suffered severe headaches, backaches, chills, and high fevers. These men the ladies sponged with cool water, trying to bring the fever down. Nausea followed. Oh, the disgusting work of emptying bedpans heavy with vomit! Changing sheets, washing. The stench became almost unbearable.

After a few days, the sick man would seem to get better, his symptoms lessened, but it was a false recovery. It raised the hopes cruelly, that was all. Almost inevitably, a rash of hard red lumps appeared, first on the arms and legs, then on the chest and face. As the rash turned to blisters, it hurt unbearably. At this point, Doc Wheeler advised the ladies to keep the sores clean and pray the blisters and the patient didn't become infected.

Mariah soon lost any embarrassment over a man's naked body as she washed out sores and swabbed down the men. Though she used as gentle a touch as she knew how, some patients screamed when the soapy water hit their wounds. Others sobbed and begged for mercy. She pumped and boiled water until her arms felt like lead. She washed red, blistered bodies for so long that when she closed her eyes, red dots swarmed before her. She smoothed brows, changed compresses, spoke words of comfort until her voice gave out. Neither she nor Molly slept more than a few hours at a time for days and days and days on end. And still the men died in rapid succession. Fresh graves with pine crosses sprang like rows of corn up the hill in the once tiny cemetery outside town.

Should a victim survive for near to two weeks without developing a secondary infection, the blisters scabbed over and left pitted scars, but the ill one usually survived.

Mariah lost track of time. She couldn't remember when she'd last changed her dress—probably weeks ago. Days and nights blended together until the day Phil brought Dallas in. The sight of Dallas fevered and sick split a cleft in the continuum of time. From then forward, Mariah fought the battle of her life to save him as time marched on both incredibly slowly and far too quickly.

Though a week's growth of beard disguised him, Mariah recognized Dallas the moment her gaze touched his. He leaned heavily on Phil's arm as they came through the hospital door, backlit by sunshine. Dallas's dark hair plastered his head, sweat beaded on his brow, and his shirt stuck to his body, still hard and muscular despite the ravages of disease. When they stepped into the room away from the light, she saw telltale dark circles beneath his eyes and red pox on his arms beneath his rolled sleeves.

She froze, paralyzed with fear a second, no longer. Then she dropped the clean sheets she carried and met them at the door, wrapping Dallas's free arm around her shoulders to take some of his weight off Phil. Her quick gaze caught sight of infected pox, and for the first time in days she felt dizzy with nausea herself. Heaven help her, her worst fear had materialized!

"Phil, in heaven's name, why did you wait so long to bring him in!" Mariah's fears manifested as anger. She lashed out at the nearest target. Dallas was just too weak to accuse. Deep down, she knew blaming Phil wouldn't help, but she couldn't stop herself.

Dallas gave her a pleading look. "Don't go blaming Phil, Mariah. It's only because of him I'm here now. I fought coming. Didn't think it was serious. Thought I could fight it myself." His words came in weak gasps punctuated by deep coughs.

Mariah feared he had pneumonia already.

"He is a stubborn cuss. Had to haul him here, I did." Phil nodded. His usual buoyant humor had been replaced by an uncharacteristic graveness.

"Let's take him to the back. There's an empty room there with fresh sheets. I just changed them myself."

They maneuvered Dallas onto a bed in the last room on the first floor. After they settled Dallas in, Phil and Mariah met in the hall just outside Dallas's door.

"I'm sorry for blaming you, Phil." She paused, tears dancing in her eyes. "I'm just so frustrated, so scared." She started shaking.

Phil wrapped his big Irish arms around her. "And tired and overwhelmed, no doubt. Listen, lassie, I have to tell you, he didn't want to come, didn't want you to see him like this. I told you, he has a strange code of honor. He worked down in the hole until he collapsed. I think he would have died out there on the claim if I hadn't hauled him in here against his will. He was just plain too weak to fight me."

"You did right bringing him here now. He's awful sick, but I'm going to take care of him and fight this thing with everything I have in me. Listen, Phil, do you know how to get hold of Jerrod?"

Phil nodded.

"Wire him and tell him that Dallas is mighty sick."

She dispatched Phil with a further list of errands for the hospital and then went back to check on Dallas. She found him still awake, staring at the ceiling, his thoughts seemingly miles away. He barely had the strength to look at her when she approached. She, however, had renewed energy. When Pa and Ma and her two brothers had lain dying, she'd been too frail, too young to help them. Not this time! She wouldn't lose again.

She walked directly over to Dallas and, without looking him in the eye, tore open his shirt. The thing was rags anyway, filthy and stained with infection, not worth saving. Festering blisters covered his sculpted chest. The pox was far more advanced than she'd thought.

"Damn you, Dallas Baldwin, for your own stubbornness." She blinked back a sudden tear. "When you get over this thing, you aren't going to be as pretty as you used to be."

He tried to laugh, but a cough tore through him.

"You need washing—"

"To put it mildly."

"—and disinfecting." She caught him trying a weak smile. "You won't be thinking this is funny when I'm done with you. Doc Wheeler's antiseptic scrub has had stronger men than you begging for mercy." She kept her voice stern to keep it from cracking. He was bad off, real bad. She hadn't seen anyone this far gone live through it. "You strong enough to get yourself undressed?"

He nodded.

She turned to leave, pausing to call back over her shoulder, "Good. I expect to find you naked under that sheet when I come back. Drop your clothes in a pile next to the bed. They'll have to be burned." She walked straight out without waiting for a reply. Molly caught her in the hall.

"I hear Phil brought Dallas in. I'll have Clara tend him."

Mariah shook her head. "No, he's mine."

"You sure?"

"As anything. But I need Doc Wheeler to see him. He's in bad shape and I need the doc's advice on what to do."

"He's upstairs. I'll get him for you and meet you in his room. Where'd you put him?"

Ten interminable minutes later, Doc finished his examination while Molly and Mariah waited in the hall. Doc came out of the room shaking his head.

"He won't last the night. The fever's spread to his chest; most likely he has pneumonia." Doc Wheeler pulled a small vial filled with white powder from his pocket. "You his nurse?" he asked Mariah, then handed her the vial. "Morphine—it's a new, much stronger form of laudanum. It'll ease his pain some on his way out. Mix it with a straight shot of whiskey. It works faster that way, but be frugal with it. Too high a dose will shut his lungs down completely. Once he's settled down, come upstairs. I have half a dozen patients who need bathing."

Mariah stared at the bottle, then turned a steely gaze on the doc. "From now until he either dies or recovers, Dallas is my only patient."

The doctor's eyes went wide. "Listen, little lady— that man is a lost cause. There are others who need nursing, whom nursing might save."

Molly caught the doctor's attention and shook her head gently. The doctor mumbled something and strode off in silent acquiescence.

"Thank you for standing up for me, Mol. I'm sorry, but I can't leave him alone. He'll die. I'm the only chance he has." Mariah's voice broke.

Molly patted her arm. "No need explaining, just do your best by him."

Dallas rested on his back with his eyes closed when Mariah returned to his room with a bottle of whiskey and a glass under one arm, washbasin and soapy water in hand, and Doc's vial in her pocket. Dallas breathed shallowly. His chest rattled. His clothes sat in a pile next to the bed. The exertion of the meager exercise of removing his clothes stood in beads on his forehead. She was probably a fool to have any hope. Curse this vicious killer!

She set her supplies down on the nightstand and carefully rolled the sheet down off his naked chest, past his abdomen. His hand clasped hers, weakly but insistently. His eyes popped open, imploring her to stop her progression.

"I'm going to bathe you, Dallas. And disinfect every festered blister. I'll be as gentle as I can, but it's going to hurt."

He grasped the sheet. She tugged gently, but he wouldn't let go—not that she couldn't have overpowered him.

"This is no time for modesty. I've seen what you got hundreds of times this week. It won't shock me any."

"Not mine."

"You any different than any other man?" She forced herself to smile.

"I didn't mean for you to see me like this. Not like this," he whispered hoarsely.

"You want another nurse?"

"No woman...in town...seen mine. Don't leave me, Mariah."

It hurt watching the effort it took for him to speak.

"We'll just start with your chest, then. I've seen that before, remember?" She talked as she bathed, trying to distract him. But he flinched at the softest touch of the washrag and set his jaw with clenched teeth. What would he do when she used the alcohol disinfectant?

"You were helping me on my claim. The day was hot and you took your shirt off and I sat back and admired the fine play of your muscles as you filled the sluice box." She thought he smiled. She couldn't tell for certain. She finished washing up the area he'd let her uncover. "You want a drink, Dallas? I'll just give you a little whiskey with some medicine for the pain mixed in."

He didn't answer. She followed Doc's direction and mixed the morphine. What choice did she have? He fought so bravely to keep from letting her see his pain, from screaming or groaning. Heaven help her if she killed him! He took the whiskey easily enough.

"Roll onto your stomach now, Dallas, and we'll take care of your back."

He succeeded with effort, but his back remained taut as she washed and then dabbed with the alcohol.

Half a dozen times she nearly told him to go on ahead and cry out, but she let him have his dignity.

"I'm going to have to see that bottom of yours now, Dallas."

He was getting drowsy. The morphine must be working. He let her pull the sheet completely off him, but immediately started shaking with chills. She worked quickly. He was nearly unconscious and shaking violently by the time she turned him over on his back. Without regard to lowering his fever, she covered him with a light blanket and tucked him in tightly.

He slept fitfully, moaning and coughing and mumbling. Mariah could make out very few words. Once she thought he said, "ax," another, "I killed him." Sometimes he called out her name. Through it all she held his hand and talked about nothing in soft, reassuring tones.

She bathed him every few hours and dosed him with more morphine when the pain came back. She sat next to his bed, unable to sleep, afraid that if she dozed off he'd stop breathing. In the middle of the night, he began wheezing severely and gasping for breath. His own phlegm choked him.

"Oh, dear God, oh, dear God." Her prayers got no further. Dallas turned purple. She forgot her anger at the doctor, her resolve not to call on him. "Doc Wheeler! Doc Wheeler!" She ran to the door and screamed again. Clara strode by with a washbasin in hand, shaking her head.

"He's got two men dying upstairs in the death room. He ain't going to come. I got to get up there myself." Clara brushed past Mariah to the stairs.

The room behind her suddenly seemed too quiet, as though death was settling in. Mariah turned back to look at Dallas. His chest sat silent under the covers. Curse Doc Wheeler—there wasn't time for him anyway.

She rushed back to Dallas, whose skin now looked ashen, pale, lilac gray. He lay still, with his eyes open, too weak to fight.

A small pocketknife sat on the table next to the bed. She'd watched Doc Wheeler cut holes in men's throats to help them breathe at least a dozen times. She picked the knife up and dropped it just as quickly, shaking furiously. It missed the table and clanked to the floor. Likely as not, she'd kill him trying that trick and everyone would accuse her of mutilating the body. She pulled her skirts up, and with an effort of will, propped Dallas up and slid in behind him, one leg on each side of him, skirts hiked clear to her hips. She slid a washbasin in front of him and thumped his back with closed fists.

"Come on, Dallas. Quitter! You can't give up. You bastard, breathe!"

Nothing.

She cursed him for being muscled and strong. Though she hit him ferociously, her pummeling made no difference. He didn't breathe. Frustrated, she wrapped her arms just below his ribcage, placing her fists at the base. If she could get him to vomit, that might clear his throat. She braced herself and then pulled up with the strength fear gives.

Dallas coughed and retched into the bucket before him. He gasped for air and his chest swelled—he was breathing!

Tears slid down her cheeks. He slumped back against her, unconscious, but breathing. She reached around him, managing to maneuver the basin back to the nightstand. Then she leaned back against the headboard with Dallas's weight pressing against her, listening to the hollow sound of his ragged breaths against the night.

She hadn't been aware of dozing off. Doc Wheeler's brash voice startled her awake.

"Well, young lady, if this isn't a sight to behold."

Mariah opened her eyes. A pale shaft of sunlight slid in through a crack in the muslin curtain, giving the room a wash of hope. Doc Wheeler stood before her with his shirtsleeves rolled up, circles of sweat pooling under his arms mirroring the dark half-circles under his eyes. It took a minute for her predicament to come back to her.

"It's a sight better than death." Numb from Dallas's weight resting against her, she awkwardly tried to straighten her skirts.

Doc Wheeler nodded and gave her a hand. "You're right on that account. Seen enough of that these past days." Doc helped wrestle her out from behind Dallas.

When she'd pulled free and was on her feet, Doc saw the knife on the floor. He gave her a questioning look.

"He couldn't breathe. I saw you do it before, but...but I couldn't." Mariah's body ached. Her back was sore. She stretched. "Never rest on your bustle, Doc. It makes for a terrible backache."

Doc was bent over checking Dallas, but even from the distance, Mariah could see Dallas was better. She heard it in his breathing.

For the first time in days, Doc smiled. "I'll try to remember that." He bent down to listen to Dallas's chest. "Whatever you did to get him breathing again seemed to do the trick. His lungs sound clearer." Doc straightened. "You're a better nurse than I guessed anyone could be. Looks like he just might live," he told Mariah. "Keep bathing him. Bandage up the worst of the sores and let the rest dry out. Dose him with the morphine so he can rest and call me if he gets worse."

She stayed with him all that day and night. To stay awake, she began reading aloud from a copy of Missouri native Mark Twain's latest novel, *Adventures of Huckleberry Finn*. She thought Dallas might like hearing a tale of an adventurous boy from home, that the cadence of the words, the familiar dialect and setting, might bring him back, comfort him. From time to time, she prayed, sometimes to herself, sometimes out loud. Other times she implored Dallas to live. The second evening, Doc Wheeler pronounced that Dallas would live, and sent Mariah home before she collapsed of exhaustion like Molly had earlier the same day. Mariah went, not because Doc told her to, but because she could see for herself that Dallas grew stronger each day.

She stumbled back to her little cabin, fell onto the bed fully dressed, and slept for sixteen hours straight.

CHAPTER FIFTEEN

Mariah went back to the hospital to check on Dallas. Freshly scrubbed with French-milled lavender soap, hair twisted into an elaborate knot at the back of her head, wearing a clean gown, and doused in rose water, she felt optimistic, whole, fresh, and beautiful as the riotous wild rose bush that grew along the fence outside her cabin. Happy, euphoric—Dallas lived, would live, had called her name in delirium. She didn't want to inspect too closely her raging passion for Dallas Baldwin. What it meant, she couldn't say. Would she marry him, make a life with him? Did she want to? Would he ask again? That she felt this burbling sense of joy was enough for this moment.

She carried her copy of *Huck Finn,* and a lovely bunch of wildflowers—buttercups, birdbills, ladyslippers—to brighten his room. She would read to him, lull him back to vitality, and then she would see where life led.

A renewed spirit of optimism surged through the hotel. Mariah felt the hum of triumph, the thread of hope the moment she stepped in the door. The disease waned. No new cases had been reported in days. She went directly to Dallas's room and pushed the slightly ajar door open to find herself staring at duplicate images of her heart.

Jerrod had returned. He sat with his back to the door next to Dallas's bed, leaning over, conversing with Dallas. They didn't notice her, engaged as they were in their exchange. Both men laughed in unison at something Mariah could not hear. She was struck immediately by the new differences in the two. Dallas looked weak and pale compared to the robust Jerrod. And Jerrod was unscarred, handsome as ever, but did not trip her heart as Dallas did.

Dallas saw her first. In his eyes, a brief embarrassment flashed. He averted his gaze and stared at the blanket covering his lap. "Mariah," he said very softly.

Jerrod turned. His eyes lit up at the sight of her. He was on his feet immediately. "Our angel of mercy!" Delight resonated in his voice, almost calculated. "Look, Dal, your savior has come to visit." An instant later, he gave her a bracing hug, pressing her against him a little too tightly right before Dallas's eyes.

Mariah blushed and stepped away from him. "Jerrod, you're back."

"Phil's telegram scared the hell out me." He sounded suddenly serious. "I took the first train out. God bless you, Mariah. I've heard the whole tale of what you did for Dal. We can't ever thank you enough." He extended his arm, a welcome into the room.

"No thanks necessary. I was just doing my job." She went to the bedside. "How are you feeling, Dallas?"

"Old, very weak, but alive." He looked at her searchingly; pain and suspicion played in his eyes, disfiguring the joy she'd hope to see. His manner seemed guarded. Did he suspect Jerrod's feelings for her? She wished that he'd been alone, that she could speak to him in private and explain.

She spoke cautiously, impersonally, and laughed nervously. "I know. It feels like you'll never be yourself again. But you will. It may take time—"

"Yes, that's what the doctor said as well." Dallas seemed uncomfortable in her presence. "I haven't thanked you myself, Mariah," he said. "I'm in your debt."

She felt herself blushing again. "We all, those of us who the disease skipped over, did what we had to." She forced a smile. "I brought you flowers. You've been too sick to notice, but spring has taken hold. Flowers are blooming everywhere." She put the buds in a drinking glass next to the bed. "I brought the book I was reading to you when you were so sick. Do you remember? I thought I might finish reading it to you now, but you have Jerrod to keep you company." She set it on the nightstand.

Jerrod came up behind her. "Mark Twain—a good old boy from home. A fine choice, Mariah. I'll read it to you later, Dal."

Unease stifled the warm meeting with Dallas that Mariah had anticipated. Suddenly, she longed to escape. "You look tired, Dallas. I don't want to wear you out. You need your rest. I just wanted to see how you were doing. I'm glad to find your health improving." Mariah smiled, preparing to leave. What use was there in staying?

Dallas grabbed her hand suddenly. "Wait. I have to know, Mariah. Why did you do it? Why save me when everyone else, even the doctor, had given up?" He gave her a searching look, confusion and hope mixed in.

Emotions stumbled inside her, tangled in the bracken surrounding her heart and head. She felt Jerrod stiffen behind her. She caught herself, more confused now than ever. Finally, she found her voice.

"I had to believe in a dream, Dallas. I wanted to see one lucky person go on to live the golden life. You found the mine. You're so close to having wealth and power and fame. I couldn't let it die. It all seemed so unfair. Smallpox took everything from me. I couldn't let that happen to you."

"I see." Evidently it wasn't the answer Dallas expected. He stared at her for a long moment, his expression masked.

"The trial starts next week," Jerrod said, breaking an awkward silence. "Soon, very soon, he will indeed have it all." Jerrod smiled.

Dallas fell back onto his pillow and closed his eyes.

"You're right, Mariah. Dal needs his rest. I've kept him up too long." Jerrod took her arm and guided her from the room, closing the door behind him.

In the hall, he took her in his arms and tilted her chin up to look into her eyes. "My God, Mariah. I owe you everything. Dal is like the other half of me. How could I live without him? I should have known you'd do this for me." He kissed her then, right in the hallway where anyone could see.

She stiffened. He separated from her suddenly. "Forgive me. I couldn't help myself. I've missed you so badly." His words sounded tender, but jealousy raged in his expression. "We'll have to keep our distance for a time. I haven't had a chance to talk to Dal about us, the three of us. He has enough on his mind for now. You understand?"

Mariah nodded.

After that, although she stopped by the hospital frequently to check on Dallas, she didn't get an opportunity to speak with him alone before he went back to the Bunker. Judge Buck moved the trial date back until June, but preparations for it kept Jerrod and Dallas busy and out of sight.

The trial began in early June in the stuffy little second-floor courtroom of the Shoshone County courthouse in Murray. Tobacco-chewing Territorial Judge Norman Buck presided. On the streets of town, near-riots erupted as miners debated the pros and cons of the case, and the trial stretched into weeks.

Phil and Jake had their own strategy for winning, but it wasn't carried out in the courtroom. They bought drinks for any and every miner who'd listen to their plight and sympathize with them. Their plan seemed to be working. The average miner stood solidly behind Noah and partners. Miners who dared side with Peck and Cooper, or sympathized with them in any way, were ostracized and threatened with violence by the masses.

Phil and Jake continued buying drinks with abandon for anyone who backed them. They felt a kind of euphoria, a certainty they'd win. Soon they'd be rich men. Phil greeted all his drinking compatriots with a hearty "hail, fellow." The phrase reverberated through town.

"What makes you so confident, Phil?" Mariah asked him one day.

"Mariah! Can't you see? The people of this town are squarely behind us. The men on that jury couldn't do no different than vote in our favor. No one likes those tight, penny-pinching bastards Peck and Cooper." He slugged down a beer in only a few gulps.

"But should public opinion guide law? Don't the jurors have to vote based on the evidence?"

The trial had been going well, though lawyers for both sides had their antics. Noah's side claimed that the meager grubstake provided by Peck and Cooper lasted no more than a day or two. The opposition procured a list from Jim Wardner, who'd originally filled the grubstake order, but who had become a partner in the

Bunker Hill and Sullivan just days after it was discovered.

Peck and Cooper's lawyers brought in a wheelbarrow filled with supplies from the list brimming over the top. Ample food to sustain a man for two to three weeks, they asserted.

Jim Wardner kept a low profile. He spent most of his time out at the mine managing a crew of forty men excavating the newly discovered thirty-six-foot vein. Wardner had kept the Bunker going when it seemed ready to fail. He'd found a market for the ore in San Francisco when no one else would buy, and when that ran dry he struck a deal with the governor of Montana to mill the galena so they could sell it elsewhere. He had more money, and as much sweat equity, tied up in the mine than anyone. Mariah guessed Jim maintained his head. He'd seen them through the impossible. She assumed he thought they'd come out ahead in the end.

Dallas had recovered from his smallpox. He'd filled out and was clean-shaven again. His scabs had fallen off, leaving round pink scars like polka dots on his body. Dallas, Jim, and Jerrod kept busy consulting with their lawyers. Mariah saw very little of them other than from a distance in court.

"Damn those bastards," Dallas remarked to her once on a rare occasion he'd come to Jake's. "They're making us out to be liars and cheats."

"Dal never lies," Jerrod added. He smiled, but a sardonic expression drained it of any warmth. "His reputation is too important to him. I've told him a hundred times—what the hell does it matter what they say about you as long as you win? Hundreds of thousands of dollars should compensate him for the blot on his honor."

Dallas looked directly at Mariah and said, softly but vehemently, "I don't cheat. I don't lie. And I always keep my promises. Remember that." The passionate look in his eyes took her aback. "Once my name is cleared—" He didn't get the opportunity to finish the thought.

"Buy me a drink, Dallas Baldwin. You've got my vote." He was interrupted by another miner, as he'd been so often lately. The partners were the biggest celebrities in town.

No matter. A heady breathlessness overcame Mariah. A glimmer of the old Dallas had sparkled. He could have meant anything—*once my name is cleared, I'll show this town,* for instance. But the look he'd given her was personal. Maybe it was only vanity, and she had been vain concerning his early devotion to her and piqued when it seemed to have disappeared, but she knew he spoke regarding her. It was the first tiny glimmer of his interest since last fall.

The others might have been worried, but nothing damped Phil's hopeful outlook. Then came the day in court when one of Peck and Cooper's lawyers, William Stoll, produced the original location notice posted by Noah Kellogg dated September 3, a full week before the partners' posting of September 10.

Noah was called as a witness and had to write his name for comparison. An exact match. The evidence was shown to the jury.

Mariah sat, mouth like cotton, hands trembling. They'd certainly lose now. The judge could turn it all back over to Peck and Cooper. Dallas would be a poor man again, and worse, a man convicted of being a liar and a cheat. She turned to watch Dallas, but all she could see from behind was the ramrod stiffness of his posture.

The jury went out. Every tick of the clock sounded eternal. Mercifully, the jury came back quickly.

"Will the foreman read the verdict?" Judge Buck said solemnly.

"Yes, Your Honor. We, the jury, find for the defendants."

The crowed roared, drowning out the rest of the proclamation and shaking the windows of the courtroom. Judge Buck looked almost comical banging the gavel furiously, but silently in the face of the thunder of victory in the room.

Mariah shook her head, stunned. They'd returned a decision for Noah, Jake, Phil, Harry, Con, and Dallas on the first ballot.

Suddenly, the crowd, acting of one mind, swept Noah, Phil, Jake, Jim, and Dallas up and carried them out of the courtroom, down the stairs, and into the street on shoulders and backs, whooping and hollering.

Mariah stood shakily and followed them out.

Almost instantly, liquor flowed freely in every saloon in town, not the least of which was Dutch Jake's. As soon as he managed to dismount from the crowd and throw the doors open, the crowd surged in to his chorus of "Drinks on the house! On the house, boys!"

Gran's manuscript ended there.

"That's it?" I said to her as I flipped the last page over. She'd come into my room to check on me and been delighted to find me reading. "Where's the murder?"

"Oh, it happened the next morning." Gran pointed to a folder stuffed with photocopies of old newspaper stories and Mariah's journal. "It's all there. You can read the details for yourself, but they won't tell you much.

"That night everyone in town drank themselves silly. It was the biggest bash Murray had ever seen. Dallas and Jerrod were drinking and gambling, too. The next morning, for reasons I can't discover, Jerrod left town early. Mariah herself claims to have gone out for an early morning walk, not connected to Jerrod's departure. She heard the sounds of a rock slide before she left town, and, needing to walk off the effects of the night, went to investigate." Gran nodded toward me. "We really should take a drive out there. You should see those tailings for yourself. They'd give you some idea of how things happened."

I was in no mood for a drive, but I nodded just to make Gran happy.

"A rock slide came down on Jerrod, covering him. That's Mariah's story, anyway."

"Wouldn't a rock slide be rather obvious?"

"Hmmm, yes, that's not what was disputed. No doubt the rocks came down on Jerrod. But how did Mariah escape unscathed? The details of her story didn't add up."

"No?"

Gran shook her head. "She claimed that when she found Jerrod, the slide had already happened, that he'd already been buried. She ran down the hillside and bloodied her hands digging him out of the sharp basalt rock barehanded. She was cut and bruised and covered with blood when they found her."

"How did she know he was down there?" It seemed a natural question.

"That's what everybody wanted to know. She claims she saw his horse first and then his hat lying some distance away, blown off by the wind created by the slide, and she surmised what happened. She ran down the hill, crying out his name. When she came to the spot where he lay, she saw his fingers sticking out from beneath the rock. Horrified, she began digging, unmindful of the harm to herself or the danger of another slide. She managed to uncover his head, but he was dead. She went for help immediately, and ran into Dallas on the trail. He took her back to town to get help."

"Didn't anyone in town hear the slide?"

Gran smiled. "Oh, my smart girl. Indeed they did, and that's part of Mariah's problem. Explosions and sounds of rock slides were nothing new in a mining town, and truthfully, after that night of drinking and carousing, no one was up early or expected anyone to be out on the tailing. But no one in his right mind would have been mining that morning. Several people reported hearing the slide. Unfortunately, several other people, mostly men stumbling home after a night with Molly's girls, reported seeing Mariah leave town before they heard the sounds of the slide."

"That implies, what—that she somehow started the slide?"

"Maybe. The tailings were unstable and unsafe. What Jerrod was doing crossing them, no one knows. Mariah could have stood at the top of the hill and started the slide, though it's not likely. The consensus around town seemed to be more along that lines that she didn't get help for him immediately. Or, more damning still, they found Jerrod with his head unburied, but it had been smashed by a large, blood-covered rock found lying near him."

"The rock she pulled off him?"

"Maybe, or maybe the rock she used to kosh him over the head and finish him off."

"Why?" I asked. "What was her motive?"

Gran sighed. "I thought you'd know the answer to that one, Dani. Greed. The town branded Mariah a gold-digging woman. Isn't that what you think?"

"No. I like Mariah. I don't see her that way. Anyway, how would killing Jerrod put her in the money?"

Gran settled herself in her chair. "I'm muddled. I forget that I haven't told you all the facts. The night of the big celebration, Dallas, Jerrod, and Mariah all celebrated at Jake's. Dallas got involved in a card game for stakes neither Jerrod nor Mariah liked. Jerrod and Dallas fought and Jerrod took Mariah home. Terrible Edith reported seeing him leaving Mariah's cabin early in the morning. Edith made certain indecent insinuations about what had being going on between the two. She claimed Jerrod left smiling.

"Jerrod himself seems to have been unable to remain discreet. After leaving Mariah's, he went back to town and started drinking and bragging about his conquest, so to speak. A few hours later, Dallas went to Mariah's cabin. Edith heard them shouting at each other, but she couldn't make out the words. Dallas stormed off. So you can see what the town thought—Dallas and Jerrod were fighting over Mariah. She got rid of Jerrod so that she could catch Dallas, the rich one."

"But that doesn't make sense. She knew that Dallas was rich before she slept with Jerrod. And if Jerrod and Dallas were so close, wouldn't Dallas blame her, hate her for killing Jerrod?"

"You'd think, but he married her as soon as they'd removed Jerrod's body from the tailings. He married her that very day. The townspeople were somewhat vindicated just a few hours later, when Judge Buck, disgusted with the jury's blatant disregard for law, overturned their decision and found for the plaintiffs. For a while it looked like Mariah had been skunked, left married to a penniless gambler. But Dallas and company still had enough clout to see that Mariah was never charged with a crime.

"The partners appealed to the Supreme Court, which split the ownership of the Bunker Hill between Peck and Cooper and the partners, Noah getting the lion's share. But that all didn't happen for another year. Eventually Dallas and Mariah were quite wealthy. And before the final decision, they had a new baby to add to their happiness. Their money has carried through all the way to me." Gran smiled and patted my arm.

"And that baby was the very first Molly, named for Mariah's good friend Molly b'Dam. She was the mother of generations on, all of us with a bit of Irish in us, all of us Erin's daughters."

"We're Irish?" I asked.

Gran laughed. "A bit. Like most Americans, we're mutts. Mariah's maternal grandparents were from Ireland. Haven't I told you that before?"

"No, Gran," I said.

"I'm getting forgetful. I do hope I haven't left out any other important details." Gran shrugged and continued her original thought. "I suspect that first Molly was both blessing and curse to her parents."

I snorted. "Aren't all children?" I was thinking of the one I hardly believed I carried in my womb.

"Some would argue with you there, Dani, but this one assuredly was. You see, Dallas and Mariah never had any more children. She didn't get pregnant again even once more. I suspect that the smallpox had made Dallas sterile, though they wouldn't have known that. No, I think Jerrod had to have been that baby's papa. It couldn't have ever been proven. But I think Dallas and Mariah figured it out eventually. So poor little Molly was a reminder of betrayal, of a straying heart and speculation."

I felt sick. Suddenly Gran's admonishment early on, that helping her might do me good, made sense, though neither of us had any idea about the pregnancy. A story of betrayal to learn from, but had I?

"Surely the marriage was a good one?" I could barely ask.

Gran nodded solemnly. "Everyone said so. Dallas remained devoted to both of his women for his entire life. He and Mariah seemed to love one another deeply, but what a cross to bear." Gran gave me a head-tilted little bird look. "So, what do you think, Dani—can you figure out for certain whether Mariah killed Jerrod?"

CHAPTER SIXTEEN

Just after the museum closed for the evening, Gran's doorbell rang. Gran and Lucy were out back, so I answered it. Ann Wilson had stopped by to drop off a thin folder for me. She looked the way historians look when they've turned up something new—excited and cautiously optimistic.

"It came in just before closing." She smiled with the pleased look of a three-year-old who's just handed you a dandelion. "It's not much, just a bit about a Jerrod Baldwin. A *very telling* bit. Baldwin's a common name, but I'm sure this is your guy." She thrust the folder at me. "Happy reading. And you'll let me know how this fits in with Maggie's story?"

I thanked her and assured her I would. I resisted the urge to plow through the new information first and instead added it to the bottom of my pile of research to comb over. My method may have been madness, but I had a sequence to the way I was working through the material. I wanted to know all Mariah had to say first.

I spent the evening reading Mariah's diary and the folder of research Gran already had. It beat thinking too closely about my own life. But I couldn't see anything that Gran hadn't. Mainly, reading it allowed me to avoid facing my fears and obligations. I just felt too weak. Too many questions remained unanswered.

About nine o'clock, I took a break and checked my phone.

Finally! A reply from Sean. *Appreciate your honesty. We need to talk whenever you're ready.*

Soon, I thought.

A wave of nausea swept over me. The denial of the day gave way to a strange grief mixed with joy. Finally, after all these years I was going to be a mother. A dream realized. A dream destroyed. A marriage broken. A scandal started. History repeated. Me and Mariah, two of a kind.

A baby—I thought of the joy it was supposed to bring Sean and me, but now it just might be the breaking point of the marriage. An inconsolable sadness overwhelmed me. I had to tell Sean about the baby. I owed him that much. He'd probably decide for a divorce. I couldn't blame him. I wept again for my baby, the baby who needed a father.

I inelegantly wiped my tears with the back of my hand. An inky streak of mascara stained my fingers. Why hadn't I ever learned to wear waterproof?

I tried Sean's phone. He didn't answer.

I turned my attention back to Gran's hundred-year-old mystery. If I was leaving in a few days, I needed to get cracking. Without much optimism, I picked up the folder Ann had left for me and began reading.

She'd left photocopies from an old book that had been printed by a university press back in the 1950s—a history of the author's great-grandfather, a legendary lawman in the West. Lawman? What connection did Jerrod have to a lawman?

The first page was a cover teaser. My heart raced as I searched for Jerrod's name.

Read about little-known outlaws like Jerrod Amherst Baldwin, 1856-1886, a coward who rode with the Wakefield Boys during their brief bank-robbing spree in Missouri in the late 1870s. Read a historical eyewitness account of this outlaw from the journals of William Tillman.

I took a deep breath, trying to calm my excitement. Could this be the same Jerrod? The dates fit, but the bank robbing? On the next page, the author's great-grandfather, William Tillman, offered this portrait of Jerrod:

Baldwin was one of the handsomest outlaws I ever knew—six feet tall, he weighed about one hundred and eighty pounds, and every ounce was lean muscle. He had a serious countenance that seemed respectful and a quiet, charming wit that ladies found irresistible. Unfortunately, he had a fatal flaw, one a person wouldn't expect in a man who'd chosen bank robbing as a profession—he was a coward.

As long as the Wakefield Boys' robberies went smoothly and no one resisted, Baldwin acted with the flamboyance of a true outlaw, brandishing his gun and shouting commands at cowering tellers and bank customers. But on the afternoon of March 4, 1881, the Boys held up the Liberty Bank. One of the tellers managed to conceal a gun and shoot Tex Wakefield in the head.

As gunfire erupted, Baldwin, who'd been emptying the safe, panicked and bolted from the scene, which probably saved his life. Three of the Boys were killed in the bank that afternoon, and the others, including Baldwin, were rounded up later that week. The cash, over $10,000, disappeared. I believe to this day that Baldwin hid it somewhere, but he never did own up to it.

He was tried and convicted of being an accessory in a bank robbery, but he got off with the minimum sentence. Baldwin had a double cousin who lived nearby and looked very much like him, almost a twin for looks. Baldwin's attorney argued that either man could have been the one at the bank that afternoon. Jurors couldn't tell photographs of the two apart. From all accounts Baldwin's cousin was a law-abiding man, but this trick served to introduce doubt in the jury's mind. Baldwin's charisma seemed to sway them. Not wanting to unduly punish a man who might be innocent, they gave him minimum time.

Baldwin was released in the spring of 1885 and immediately headed to Idaho Territory to join the gold and silver rush up there. The bank hired me to track him and see if he led me to the stolen cash. He never did.

Frustrated, in June of 1886 bank officials sent me to Idaho to see if I could get any information out of Baldwin concerning the stolen money. But I arrived too late. The morning I set out to question him, he was killed in a landslide outside the town of Murray, Idaho. With him died any knowledge of the stolen money. It never was found.

Handsome. I liked that. Evidently, so had Mariah. Charming, good with the ladies, quiet, respectful—I could see how Mariah could be seduced by him. But Jerrod an outlaw? And a cowardly one at that? It contrasted with the picture I'd had of him.

Stunned, I sat woodenly on the bed. Had Mariah known?

A scenario danced through my head. Quick visions of Mariah unable to sleep after the events of the day and night, of getting up early and encountering a lawman named Tillman.

The passage answered so many questions. Jerrod must have realized that Tillman followed him and decided to leave town rather than face him. So he set off early, going across the tailings to make better time. Maybe he figured that he'd lose Tillman and eventually go for the money. If what Tillman wrote was true, maybe Jerrod was just running out because he didn't want to face Dallas. Maybe he was a big coward, which made me wonder about his little story to Mariah about killing the Yankee. Had he superimposed Dallas's actions on himself? Jerrod Baldwin, liar and coward, a lot like a modern man I knew.

It was past ten thirty at night. Gran would be in bed. She'd be ecstatic with what I'd turned up. But pleased as I was with myself, I decided it could wait until morning. I tried Sean again, but got no answer, so I went to bed.

I slept fitfully, haunted by weird, disjointed images and sudden rushes of panicky fear and guilt. I sat in the dark with myself, surrounded by the silent images of night, trying to decide what I wanted out of my life. Several things became clear—I wanted my baby, no matter who its father was. I wanted time to enjoy and raise this baby. And, most startling, I wanted to give my marriage another shot. I wanted Sean back, if that were possible.

First, I had to own up to my mistake and ask for Sean's forgiveness. Exorcise that which I didn't want to face. Our marriage fell apart long before my affair because of both of us, but I needed to accept my share of the blame. Next, I had to tell him about the baby. No matter what Sean decided, I had to be a woman of integrity. I meant to live the rest of my life being the decent, honorable mother my child deserved.

Two a.m. I got up and steeled myself to talk to Sean. He picked up on the third ring.

"Hello." He sounded fully awake. Sean had never been an early-to-bed guy. Hearing his deep, steadfast voice, I felt a new measure of fear. I had to force myself not to chicken out and hang up.

"Sean."

"Dani? I was hoping you'd call." He stumbled over his words. I heard papers crinkle in the background and an electronic hum. He must have been at his computer.

"I'd have thought the opposite." My voice broke.

"Dan, come on, I haven't given up on us."

Tears blinded me. "We need to talk, in person."

"Yes, I agree." He hesitated. "Are you coming back to Seattle?" He paused. "Are you coming home soon?"

"I don't know. I think so. Nothing's definite." I bit my lip. "Sean, we need to meet on neutral ground—"

"Name the place and time, Dani, and I'll be there."

Poor Sean. He sounded willing, but cautious.

"How about Spokane? I'll come. We can meet at Riverfront Park. Do you remember? I proposed to you there—"

"Sean." This hurt so much.

"I have a big design review tomorrow. It'll probably run late. How about the day after, by the carousel, one o'clock?"

"Sure, yes, fine."

"Good."

An awkward silence followed. There wasn't anything more to say on the phone, but neither of us wanted to break the connection, tenuous as it was.

Finally, Sean said, "I miss you, Dani. See you day after tomorrow." He hung up. I sat staring at the silent phone. Day after tomorrow, come what may.

Dreams, like a siren's song, called me to those tailings at Murray. I was not a reincarnation of Mariah, but we were linked by blood, by history, by circumstance. Something had happened out on those tailings. Something terrible. Something tragic. Something indefinable that changed Mariah forever. In all her diary entries, she never mentioned the incident. I had to go there, had to see.

Unable to stay in bed any longer, I got up at five and promptly threw up. So this wasn't going to be an easy pregnancy, what in life was easy? Crackers, I'd heard they helped.

My shower and blow-drying woke Gran. I had just tied my tennis shoes when she came into my room.

"You're up early."

"I have to go to the tailings." I smiled, trying to keep the urgency out of my voice. "Mariah's been calling me."

"I see." She seemed to understand.

"I found something out about Jerrod, Gran. Did you know that he was a convicted bank robber?" I blurted out the news like an overeager little kid.

Gran gasped.

I laughed again and nodded. "The information Ann and I ordered arrived. She dropped it by last night." I handed her the folder.

"Oh, Dani! This is a discovery." She tapped the folder.

"Indeed it is. Now I have to be off. I'm hoping that seeing the scene will clue me in to what went on that day."

"Yes, good thinking. Did Mariah know, do you think?"

"I have a feeling she found out just before he died." I stood up.

"Drive carefully."

"Always."

"Pick some flowers on your way out," Gran said. "Take them to Molly. The cemetery is easy to find."

Murray is about two hours east of Spokane. Most of the drive is a straight shot across I-90, but the last miles are up a winding two-lane road. The going is slow. Dead mines and dying towns dot the way.

It was light before I left. I have always loved the long shadows and deep, vibrant colors of early morning before the force of the sun washes them out. This morning was clear and beautiful, perfect. I drove with the windows down, letting the cool breeze clear my head. Traffic was light, still early for most morning commuters.

Gran had told me that you come to the tailings and then the cemetery before you get to town. Putting off my anticipated epiphany, I headed straight to town, arriving just before seven. I wanted to see Mariah's venue first. I should have spared myself the trouble—a full-fledged ghost town would have been less disappointing. All that remained of the town, which had once housed thousands, were a few beleaguered buildings. Other than the historic courthouse, which had a sign proclaiming it as such, little remained from the period. Everything else looked contemporary. The courthouse itself, weathered gray and listing, looked less than prosperous.

Involuntarily, I turned my gaze to the second floor and pictured that last great day of Jerrod's life. How had he felt hearing of his cousin's victory? Happy? Triumphant? Jealous?

According to Tillman's account, Jerrod had ten thousand dollars stashed somewhere—was he frustrated that he'd never be able to claim it? Did he see the path clear now for Dallas and Mariah to get together? Was that why he seduced Mariah that night? Did he love her? Did he do it to reclaim some sense of power over himself and his cousin? Was he jealous of Dallas's attentions to another person?

I walked past the courthouse and looked across Pritchard Creek to what must once have been Gold Street. Nothing remained of Molly's cabins, but in my mind's eye I saw them clearly. I stood a minute, letting my thoughts wander. The tailings called. The rest of the town held no interest for me, just a couple of homes built last century, one with a neatly kept flower garden blooming furiously. I would have liked to walk the route from Gold Street to the tailings, but as I was hopelessly directionally challenged, I opted for the road and the car.

I parked in a wide, graveled spot just off the road and stood on the shoulder, looking down the hillside, past the trees to the ominous tailings below.

A modern environmentalist would have been horrified by the destruction wrought by the gold rush. I was amazed at the power of water and hand digging to reshape the landscape. A river of rock filled the valley for as far as I could see, completely obliterating any natural vegetation or trees. On either side a heavily wooded hillside sprang, guardian of the wasteland.

I gingerly picked my way down the steep hillside canopied with white pine, out to the middle of the slag. I sat down in the middle of that river of rock on the largest stone I could find and listened to the pines whisper in the delicate morning breeze.

"Tell me your secrets," I said. "What happened here and why?" They only murmured.

I looked at the stones surrounding me. Red veins of iron ran through many of them. I picked up one particularly sharp one and turned it over in my hand. I shivered, thinking of these sharp, vicious rocks raining down on Jerrod, of his blood mingling with the iron strains, lending them the red stain of his life. Here in this century, everything seemed serene and stable. How deceptive life could be.

Returning my gaze past the pines, to the horizon of blue overhead, I half expected Mariah to appear. Of course she didn't, but sitting quietly listening to my own heart, holding the experience of my lifetime and the details of her life, her story came to me in vivid detail. I didn't care whether it was only my own mind's musing, pure fiction or fact. To me it was truth. I gained strength from it. Through the prism of Mariah's life, the rainbow of my own appeared, and I knew how I must live.

It all started back in town on the night Jerrod seduced Mariah. Seduction I understood well enough.

Trying to get close to Dallas proved futile. A human stream of ebullient miners surrounded him. Mariah picked her way home past the revelers. Dallas would come for her in his time. Her heart pounded wildly. Dallas Baldwin was a rich man! He had something to offer her now. Impetuous, spontaneous Dallas Baldwin would surely propose again tonight! Her heart danced.

At home she shut her door and pulled her curtains closed. Slowly and luxuriously, she took a sponge bath and applied a light rose scent where Dallas would be most likely to smell it. She pulled her own stays as tightly as she could and dressed in her finest gown—a lightweight China silk with a bretelle-front bodice made entirely of torchon lace. No one would mistake her for a hurdy-girl tonight. She dressed for Dallas's eyes alone. Once married, she vowed to cast all memories of dance hall days from her mind, edit them out of her life story altogether.

Late afternoon slid into evening, and evening light peeled away into night before anyone called. When the man came, it wasn't the one she anticipated. Jerrod stood on her stoop.

"Mariah, why are you hiding?" He sounded jovial. "Come out and celebrate our victory."

She hesitated. He stretched out his hand.

"Just let me get my shawl." Her tone was flat. She didn't try to hide her disappointment, even as she took Jerrod's arm and wandered out.

Passed-out drunks littered the streets. Music and merrymaking pulsed from every building. Jake's glowed like a jewel, lit with every candle and lamp Jake could find. Jerrod pressed through the crowd, holding Mariah tight against him, and fought his way to the interior. Dallas sat at a table playing poker with a desperate intensity. In deference to his poker hand, he didn't acknowledge their arrival.

"Damn him." Jerrod's face was hard. "He'll lose everything we've worked for. I told him to get out before I went for you."

Mariah's heart sank. Dallas had promised her that he'd stop, that he wouldn't risk their interest in the mine. *Gambling men never change*, her mother had once told her. *Stay away from them, Mariah. You won't find any security with a gambler. They'll lose everything you have and leave you empty and dried up. Good times never last and one win is never enough. A gambler is always looking for the thrill of higher stakes.*

"Can't you stop him, Jerrod?" She leaned close to whisper in his ear, hoping he'd hear her above the din of the crowd.

He scowled. "Let me get you a drink, darling."

As much as Dallas ignored her, Jerrod flattered her with attention. Mariah spent the evening dancing and drinking with him, wishing with some guilt that he were Dallas. But as the night wore on and Dallas didn't see fit to more than nod an acknowledgement to her, a sort of jilted feminine ire welled up. The light feeling of victory faded, replaced by loss and defeat. If Dallas loved her, why would he let his cousin escort her so boldly?

Her answer came from her own conscience as she sat next to Jerrod, drinking yet another shot of whiskey, a sudden realization. Of course, Dallas and Jerrod had decided who got the girl. Clearly, Jerrod had won. That was why he had come for her. That's why he flirted so openly now. This was his public declaration.

How they came to the decision, Mariah couldn't determine. Had they tossed a coin, debated and settled with reason and logic, fist-fought? Had Dallas merely conceded that his feelings for her had receded as easily as those of his earlier attachments? She never would understand the relationship Dallas and Jerrod shared. Maybe no one else could. She suppressed her first reaction to upbraid them, scourge them with scathing words. Instead, she weighed the situation, turning her gaze on Jerrod, who stared intently at her.

He was as handsome as Dallas, reliable, responsible, with money of his own, and at least a small share of the Bunker would be his. She wasn't likely—indeed, she hadn't among all the men of her acquaintance—to find a more suitable man who pleased her more. Why should she throw the man out with the bath water?

In that instant, as she stared into the depths of Jerrod's eyes, she issued him an invitation as only a woman can—with a look in her own eye, a toss of the head, a moistening of the lips, a thrust of the bust. Then she looked demurely down. Jerrod smiled openly. Message received.

Dallas suddenly hooted and scooped a pile of money in front of him.

Jerrod scowled. "I won't sit here and watch that fool gamble all night." He scooted back out of his chair. Mariah took his hand.

"Then don't," she said. "It's hot and stuffy and crowded here. I'd like to go home."

Jerrod stood. "As the lady requests." He extended his hand and helped her up. "I'll just tell Dallas we're going. I'll be right back."

Mariah watched as he went to Dallas and whispered something to him. Dallas shrugged and then nodded, confirming her assumption—she was Jerrod's now.

Outside, the cool air felt good. The pines whispered around them. When they got to her cabin, Jerrod lounged insouciantly in the doorway, lingering, waiting for an invitation. He played with the hem of his coat and smiled up at her. "You look beautiful tonight, Mariah—so pretty you make my heart ache."

"You're a fancy talker, Jerrod Baldwin. Why should I believe your little flatteries?" She laughed.

"Because they're true." He stepped into her. She thought he was going to kiss her, and tilted her face up to meet his. Instead he said, "May I come inside?"

She stepped back to let him in. Just inside the door, he pulled her into an embrace that took her breath away. He kissed deeply, open-mouthed and rugged. He ended the kiss as abruptly as he'd begun it, taking her hand in his and looking eagerly into her eyes. "I love you, Mariah."

The declaration she'd hope for, but not the man. She had no idea how to answer him. She couldn't bear to lose him, too. Giddy from alcohol, she giggled.

"You find my declaration amusing?" He spoke lightly. He again took her chin in his hand and looked intently into her eyes. "The alcohol brings out the youth in you, Mariah, and it's damned attractive." He kissed her softly on the lips. "But I am serious. I am not as rich as my cousin might be now, but I have a small fortune back home. I'll be leaving in a few days to claim it. When I come back, I intend to make you my wife."

It was all so silly, so terribly funny—her good friend Jerrod proposing to her. Yet in the moonlight sifting in through the window, he looked devastatingly handsome. A day's beard shadowed his face. The whites of his eyes glinted against the dark, and in them she saw only passion. It was more intoxicating than alcohol. Soft, muted sounds of lovemaking drifted down the row from Gold Street—beds thumping, grunts and moans on the wind—cheap, gaudy sounds that stirred in her a reckless desire to throw caution away and imitate them here this night with this man. He needn't seduce her, if only she, in her giddiness and innocence, knew how to seduce him.

He spanned her waist with his hands and moved her next to the bed. "Will you wait for me, Mariah?"

She couldn't answer. She didn't want to. Laughing, she stepped into him, placing her foot between his bracing stance. She threw her arms around his neck.

Tangled, they fell onto the bed, laughing, hot and ripe for each other. He rolled on top of her and kissed her leisurely, as if all the night were theirs. A strange and powerful feeling swept over her, half fear, half elation.

He kissed her neck as he unfastened the lace-covered buttons of her bodice, kissing the skin he exposed. She matched him button for button on his own shirt. Piece by piece, their clothing fell away until he wore only his pants, and she her chemise and pantaloons. He reached between her legs and rubbed her until she felt fire, hot and weepy and weak as a rag doll. She moaned involuntarily. He stood suddenly and shed his pants to stand before her erect and ready.

"Oh my heavens, Jerrod, you're too big. You'll kill me with that thing. It'll never fit." She spoke spontaneously, without thinking.

He laughed, rich and deep. "You flatter me, Mariah. Believe me, darling, you'll be pleased with the fit."

He was on her again pressing himself between her legs, easing himself into position, kissing her with an intensity that left her breathless. As he cupped her breasts and pinched her nipples, a deep, frustrating need engulfed her. He must have sensed her readiness. With one long, hard thrust, he was in her.

The pleasure ended abruptly, replaced by a white-hot shot of virgin's pain. She cried out, "Stop, Jerrod. Oh, stop."

Her words came out breathy and soft and only seemed to goad him on. He thrust wildly, indifferent to her pain. She whimpered, seared by pain, and arched beneath him, trying to escape. Mercifully, he finished quickly, stiffening and grunting and finally collapsing on her. His sweat stung her skin as he held her close.

He rested inside her. Even as her tight body gripped him, it ached and throbbed. "Please, Jerrod, come out."

He kissed her forehead and obeyed, pulling her into the crook of his arm. "I'm sorry. I forgot a woman's pain the first time. It'll get better, darling. I promise."

They lay quietly next to each other for some time. Finally, Jerrod stood up and got dressed. "I have to be going. Wouldn't want your reputation sullied." He eased out the room to the doorway. "I'll see you tomorrow." He blew her a kiss and disappeared into the night.

She lay there a long time before getting up to put on her nightgown. When she stood, a warm stickiness slid down her legs. What had she done? A quick, unexpected remorse swept over her. She stared down at her mattress, at the dark stain in the center, the proof of virginity lost. Then she crumpled into a ball on top of it, gathering her knees to her chest, and cried silently until the soporific effects of the alcohol took effect and she drifted off into a troubled sleep.

A loud pounding on her door woke her. "Mariah, I know you're in there. Mariah!"

Fighting the haze of sleep and alcohol, she went to the door to find Dallas looking wild and haunted and distraught. His hair stood on end, combed there by his own restless fingers, which even now played. Blood dripped from the corner of his mouth. His lip was fat and swollen. He smelled of alcohol, cigars, and cards. The sight of him sobered her.

"Dallas, good heavens! You've been in a fight. Let me get you a cool cloth to clean you—" She was stopped mid-sentence by the stiff set of his jaw and the steely look in his eyes. He looked not at her, but past her to the condition of the room. A quick, biting fear overtook her.

He took in the room with one swift, sweeping gaze that came to rest directly behind her. When she turned back over her shoulder, she saw the object of his attention—her obviously rumpled and stained bed.

"God damn it, Mariah!" His words blistered. She'd never heard him raise his voice so indiscreetly or sound so venomous. "Harlot! Did you have to lie with a dog?" he shouted.

Suddenly she understood. He'd been fighting with Jerrod—over her. But how on earth could he have found out, and so quickly?

"Dallas, lower your voice," she pleaded. "What in heaven's name—"

"Don't play innocent with me. How could you do it? Sleep with my own cousin when I loved you so." His voice cracked. He looked haggard.

"Love me so?" She kept her voice soft, but she couldn't hide the tremble. "You call sneaking into town last winter and sleeping with that whore Edith loving me?"

"Edith? What are you talking about?" He seemed sobered, if somewhat confused, by her accusation. "I told you long ago—I never pay for pleasure. Never have, never will."

"Then why did Edith say you did?" The tremble affecting her voice worked its way to her hands, her heart, her whole body.

"Take a wild guess. Who looks like me and lies like he was born to it?"

Mariah felt too stunned to answer. No, not Jerrod. He wouldn't. "The whole winter you never wrote me a line—"

"Damn! Damn! Damn!" The anger worked its way back into his voice. He kicked the step. "I sent you plenty. I sent you one tonight to wait for me after the celebrating. I sent it with Jerrod. Then while I sat playing Jerrod's hand of cards, trying to bail him out of trouble... Shit!"

The lump in her throat grew so large she felt like she'd swallowed her heart. Tears stung her eyes. "I don't understand. I thought Jerrod won. I thought he had your approval to court me. He's been attentive all winter while you made a point of ignoring me—"

"What do you think we are, rutting bull moose who lock horns over a girl? That we decide who gets the girl among ourselves. That I lied to you, that I have no feelings, no heart." He spoke with venom.

She grabbed him by the lapel of his coat and looked up into his eyes, pleading. "I don't know what to think. Who's telling the truth, you or him? You two are almost like halves of the same man and not. You're tangled and entwined, and who knows where one of you ends and the other begins? Who knew what you thought? Jerrod said he'd had your permission to court me. Why should I believe him to be a liar? He flirted openly with me before your very eyes this evening and you did nothing, said nothing. When he made his proposal to me tonight, I thought that meant your feelings had gone. And"—she fumbled for words and fought back tears—"I thought that if I couldn't have you, I may as well have him."

Dallas stood very still, his expression inscrutable. Mariah couldn't stand the silence.

"With so much to celebrate, with your fortune made, I thought tonight that if you still cared about me, you'd renew your proposal. When you ignored me, Dallas..." She couldn't finish. Tears clouded her vision.

"I thought you were waiting for me. I thought you understood." He spoke very quietly. "I thought you'd wait for me at least one day. What a fool I have been." He pulled her grip loose from his coat and turned to leave. When he reached the bottom of the stairs, he turned back to her.

"I never should have trusted Jerrod. A mutt will always be a mutt. I thought he'd changed, that he'd look out for my interests, like I've always done his. That's why I tolerated his flirting with you. It kept you out of reach of other men. Jerrod understood my intent, so I guess his actions were deliberate." He paused to take a deep breath and look up at the stars.

"I underestimated his envy. He never has taken my successes with grace, and he's always been jealous of the women in my life. In hindsight, it was a lethal combination. He is a dog, Mariah. Someday you'll find out just how much of one." He touched his swollen lip and wiped at the drying blood. "You've killed me, Mariah."

Then he turned and walked away without another word.

She listened to his footfalls until they receded. What had she done? What in heaven's name had she done?

CHAPTER SEVENTEEN

Mariah rose early the next morning. Truly, she'd never really gone back to sleep. In the creeping paleness of dawn, the whole affair seemed like a potent nightmare. The rawness between her legs reminded her otherwise. Her head pounded with the afteraffects of too much alcohol and too many tears, but her thoughts ran amazingly clear. She had to confront Jerrod.

She bathed in the frigid water of Pritchard Creek. Later in the day she'd have to see Molly about a remedy for preventing a baby after you've already done the deed. Molly would know. In the meantime, she meant to wash away as much of Jerrod as possible.

Just before six, Mariah went to the boardinghouse where Jerrod lived. A tall, dark blond stranger with startling blue eyes came from the opposite direction and met her at the steps. She'd never forget the clarity of those blue eyes. They turned up the stairs in unison. At the top, he opened the door for her politely.

The lady keeper of the house, Mrs. Smythe, was already up making her boys breakfast. She looked surprised to see two guests arriving so early.

The gentleman spoke first: "I'm sorry to intrude, ma'am." He pulled a badge from his pocket and showed it to Mrs. Smythe. "I'm a lawman from Missouri. My name is William Tillman. I'm looking for Jerrod Baldwin. I was told he lived here."

Mariah stifled a gasp. What did a lawman want with Jerrod?

Mrs. Smythe looked from one to the other. "I don't want no trouble, and from the looks of both of you I'm not so sure I'm not getting it." She eyed his badge carefully. "What do you want with Mr. Baldwin? Is he a wanted criminal?"

Mrs. Smythe had asked the question on Mariah's mind.

"Not anymore. He's served his time, ma'am, for bank robbery. The money was never recovered, and rumor has it that Baldwin knows where it's hidden. I've been hired to convince him to return it." He spoke with the same accent as Jerrod, lazy and deep. He dimpled when he smiled. "There's a reward for the money's recovery. My employer is willing to divide it between anyone who provides useful information. That could be you, ma'am."

Mariah's heart pounded wildly—Jerrod, an outlaw! She remembered Dallas's words, making sudden sense of them.

Mr. Tillman turned to her. "Do you know him, ma'am?"

"Yes, sir."

"He ain't here," Mrs. Smythe said suddenly.

Mariah opened her mouth to speak. Mrs. Smythe silenced her with a look of reproach.

"He packed up his things and headed out at first light this morning. Oh, an hour or so ago."

"Everything? He's gone for good?" Mariah felt weak.

"Appears so." Mrs. Smythe turned back to her stove to stir a pot of mush she had cooking.

"Did he say where he was going?" Tillman asked.

"No."

"Which direction did he head?"

Mrs. Smythe pointed.

"Thank you, ma'am." He turned to look at Mariah. "I take it you're looking for him, too. Either of you gets any information, I'd be glad to hear it. I'm staying at the Pine Tree Hotel." He turned on his heel and left.

Mariah watched him break into a run once he hit the street. No doubt he'd be riding out after Jerrod.

Mrs. Smythe turned her gaze on Mariah. "I stretched the truth a bit. He left not five minutes ago." She went to the window and watched the lawman disappear. "Could be I was mistaken about the direction he went, too." She pointed. "I'd guess he headed toward the slag heap. A swift woman on foot should be able to catch him. It'll take a while for his horse to pick its way through the woods and across that river of rock." Mrs. Smythe smiled. "I never have liked the law."

She gave Mariah a warning look. "Don't you dare turn that charming man in! He's already taken a beating from his cousin for your sake. He don't need any more of your trouble."

Mariah was panting as she reached the hilltop above the tailings. In the valley below her, Jerrod led his horse across the bed of rocks. The horse stepped gingerly, picking its way over boulders and stones of varying size.

"Jerrod Baldwin, you coward!" she yelled, and waved. The force of her words echoed off the hills. *Let the lawman hear me. Let everyone hear!*

Jerrod turned to look up at her, obviously startled to see her there.

She started down the hill toward him. He tethered his horse in the midst of the valley, placed a heavy rock on the reins, and made his way up the hill toward her. Tiny rocks scattered with each step he took, tumbling down to the valley floor below, marking his path. They met just where land became rock and slag. She stood uphill from him, firmly grounded, powerful in her stance.

He'd made a remarkable change of appearance from just a few hours before. She didn't hide her scrutiny as she catalogued his injuries. His left eye was black and swollen. There was a gash on his cheek that was trying to scab over. Dallas had given him a fair beating. For just an instant, a stab of sympathy passed through her.

After all, he'd been her good friend through the winter. But the man whose character she'd discovered these last hours bore no resemblance to the man she had believed him to be. The feeling passed quickly. She stayed her hand from reaching out to touch and comfort him.

"Coward? Dal must have gotten to you." He laughed bitterly, hardly seeming surprised to see her out so early in pursuit of him now that he knew what she knew. "You wouldn't be calling me names if you'd seen me fighting over your honor last night." He reached up and rubbed his own cheek, trying to elicit sympathy.

He lied at will. Fighting over her honor? After he'd bragged about his conquest of her in the most public of places?

"When I got back to the bar, Dallas was drunk and coming off a loss at cards," he continued. "As I pulled him away from the table to keep him from playing again and losing more, he swung at me, taking me clear off guard and knocking me almost to my knees." Jerrod pointed to his eye. "You can see the result. Dallas doesn't like being told what to do, and drunk, he's mean. He was jealous. Like he's always been of the women in my life. And sore that for once I'd won the girl, even though he was no longer interested. And believe me, Mariah, he had no further intention of courting you." He gave his tone a fine imitation inflection of righteousness.

"Dallas has an easy manner that women have always found appealing. But he tosses them aside easily. Don't let his indignation fool you. When he started spewing insinuations and insults, accusing me of stealing his girl, you, I fought back." Jerrod reached for her hand.

She pulled back, leaving him to further tangle himself in lies. How well accomplished he was at deception. He spoke smoothly, but she recognized the lies for lies now. Dallas loved her. She knew that much.

"I'm glad you weren't there, Mariah. It was no sight for a lady."

"If it's true, I suppose not." Mariah stepped directly into him, trying to hold her temper as she stared him down. "But what have you told me that *is* the truth?" Despite her best attempts at calm, her voice pitched shriller and higher with each word. "You tell me that you fought for my honor." She pointed down the hill toward his horse. "Yet your horse is fully packed for a long journey. So what was your intention—use me like a whore and sneak out? You are a coward and a liar, Jerrod Baldwin."

"I told you I'd be leaving to handle business affairs and check on my investments." He tried affecting a charming smile, but it fell flat in Mariah's sight and looked ridiculous against his beaten face. How he had ever managed to beguile her, she couldn't understand. His smile plainly veiled a wicked and cowardly heart.

"Without saying goodbye?"

He had the scant decency to look sheepish. Or try to. "I would have. But I wanted to avoid another confrontation with Dallas. I'll be back when things calm down."

"Don't bother on my account." Her anger broke loose. She shoved him in the chest. Hard. With everything she had.

He didn't budge. "God damn it, Mariah!" He took her roughly by the arms. His fingers dug into her flesh. "Clear your infatuation with Dallas out of your mind. You think he's ever going to want you now, knowing what went on between you and me? I've known him all my life. He won't." He may as well have added, "You're mine now." His expression said it well enough. "If it's only his gold, I can promise you money."

His words infuriated her. She tried to shake him off. "I'm not one of Molly's girls to be bought and sold at a man's whim."

He released her suddenly, sending her sprawling backward. She righted herself, straightened her skirt, shoved her chin up, and glared at him. "You can rot in hell, Jerrod Baldwin." She turned on her heel and, lifting her skirts, scrambled up the hillside with as much dignity as she could manage. She heard him curse and turn to leave. Heard the sound of his footfalls as he picked his way back down the rocks.

She paused to call down to him one last time. "I wouldn't be counting on that fortune, Jerrod. There's a lawman looking for you. He's been hired to find the cash you stole. You don't have more than five minutes on him."

Real fear crossed his face. Anger quickly replaced it. "Damn it, Mariah! Traitor! Where the hell is he?" He charged up the hill at her. As he stepped on a large boulder, it gave way beneath him. He stumbled and cursed.

The next horrible instant seemed like time out of place. The rock he'd tripped on had been a dam holding back a bay of rock. Once it slid out of place, it unleashed a current of rubble.

The ground beneath her feet trembled as the tailings gave way and slid to the valley floor. Screaming, she grabbed a tree for support and caught the barest glimpse of Jerrod—a glance that stopped time. For the rest of her life she would never forget the expression of surprise and horror on Jerrod's face as the hill of rock swept him away and rained down on him. In an instant he vanished, obscured by a cloud of dust.

As suddenly as it began, the echo of destruction and violence faded away. The earth grew stable and secure again. Mariah's shrill scream pierced the still air, sounding as far away to her ear as if some terrified stranger shrieked.

"Jerrod! Jerrod!"

Only the quiet whisper of the pines and call of birds answered. She slid down the hill in the settling dust of the slide, coughing and choking. Below her in the valley, Jerrod's horse whinnied and pawed the ground in panic and distress.

"Jerrod! Jerrod!" Her throat hurt from the force of shrill exertion. She grew hoarse, but kept calling as she ran and scanned the rock for any sign of him. She found him at last, carried by the torrent of rock forty or fifty feet from where he had been.

Miraculously, he lay half exposed, unconscious, face up, his head pillowed by sharp basalt rock and round core samples. Below the waist, he was completely covered. His left arm bent at an odd angle and blood oozed from a gash at the back of his head, staining the iron-laden rock around him red.

"Jerrod! Jerrod! Jerrod." Her voice grew softer with each utterance. She fell to her knees beside him and began digging wildly with bare hands, trying to free his legs. But with each rock she dug away, another slid into place. What if she started another slide?

Her hands were soon a mass of cuts covered in blood. In a flash of inspiration, she grabbed him beneath his armpits and tried to pull him free. If she could just get him loose, maybe she could get him on the horse and back to town to the doctor. But the rocks held him in a death grip and blood continued to pour from his head wound. Later, in memory, she would swear she heard every drip, the soft patter of life slipping away.

She stripped her petticoat off and wrapped it around his head to bandage the bleeding. She had to go to town for help. There was nothing else she could do by herself. Just as she started to push up to a stand, intent on running to town, Jerrod's eyes fluttered open. They looked surreal, glassy and unfocused, confused, and fearful.

She took his good hand in hers. "Jerrod, it's me, Mariah. Can you hear me? Do you understand me?"

"Mariah." He spoke her name as a whisper on the breeze.

"Jerrod, listen to me. I can't move you. I've tried. We have to get you out of here and back to town. I'm going to have to leave you and run for help."

"No! Stay...me." He answered her grip on his hand with a faint pressure, and the exertion of even so mild an act seemed to wear him out. "Don't want to die alone."

"Don't talk like that. You *aren't* going to die." Of course, she lied. He looked nearly dead already. "But I need to get help."

He shook his head. "Please."

She hesitated too long. His fearful expression won over her good sense. "All right. I'll stay. I promise. You just rest." What could she do, leave him to die alone?

She sat back on the rock and cradled his head in her lap, gently stroking his cheeks with her bloody fingers as she stared back into his eyes. "It's all right, Jerrod. I'm here."

He seemed to relax, and closed his eyes, lapsing back into unconsciousness. She considered leaving him then, and running for help, but she'd made a promise. Instead, she prayed for help to come.

His breathing grew ragged and rattled—a sure sign of death coming. The strange stillness of his body worried her. Maybe he'd lost his ability to move. Certainly, his legs were crushed beneath the weight of the stone. Doc likely would have to take them off. If he survived, could Jerrod live as an invalid?

A vile thought intruded. If Jerrod lived, he would be a burden to Dallas for the rest of his life. But hadn't he always been? Still, there would be no future for Dallas and her, not with Jerrod to care for, a constant reminder of her betrayal.

She pushed the evil thoughts away and settled in to wait for death, uncertain that her motives were pure. But death came so slowly. In the end, she couldn't bear the small sounds of his pain and the aching rattle of his chest. With the palm of her hand, she covered his mouth and nose, leaving the smallest gap for air, not willing to smother him if he had strength enough to draw breath in past her barrier, yet unable to watch him suffer longer. The rattling faded away and his chest stilled.

All her life she would wonder if she had really been motivated by mercy or selfishness, if she had committed murder or not. Had he simply died, or had she hastened it? Horrified, she rose to her feet, and, screaming for help, ran up the hill, tripping and stumbling.

In her haste, she knocked free a boulder and shrieked, fearing another slide. The rock rolled down. As she turned and looked back, she saw it crush Jerrod's head. *It doesn't matter. I can't hurt him now.* But the terror of the scene would forever play in her mind.

As if brought by fate, Dallas was the first person she met as she stumbled through the woods, crying and panicked.

"Mariah! What's happened?" He dropped the pack he carried and came forward to scoop her into his arms.

"There's been a landslide at the tailings." Her words came in gasps. "Jerrod, Jerrod's been..." She could barely get the words out. "I'm so sorry. Jerrod was crushed by the slide. He's dead, Dal."

She stood shivering before him, pulling together some shred of dignity. This might very well be the last conversation she ever had with him.

"I'm sorry, Dallas, so sorry for everything—the betrayal, Jerrod's death. It's not the time, but I have to speak my mind anyway." Her voice cracked. She told him everything, including about the lawman who was looking for Jerrod. "I love you, Dallas. I always will. I hope someday you'll forgive me."

He pulled her back against him. "Mariah, listen to me. I've been thinking on this all night. It was my fault. If I would have warned you..." He swallowed hard. "No one knows better than I do what Jerrod is. Rather than shield him, I should have protected you. You're sure he's...dead."

She nodded.

"You say a lawman named Tillman is looking for him?"

"Yes."

"I'll tell you that story someday." His voice cracked. "We have to get to town now."

Dallas and a party of men from town dug Jerrod out and brought his body back to town. Later that morning, Dallas came by to see Mariah.

"I've been thinking things over," he said. "The town's been buzzing about the three of us for some time now. This incident is only going to cause more speculation. People are already wondering what you were doing out there alone with him. Let's silence the gossip. Marry me, Mariah. Marry me this very day because I love you, and we'll put all this behind us as well as we'll ever be able to."

She leaned her head against his chest and squeezed him tight. "What will people think? How cold will we seem? How can we enjoy ourselves with this hanging over our heads?"

"You ask too many questions. I don't give a damn what people think of me marrying the woman I love. Secondly, we can't hurt Jerrod now. This is what he would have wanted anyway, my happiness. Isn't he who we're really thinking of?" Dallas choked up. It took a minute for him to compose himself. "How long would we have to wait for people to think we're respectable? A year? Six months? I need you now, Mariah. We'll heal a whole lot faster together." His voice went hoarse.

"People will think I'm a gold digger. But I want you to know that I'd marry you whether you had the money or not. The only reservation I've ever had is your gambling."

"I'll give it up," he said as he drew her to him.

I sat listening to the pines and the birds, imagining it all. They would have kissed. Sometime that day, Mariah would have taken him to the scene of the accident. Realizing what people might think, they concocted a story about Jerrod being dead when Mariah got to him. It took away her dilemma and made her look blameless. So they thought at the time. In reality, it created doubt about her and sullied her character for over a century.

It was still early in the day. Dallas and Mariah found Judge Buck and he married them. Mariah wanted a religious ceremony, but Dallas didn't want to impose ridicule on a clergyman.

Immediately, the town buzzed with the notion that somehow Mariah had killed Jerrod so she could get Dallas. Maybe she had, but not in the way they thought. Maybe her own guilty conscience showed on her face. Perhaps that was why she looked so sad in the picture taken shortly after she married, the one Gran had. The facts looked suspicious. Many condemned her.

Why would a woman put her petticoat on a dead man's head? What had she been doing out alone with him? Had he really stumbled and dislodged the rock that started the slide, or had she in anger sent one rolling down the hill after him, causing his death when she'd only meant to scare him? Why was his horse tethered so far away? Why hadn't she ridden it to town for help? What a sight she'd been when she'd arrived in town. Her cuts couldn't account for so much blood covering her. What about that rock that had crushed Jerrod's skull? Had she smashed his head in when she found him still alive? Why would a woman sacrifice her petticoat and then kill him?

Suspicion, questions, and scandal swirled around her like a powerful dust devil made of the debris of evil. Molly came to her defense and, by the sheer force of her personality, silenced the most blatant accusers and gossip.

Later that afternoon, Judge Buck, who had married them earlier in the day, overturned the jury's decision and found for Peck and Cooper. Dallas was once again a poor man. His lawyers filed an immediate appeal. Some in town thought that justice had been served after all.

Dallas took his bride back to her cabin and made her his.

Mariah wrote in her diary only that he was gentle with her. To me now, as I sat in this place of tragedy and triumph, I saw the depth of those few words. Dallas treated her as a man who loved her—gentle, eager to pleasure her, mindful of her pain. There was plenty of time later in their married life, after she'd become used to the fit of him, as she might have said, for wild, romping sex. But this day they needed tenderness, both of them. Dallas's technique contrasted sharply with Jerrod's, who had used her like a whore.

They buried Jerrod the next day. The undertaker worked hard to make the body presentable. Jerrod took the secret of the bank's gold with him in death. Bill Tillman questioned Mariah and Dallas, but neither one knew anything about the gold. Tillman left the valley quietly, without disclosing his mission to anyone else.

The rest is history, as they say. Dallas promised to take Mariah away from the gold country, but was unable to keep his promise until nearly two years later when the Supreme Court made the final decision, splitting the profit between all parties—albeit unequally, but Dallas still became a rich man.

By that time, Mariah had given birth to the first Molly of our line. Those first days after she married Dallas she prayed that at least one blood flow would come before she conceived a baby. She sought Molly's advice on what to do and followed every remedy to prevent a child, but one came before another flow anyway. Mariah bore the cross of her child's uncertain parentage her entire life.

I felt my own flat abdomen. I didn't have to face her fate. DNA testing could determine my baby's father, but did I want to know? On the other side, could I bear the uncertainty?

Molly b'Dam died before Mariah left the gold country. During the winter of 1887, she lost her energy. Quick consumption, the doctor called it. Was it tuberculosis? Maybe. She died shortly after the new year of 1888 dawned, just shy of her thirty-fifth birthday. She had been Mariah's mainstay. After her death, Mariah couldn't leave the valley fast enough.

Dallas built her a pleasant house in Spokane Falls. Twenty years later, when Mariah was barely forty, he built her the grand house Gran owns. And which will be mine after she's gone.

My thoughts returned to Mariah. In the emptiness and serenity of the valley, she seemed to be with me. I knew with certainty what had happened. What was I supposed to learn from it? Uphill, I heard the whine of a car engine as it roared into town. Life went on around me, even as it had in her day.

Clearly, Rand was my Jerrod. But maybe, with Rand as far away from me as possible, I might have a chance with Sean again. My baby had a shot at a good family life. Rand wouldn't suspect that the child might be his. Why should he?

The sound of a rock clattering startled me. I jumped as I looked up. The figure of a man emerged from the forest. For one crazy instant I imagined that Dallas came toward me, a ghost from long ago. Then reason took hold.

"Sean!"

CHAPTER EIGHTEEN

Sean waved back. I stood. Indecision rooted me in place. My mouth went dry. My hands shook. And yet I was as inexplicably happy to see him as I was surprised by his arrival. Obviously more prepared for the terrain than I was, he wore belted denim shorts, a white T-shirt, and hiking boots, and strode easily down the hill and across the rocks. Sean was an experienced hiker.

Something about his surefooted confidence appealed to me. He exuded strength. Where had it come from, I wondered? What gave him this new power? For the first time in years, I felt protected by his presence—my white knight had come to rescue me, or had he?

His hair had been recently, very recently, cut. He was clean-shaven and fit. I admired his tall, lean, muscular body as he came toward me, seeing the boy I'd fallen in love with again, as if for the first time in far too long. Where had that attractive man gone, these past bad days, months, and years? Why had I refused to see him until now? My pulse quickened with both fear and delight.

As he came nearer, the breeze waving the pines in the distance carried a hint of Sean's cologne. Had he really fixed up for me? Or did he just want me to see what I'd thrown away so callously, so casually?

He stopped a few paces in front of me and jammed his hands into his shorts pockets. The tight ball of his fists was not lost on me. The memory of Sean in the rain all those years ago came back. Although the sun beat brightly down upon us, the young, hurting man of those days stood before me as clearly as if water dripped from his hair and he'd just swung my coat over my shoulders.

"Dani," he said softly in a deep tone.

I had been wrong. He was not quite the boy of those long-gone days. A maturity and confidence surrounded him.

"What are you doing here?" I sounded incredulous, like a young girl at her first dance as I asked the obvious and mundane.

"Gran told me where I'd find you. She said you were out chasing ghosts."

Tears clouded my eyes. I laughed lightly, fighting to hold them back. "That sounds like Gran. I thought you couldn't get away? What about your project review?"

He shrugged, and with that simple gesture forever endeared himself to me. Then, for the first time in our married life, I reached out to him first, tried to win him back. I stepped into him, slid my arms beneath his and around him, and pressed my cheek to his chest, dampening his shirt with my tears.

"I'm sorry." My voice cracked as I listened to the rapid, reassuring patter of his heart.

He freed his hands from his pockets and pressed me even tighter against him. "Did you find those ghosts?"

I pulled back far enough to look up into his searching expression. "Yes, I did. And believe it or not, they taught me a thing or two about life and love and choices."

I bit my lip and took a deep breath. It was time, time indeed, that I put my feelings out to be trampled first. "It's not fair to ask, but I'd like to try again. You may not want to, though, when I've told you all there is."

He shook his head violently and interrupted me. "I don't want to hear it—not now, not ever. All I need to know is that it's over."

"Yes. It's over." I laughed. "As bad as it sounds, it was over as soon as it began."

"Good." He squeezed me. "I've come to take you home."

"*Really?*" It was my turn to ask.

He nodded. "Absolutely."

I steeled myself to be shoved away. There was no easy way to say it, but he had to know. "I'm pregnant, Sean."

He paled. His Adam's apple bobbed as he swallowed hard.

"I'll understand if you retract your offer." I forced myself to continue. "I can't lie to you. It could be yours. Or it could be his. I used protection, but..." Call me a liar, but I couldn't tell him about the condom failing.

Sean didn't reply.

I couldn't stand the silence. "The baby can be tested. We can find out—"

"No!" The vehemence of his reply startled me. It echoed off the hills, mocking me again and again.

"No," he said, more softly. He looked stunned. "I'd like to believe it's mine. You two used protection. We didn't. Why shouldn't it be ours?" He paused. "Did you know when you left?"

I shook my head.

"You're sure you're pregnant? We've had so many false alarms—"

"I haven't been to the doctor yet, but yes. The home pregnancy test was pretty definite."

"Jeez, Dani." He took a deep breath. "Do you want it?"

It seemed like a crazy and callous question, and yet I knew what he meant. Did I want this baby, knowing how it came about, knowing it could ruin us? The answer was simple: "Yes."

He paused. Sean was never quick to answer. His logical mind took time to process every angle of a situation. Finally, a small, lopsided smile sneaked onto his face. "Me too. We're going to be parents!"

I couldn't quite digest my good fortune. "You won't mind? You'll love it no matter what?" Typical me—I had to press the issue. I expected him to frown, to scold me for my insecure doubts.

His look turned both serious and contrite. "I've done a lot of thinking about things these last few days. I've been a callous bastard. I know how much you wanted a baby, and I know we tried. But I reached a point where I couldn't stand the failure and disappointment anymore. I gave up. I let you down because I guess I felt like less of a man for not being able to get you pregnant. We've been given a gift."

"But—"

He silenced me with a lift of his hand. "Don't say it. What if he looks like Rand? What if he looks like me? What if he looks like you? What if he looks like Gran and all those Maggies and Mollys of the past? Does it matter?" Sean took a step back and grabbed my hands.

"The implication of all this isn't lost on me. You slept with Rand, and then you slept with me for the first time in months out of guilt. We didn't use anything that night. I'd like to think that with the pressure off, a blessing happened. And if it didn't..." He shrugged. "The child's father isn't the man who donates his sperm, but the man who loves and raises him. If you can live with the uncertain parentage of this baby, I can live with the joy of loving it, of having a child to call mine."

So there it was—Sean's condition. He had every right to make it. *Oh, Mariah, why must you haunt me so? I have technology at my fingertips. I could know, absolutely, who fathered this child. But if you could bear it, so could I.* "As far as I'll ever be concerned, the child is ours."

He smiled. "And I'll make you a promise—I'll stop ignoring my wife for work and avoiding our problems."

I laughed lightly. "Don't make promises you can't keep, Sean. I know your passions."

"You should—you're one of them." He pulled me back into him and kissed me like he had when we were young. I could have swooned, although maybe it was only the shortness of breath that came with pregnancy. I laughed inwardly, reveling in the joy of this restored passion. Sean slid his arm around my shoulders as we walked toward the woods and the hill.

I kept thinking of Mariah and Dallas. When we reached the end of the tailings where the trees began to grow again, I stopped. "A man died here over a hundred years ago."

"I know. Gran told me the story and why you're here." He squeezed my shoulders.

We gave them a minute of silence, all of them— Molly, Mariah, Dallas, and Jerrod.

Sean broke the silence first. "Are you finished here?"

"Almost." I reached for him, sliding my hands up his shoulders, around his neck and up into his still gloriously thick hair. I pulled him into a kiss.

He pulled my blouse free of my shorts and slid his hands up my bare back. And then we did the mating dance. Parrying tongues, hot, pressing bodies, licked lips, wet kisses, mouths sliding together, open caverns of soul.

I unzipped the fly of his shorts and slid my hand in. He unzipped mine and tugged them down as he thrust into my hand. I pressed into him. He into me. Pressing, exploring, hoping, tension building. I pulled him on top of me and fell backward onto a bed of ferns and soft, fallen pine needles.

There we lay, two rutting animals making love as it was intended, primal, instinctive, and passionate. Me with my shorts around my knees. Him through the fly of his pants. My blouse hung open and loose around me. My bare breasts bounced with his movement. My tailbone ground into the earth. I was more aroused than I had ever been. I pressed my knees into his sides, wanting to lock him to me forever. I threw my head back and moaned softly to Sean and the guardian pines overhead.

I needed that union with Sean, the hot, open, intensely personal and private expression of us. Nothing else healed quite so completely. As he stiffened and grunted above me, a blinding pleasure overtook me. A scream loosed from my lips—a sound of ecstasy and love to drown out forever those tragic echoes of the past.

Sean collapsed on top of me. I kissed his neck and stroked his sweaty back. The growing heat of the day closed in around us.

"I love you, Dani."

It was the thing to say in such a moment, but the rich depth of his voice gave it a new sincerity. I was happy.

"I love you too."

His gaze slide down to my bared breasts. He smiled. "Jeez, Dani, look at those bazoombas! Have they grown! You look like a centerfold." He smiled broadly. "I like it."

"A side effect of pregnancy. Daddy-come-see-me breasts. Enjoy them. They're only temporary. Just wait until the rest of my body grows to match them." I grimaced.

He kissed my nose. "You'll always be beautiful to me." He slid from me. "Shall we get up before some nature lover discovers us?" He stood and offered me a hand.

"Yeah, I guess we should."

We rearranged ourselves into our hot, sticky clothing and, smelling of sex, hiked back up the hill to the car.

"Wish we could ride back together," Sean said, patting my rump.

"Me too." As I unlocked my door, I saw the flowers lying on the passenger seat and remembered my uncompleted task. "I have one more stop to make before I head home. It'll just take a minute. I promised Gran I'd leave these flowers on Molly's grave. The cemetery is just up the hill. You head back. I'll meet you at Gran's."

"I'll go with you."

"At the risk of offending you, I'd rather go alone."

He nodded. "I'll wait for you by the ramp to the interstate."

"See you in a few." I gave him a light kiss and hopped into my car. As I pulled away, I turned up the air conditioning to full blast.

The Murray cemetery was on a heavily wooded hill outside town. Pines guarded it against steady light and blanketed it with needles, giving it the solemnity expected of burial grounds. I pulled the car off the road and climbed out, flowers in hand. If Sean hadn't been waiting for me down the road, I might have lingered longer to look over the headstones of so many characters now familiar to me. Instead, I hurried on to find Molly.

I stumbled upon her grave all of a sudden. I guess I expected more pomp and circumstance surrounding it, a real mausoleum to greatness, a tribute in stone. What I found instead was a simple, but meticulously maintained, rectangular wooden marker with a rounded top. The inscription was carved in plain block lettering. It read:

Sacred to the memory of Maggie Hall. Molly-b-Dam. Died at Murray. Jan. 17, 1888. Age 35 years.

I knelt beside her in silence a moment, flowers in hand, as memories of her life flashed through my mind. Tears welled in my eyes. *Oh, Molly, old friend*, I thought, feeling as though I'd lost her, too. It was inexplicable and crazy. We hadn't even lived in the same time period, but seeing her grave stunned me. She'd been so much a character in my thoughts and Gran's book. She'd come to life for me. But here in the quiet wilderness of pines, I felt some of the grief Mariah must have known. Molly was dead.

Sadness swept over me. I would never meet her other than in my thoughts and through records of her life.

The shame I'd carried for years over being named for a prostitute melted away. I vowed in that instant to live like the honorable side of Molly, to live up to the name. I swept my hand lightly over the tips of the delicate, sparse grass covering her resting place, enjoying the light baby-hair feel of them.

"Thank you, Molly," I said to the quiet hush of the woods. "I wouldn't be here without you. Do you know that you saved more than Mariah that day? For better or worse, you saved generations of us, all named after you. I hope you're pleased."

I positioned the flowers across the grave in front of the marker, fussing with them, trying to get them to look just right, in reality delaying leaving her. Satisfied at last with the result, I pressed to a stand, happy that I could carry on Mariah's friendship and love for her.

"Goodbye. Rest well." I walked back to the car without turning back. Molly had lived her life—now it was time I faced my destiny.

When we returned to Spokane, Gran met us in the driveway, a serene and smug expression on her face. My all-knowing gran—how did she do it? Sean and I stepped out of our respective cars and met to link arms.

Gran clapped her hands together, so happy she nearly chortled. "So, children, what did you find? How is Molly?"

"Wonderful, great, same as ever," I said, smiling up at Sean. Gran and her double entendre. Weren't we all Mollys?

Sean, in his usual manner, remained mute.

"Good," Gran said. "Those Murray folks haven't let the grave go to ruin?"

"Not in over a hundred years. Why should they start now? The flowers looked wonderful, really perked it up."

"Well, you kids must be tired and thirsty. This heat!" Gran shook her head and clicked her tongue, but she wore her omnipresent sweater. "Let's go out back and have some refreshments. Lucy! Bring a tray to the patio."

We retired to the shade. Gran couldn't contain her excitement at Jerrod being an outlaw. "It explains a lot. Don't you think so, Dani?"

"Yes, Gran, a lot."

As we sipped lemonade and ate sandwiches, I told them what I experienced out there on the river of rock, how the story took shape, what must have happened. Gran, Lucy, and Sean listened with rapt attention. Gran's eyes glittered brightly and she interrupted often to make her own assertions. In the end, I think only Sean understood my point.

"But we don't *know* that it happened that way," Gran asserted.

"There's no way to prove it, if that's what you mean," I said. "But it fits the facts."

Gran sighed. Her expression spoke of sadness and resignation. "It may, but I'm playing historian. I can't write it that way, not without facts to back it up."

"You can put in about Jerrod," Lucy said between bites of sandwich. "That at least clears up part of the mystery. The reader will have to draw her own conclusion."

I interrupted Gran as she nodded, mouth open to speak. "You can, but is that fair? Gran, you're dooming Mariah to speculation and conjecture forever."

"She never set the record straight herself, never gave the full details of what happened that day." Gran set her lemonade down and looked at me thoughtfully. "Why do you care so much?"

"I don't know. I just do."

Sean reached over and squeezed my hand. I smiled back at him.

"I understand her," I said. "She claimed she didn't kill him. What more could she do? Lashing back at gossip is nothing more than shadowboxing. You look guilty if you do. You look guilty if you don't. She chose to keep silent. Why give the rumors any credibility?"

"You're right, Dani." Gran's gaze rested on Sean's hand holding mine. She smiled broadly. "You two look like you've resolved your own differences."

I looked up into Sean's eyes.

"We have," he said. "We're going to try to put things back together. The thing is, Gran, I like your granddaughter very much, too much to lose her."

Gran may have thought that Sean understated his feelings. Mere like, what was that? But I understood the deep emotion beneath it. To love someone, you must first like him very much indeed. And if you ever falter, ever misstep on the rocky field of love, you can always fall back to that, build on that again, until you're so strong in your love, you no longer feel vulnerable.

There was an inevitable pause in the conversation. Finally, I said, "It seems I'm finished here, Gran. I can't give you any more help with the book. Early tomorrow, Sean and I are heading home to Seattle."

Gran didn't argue. We filled the remainder of the day with preparations to leave, quiet walks and discussions, and a celebration dinner that evening. That night Sean retired with me into the little green and white sprigged bedroom. We rocked that little bed, banging the headboard to the wall for all it was worth, not caring if Gran or Lucy heard. For my part, I think Gran expected it.

I still worried about Sean and me. Would we really survive this? Bouncing each other's bones was one thing, rebuilding a trusting relationship another. As far as I could see, the survival of our marriage hinged on two things—whether Sean could genuinely forgive my infidelity and whether I could truly express my regret and apologies. Could I live with the restitution I had to make? Could I stand strong and sympathetic when distrust danced in his eyes? Could I express my regrets when my indiscretion flew at me in the heat of an argument? Could I never, ever so much as hint that the baby might not be his? That I wanted to know who the real biological father was? I'd never thought about it before, but while transgressions can be forgiven, consequences linger.

As I lay there worrying, I heard Sean's slow, even breathing. I stared for a long time at the firm line of his jaw and his strong profile, and ran my fingers lightly through his thick hair. In our favor—Sean had always been able to forgive, both the little things and the big. And as for me, I was determined to pay penance. To love him as he should be loved. To remain true. I thought of Mariah and Dallas. We had history in our favor. We just might make it yet. I hoped we made it.

I curled up behind Sean and drifted off to sleep.

Erin's Daughters is largely a work of historical fiction. Molly b'Dam, Phil O'Rourke, Terrible Edith, and Noah Kellogg are all real historical figures who shaped the history of Idaho's Silver Valley. Mariah, Dallas, and Jerrod are fictional creations of mine. Many of the events I described actually happened. I tried to stay true to the facts and the personality and characters of the people involved as presented in the research I did. But any interaction between my fictional character and the real historical figures is obviously made up. And in many cases, we don't have the actual conversations between the real people so I had to improvise.

Molly b'Dam was the original for the stereotype of the madam with a heart of gold. The miners and people of her day loved her. Many acts of her kindness and courage are recorded. There's even a museum in town dedicated largely to her. If you visit Murray, Idaho, today you can visit her grave with its plain wooden mark, still lovingly maintained by the people of Murray.

Gina Robinson is the award-winning author of the historical romances *The Escort, The Last Honest Seamstress, The Union* and the Agent Ex series of humorous romantic suspense novels. She's currently working on a new contemporary romantic comedy serial, *Switched at Marriage*.

Connect with Gina Online:

My Website: http://www.ginarobinson.com/
Twitter: @ginamrobinson
Facebook: www.facebook.com/GinaRobinsonAuthor

www.ingramcontent.com/pod-product-compliance
Lightning Source LLC
Chambersburg PA
CBHW060539180626
46817CB00002B/647